TREASURES OF THE HEART BOOK 1

COLORADO TREASURE

WHAT PEOPLE ARE SAYING ...

When you think of Scarlett O'Hara, or Jo Marsh and her sisters in *Little Women*, you'll remember Victoria Silverthorne in *Colorado Treasure*. You'll judge other heroines by Victoria's compassion, courage, and faith. Derinda Babcock plunged Victoria into the murky depths of finding family and turned Vicky's world upside down. Why had she been sent to Mary and John Keeson instead of her paternal uncle after the death of her parents? Why did she have to find out about her Silverthorne connection from a newspaper article? Blossoming love and a thirteen-year-old deaf boy are the spices that flavor this story packed with lies, revenge, and organized crime. Learning some Spanish and sign language rounded out this unforgettable saga. Derinda Babcock — we're ready for your next novel.
—**Linda Harris**, author of *Mansion of Stolen Hearts*, Harvey Girls Collection, (Winged Publications, Forget Me Not Romances), *Treasure Among the Ruins*, Book 1, *Voices in the Desert Series* (Winged Publications, Forget Me Not Romances, 2017), *The Lye Water Bride*, *California Gold Rush Romance Collection* (Barbour Publications, 2016)

Sweeping vistas meet personal discovery, evolving relationships and a healthy dash of intrigue in this wonderful story of a girl searching to find the truth about her family and her past. Enriched with a cast of characters who made me want to jump into the book and spend an afternoon with them, I loved every little bit and piece. I was drawn in and taken for a wonderful ride. This book truly lives up to its namesake as a Colorado Treasure!
—**T.E. Bradford**, author of *Dragon Between Worlds* and *Child of Prophecy*

I just finished reading *Colorado Treasure* and already look forward to the release of the next book in the trilogy. The book held my attention because the author weaves many issues and side stories into the tale. I found elements of a love story, high drama, tragedy, sadness, joy, history, crime, morality, and faith. The story was a fast read and left me feeling good at the end. I couldn't ask for more. I highly recommend this book.

—Gary Waples, Reader

TREASURES OF THE HEART BOOK 1

COLORADO TREASURE

DERINDA BABCOCK

ELK LAKE PUBLISHING INC.
Plymouth, Massachusetts

Cover and Interior Design: Derinda Babcock

Editor(s): Sue Fairchild, Deb Haggerty

Author Represented by Hartline Literary Agency

PUBLISHED BY: Elk Lake Publishing, Inc., 35 Dogwood Dr., Plymouth, MA 02360, 2019

Library Cataloging Data

Names: Babcock, Derinda (Derinda Babcock)

Colorado Treasure / Derinda Babcock

216 p. 23cm × 15cm (9in × 6 in.)

Description: Fifteen years ago, Victoria Silverthorne's parents died under mysterious circumstance. She is determined to find answers, but someone is determined to prevent her from doing so.

Identifiers: ISBN-13: 978-1-950051-83-0 (trade) | 978-1-950051-84-7 (POD) | 978-1-950051-85-4 (e-book)

Key Words: American Historical, Clean and Wholesome, Relationships, Mystery, Inspirational, Twentieth Century, Deaf, Mexican-American

LCCN: 2019943581 Fiction

DEDICATION

To Dwight—
One of the treasures of my heart

ACKNOWLEDGMENTS

Johnathan Naranjo and Leslie Villalobos
Thanks for your enthusiasm and good-humored willingness
to give up a Saturday to pose for the interior soft cover of this book

Deb Haggerty, Editor-in-Chief, Elk Lake Publishing, Inc.
and
Sue Fairchild, Fiction Editor, Elk Lake Publishing, Inc.
Thanks for being on my team.

ONE

Victoria Silverthorne watched the train approach the Amarillo station and grasped the handle of her carpetbag until her knuckles whitened. She didn't like the churning in her stomach. She looked at the sky. *Am I doing the right thing, Lord? You gave me peace about this decision months ago, so why do I doubt now?*

She searched the faces of the people who had come to see her and her friend, Abigail O'Brien, leave for Denver. Mary and John Keeson stood on the platform next to Elizabeth and Miguel Morales. Though she'd lived with Mary and John from the time of the tragedy fifteen years ago, her heart accepted Miguel and Beth as parents. She glanced at their son, Antonio— *Ah, Tony.* Victoria did not consider him as a brother. She glanced at her childhood friend, and the acid threatened to climb into her throat. His clenched fists, blazing dark eyes, and rigid posture indicated he still hadn't accepted her decision to leave.

She glanced at Mary. The woman's lips and square jaw hadn't relaxed since Victoria had broken the news. Next to Tony, she'd dreaded telling Mary the most. Mary's intent blue stare could make the naughtiest boys squirm. *Why doesn't she turn that stare on John every now and then? Is Mary truly blind to his unkind actions and words? Does she ever say anything to him in private to encourage him to curb his tongue and treat others with more respect?*

Most of her people had voiced their objections to this trip, some more strongly than others. She'd known they would, which is why she'd waited until the after church picnic one Sunday to tell them. She took a deep breath now and closed her eyes in remembrance. The scene and all the events leading up to her departure hadn't dimmed.

COLORADO TREASURE

After everyone had eaten, and families and friends had gathered in clusters on benches or blankets spread on the lawn to enjoy the warm June day, Victoria finally found enough nerve to speak. She brushed back a stray tendril of hair and prayed her voice wouldn't shake as much as her insides. Why did she feel so nervous? She was twenty years old and her own woman.

Arnie Gilford and Sam Johnson joined the group, and during a lull in the conversation, Victoria spoke. "I got a telegram from my uncle in Denver." She continued before her courage failed. "He invited me for a visit, and I've accepted." *I only wished I'd known about them earlier. Why did I have to find out about my aunt and uncle from a newspaper article instead of from Mary or John?*

Her announcement silenced all conversation. Victoria's mouth tightened at their expressions. She slanted her eyes toward Tony and watched his shock quickly turn to anger. If she said anything else, he'd probably explode through his skin or shoot a string of rapid-fire Spanish words at her, which is why she'd waited until her plans were in motion to tell him. John glanced at Mary, who pinched her lips together. Mary looked at Sam who scrunched up his face and said, "Why? Denver's a long way from here."

"I have to, Sam. The nightmare of that day fifteen years ago returns to haunt my dreams almost every night now. I need answers. Maybe my uncle can provide them."

Sam and Arnie both nodded. They knew. They'd been in the mountains with her and had also watched her parents die.

Tony spoke then as anger tensed both his body and voice and thickened his accent. "So, you would endanger yourself to travel hundreds of miles to meet a man of whom you know nothing, who may or may not be able to answer questions you have, because of a dream?" He clearly thought the idea nonsensical.

"You still don't understand. This nightmare isn't just any dream, Tony. Every night, I return to that high mountain valley in southwestern Colorado. I relive the moment when the mountain fell and buried my mother and father alive." She shuddered. "The nightmare haunts my dreams whenever—" She stopped the words and forced them back into her throat.

"Whenever what?"

Whenever daytime thoughts of my uncertain future create unrest and dissatisfaction.

"Never mind."

"You should not leave. Denver is a dangerous place."

Victoria lifted her chin and looked into his umber-colored eyes. She clasped her hands behind her back, so he couldn't see how they shook. "That's a risk I have to take. I don't think I'll be in much danger, but I'll be careful."

Tony crammed his hands into his coat pockets and paced back and forth. He looked at his father and spoke in rapid Spanish. Though his back was to Victoria, she caught enough of the conversation to know he was asking Miguel to "talk some sense into this foolish woman."

Miguel glanced at her before clasping Tony's shoulder. "We will speak of this at a more convenient time, in a more appropriate location, Antonio." He tilted his head toward several curious townsfolk who gazed at them. Many whispered behind their hands. Some pointed. Lawrence Lucky, the town's newspaper editor and only reporter, looked especially interested. Victoria sighed. *Can't they mind their own business? Just once?*

"Time to go." Mary's tone brooked no argument. "John, will you get the wagon?"

He nodded and rose. Victoria watched as he headed toward the wagon. He twirled the corner of his left eyebrow between his thumb and index finger, a sure sign of his distraction. She couldn't imagine her trip to Denver caused his abstraction. *Perhaps he's planning a party to celebrate my departure? Or maybe he's considering ways to keep me from returning?*

She stiffened as the newspaper editor approached and engaged John in conversation. Though likable enough, the man had an uncanny ability to smell a story brewing as easily as Arnie's black mule sensed storms.

Victoria sighed. How many more years must she live before the people of the town no longer viewed her as a person of interest and a prime target for gossip? In her weaker moments, the injustice of their actions poked through the protective barrier she'd raised.

I hope John keeps a still tongue between his teeth. She grimaced. *Right, when has he ever done that?*

Her thoughts returned to the present, but only long enough to scan the faces of those who waited with her and to stare down the tracks. She caught John's stare, and he quickly wiped a smug expression off his face and turned away from her. *How did John and I get to this point? We barely talk or tolerate each other's presence now. What has made him so willing to tear down the character and reputation of others? Has he always acted this way, and I was too young to pay attention?* She began to pace and thought about his recent words and actions.

Before Victoria made her big announcement, she'd been up most of the night trying to escape another of the painful memories of her parents' deaths. There didn't seem to be any purpose in tossing for hours, so Victoria rose and dressed. She reorganized her already orderly room in an attempt to find something to occupy her time until Mary and John stirred.

When the Keesons' bedroom door closed, and she heard their footsteps descend the stairs, Victoria glanced once more in the mirror and grimaced. She couldn't do anything about the dark rings under her eyes, so she'd best prepare for Mary's comments. She stood and brushed at the wrinkles in her long skirt.

Mary's eyes met hers as she stepped into the kitchen. "Heard you fiddlin' around 'til all hours of the night. Had those dreams again?"

Victoria nodded and helped Mary bring breakfast to the table. She filled Mary's bowl with oatmeal and then reached for the freshly-churned butter.

Mary slid her squatty frame into the chair next to Victoria's and grimaced. "Goodness, child. You know I can't eat this much." She eyed Victoria and shook her head. "How you can eat as you do and never gain beats me. I think you must have a tapeworm."

Victoria had heard this comment so often the words didn't register. She continued to puzzle over questions the dream evoked—questions she hadn't thought of until last night.

"Mary, how well did you know my folks?"

Mary stilled. Victoria sensed the older woman's surprise and suspicion at her question. Mary picked up her spoon and dipped the utensil into the oatmeal, eyes downward. She took a bite and chewed slowly. Victoria suspected the woman examined her question for motive. When she finally spoke, her face and tone sounded noncommittal.

"Not well. Your ma and I were first cousins. That's why they brought you here to me after the accident."

"Who brought me here?"

"Don't you remember?" Mary's steady blue eyes searched Victoria's face.

"No, I don't. The last thing I remember was Sam and Arnie trying to dig through tons of rock and dirt ... Sam and Arnie. Did they bring me to you?"

Mary nodded as she took another bite of her oatmeal.

Victoria toyed with her spoon and studied the woman seated across from her. Mary always parted her hair in the middle and twisted the locks into a bun at the nape of her neck. Every strand had a place, none allowed to fly about her face. The dark, nondescript cotton dress she wore had seen several years of service and would see a few more. Mary believed a garment's age didn't mean the clothing could be retired before its time. Mary reminded Victoria of one of the plow horses the men used to clear the fields in preparation for planting. The horses plodded through their tasks at one speed all day long, refusing to allow anything like a stubborn stump to stop their work.

"But how did they know to bring me to you? How did they know you and Ma were related?"

"Land sakes, child. How should I know?"

Victoria recognized the irritation in Mary's voice, and she knew from experience continued questioning would do no good. Mary could get stubborn when she wanted to, especially when this topic arose.

"Mary, why do you get all riled when I ask you questions about my parents?" Victoria tossed her head and clinked her spoon against the bowl.

"I just don't see any point. What good does dwelling on things in the past do? You should focus more on your future and let sleeping dogs lie."

"My future?"

Mary nodded and studied Victoria's face. "Do you plan to live with us the rest of your life?"

Victoria couldn't speak for several moments, trying to swallow the sudden lump in her. "Do you want me to leave?"

"Don't be silly, Victoria. You're good help, and this has been your home since you were five. I'm just thinking ahead. John and I aren't getting any younger."

Victoria tried to imagine what life in the Keeson home without Mary would be like but couldn't get beyond the churning in her stomach at the thought.

They both looked up as John entered and closed the street door. The way his loose clothing hung on his medium frame reminded Victoria of an elegant scarecrow. He brushed his sparse gray hair from the side so longer strands covered the bald spot on top of his head. He tossed his black jacket over the chair, tugged at his suspenders, and strode to the two calendars hanging on the pantry door. He ignored Mary's motions for him to sit down and eat, flipping to a date in last year's calendar instead.

"Aha. Just as I thought." John smirked at them and brought the two calendars to the table. He sat down and spooned oatmeal into his bowl. "Look here, Mary." He grinned and pointed at a date on last year's calendar with his bony finger.

"What, John?" Mary's tone indicated her interest and patience. Her attitude always confused Victoria. How could Mary speak with such kindness to her husband when he acted in unkind ways to others?

The smugness in John's voice raised the hairs on the back of Victoria's neck. "Maybell Keller. She married that Ray Rannaker feller on November 12, 1893. Well, she was just brought to bed with a nine-pound son, and it ain't been but seven months since the weddin'."

Victoria choked and glared at John. He noted the wedding date of every young woman in town, and then compared this with the birth date of their first child. He made sure everyone who came into the store knew if a decent interval of at least nine months didn't separate the two.

"What a disgusting hobby you have." Victoria stood and collected her dirty dishes. Disapproval stiffened her body as she washed and rinsed them in the tubs then placed them on the drain board to dry. When Victoria turned back to the couple, John wouldn't meet her eyes. Her eyes had always made him uncomfortable, especially if they sparked with flinty green anger as she was sure they did now. Her coloring also increased his discomfort. He probably agreed with the townsfolk that the combination of emerald eyes and black hair gave her a witch-like appearance. She pushed down the sense of hurt his lack of affection continued to cause. She should be used to the feeling now. John had never stood up for her against them in all the years she'd lived with him and Mary.

"I'll be in the store if you need me. I may walk to the ranch after work to visit Beth. Don't wait for me." The store attached to the Keesons' living quarters, but Victoria chose to go out the street door. She needed air.

She closed the door with a snap and looked around, frowning. Though her eyes panned the weathered, false-fronted buildings of the town's two hotels, three saloons, bank, newspaper office, and livery barn, and unconsciously followed the movements of the townsfolk as they went about their business, she focused on her thoughts. One of these days, John's insensitivity would be his undoing, and she hoped she was around to see the event.

Victoria's conscience pricked her, and she lifted her eyes to the sky. "I know … I know, Father. Please forgive me for that unworthy thought. You've commanded me to love him, but this is so hard, especially when John uses his mouth to hurt others. I'm losing the battle, Lord—"

"*¡Hóla, brujita!*" She looked toward the sound of the soft, slightly accented voice, and watched as Tony dismounted from his large chestnut gelding, Hercules. His short, curling black hair, umber-colored eyes, and sun-browned skin hinted of his Mexican heritage.

Shards of angry green must have remained in Victoria's eyes when she looked at him because he grinned, raised his gloved hands as if to ward off a blow, and backed up a step.

"Hóla, Tony. Don't call me a witch, even if you use the word affectionately. I hear enough of the same from the townsfolk." She waited for him to step up beside her on the boardwalk. "What are you doing in town this morning?"

He smiled and dusted his denim jeans with his black hat. "The boss wanted to know if his fencing wire arrived, and because the day is so fresh and inviting, *and* because I knew you worked today, I volunteered to come to town to check."

Victoria grinned at his virtuous expression and her anger evaporated. "I hope such sacrifice is rewarded. Yes, the fencing came yesterday. The rolls are in the back room. Come with me. I'll show you."

Victoria unlocked the door to the general store and scanned the orderly row of bins, boxes, and shelves. She noted the tables of artistically displayed items offered for sale as she walked through to a large storage room. The place smelled subtly of potpourri, molasses, grain, leather, and licorice.

"Here." She pointed at the shiny new rolls of barbed wire. "Did you bring the buckboard?"

"*Sí*. I will bring it *al rato*." With unhurried movements, he signed the bill and looked at her. The corners of his mouth twitched into a grin. "So, who is the poor soul upon whom your wrath has fallen so early this morning?"

"I don't know what you're talking about."

"Do not lie to me, *señorita*. I, who have often suffered from the outpourings of your anger, recognize the signs when I see them."

Victoria laughed in spite of herself. "If you weren't so nosy, and would occasionally mind your own business, I wouldn't get so angry with you."

"Ah, but you are my business. Who else would dare to try and guide you into the paths of wisdom, eh?" He sighed and rolled his eyes heavenward. "And what thanks do I get? Nothing. Nothing but abuse and fiery green looks. This is enough to try the patience of a saint."

"I'd like to know where someone only twenty-five years old has acquired so much wisdom he thinks he can tell me what to do? Face the facts, Tony. You're a—"

John walked into the store then, and Victoria stiffened. Her chin lifted.

Tony looked from her to John and back again. "Aha. Now I am answered, am I not? What has he done now?"

"Be quiet, Tony," she hissed under her breath, and then spoke to him in a louder, more clerk-like voice. "Will that be all, Mr. Morales?"

Tony looked from John to Victoria again and his grin stretched all the way into an attractive, knowing smile. "*Sí*, for now. *¡Hasta pronto, brujita!*"

Victoria ignored his last comment and entered the charge in the ledger. She noted the tightness around John's mouth and eyes as he watched Tony leave.

"That young man is too cocky for his own good. I wish someday soon—"

"Yes? What do you wish?" Victoria stared at him with unblinking eyes, daring him to continue.

"Never mind. But you shouldn't treat a half-breed with such friendliness, Victoria. It's just not done around here—even if you did grow up with him. The townsfolk will talk."

The injustice and hypocrisy of John's words silenced her. She clenched her lips together so the words she wanted to say wouldn't spew out. She breathed another prayer for self-restraint.

The door opened and they both turned.

"Howdy, Miss Vicky. John." Sam's drawl made both Victoria and John smile.

"Good morning, Sam. What can I do for you?" No trace of John's dislike remained in his voice when he spoke to Sam.

"I need some of Mary's canned peaches."

"Sure thing." John reached for a jar.

Victoria looked at her friend and wondered if the stained, nondescript leather vest, the dingy white cotton shirt, and the faded denim blue jeans he always tucked into the scuffed, down-at-the-heels cowboy boots were the same ones he'd been wearing fifteen years before. They couldn't possibly be, yet Sam's attire remained the same three hundred sixty-five days of the year. He only added a bolo tie and a clean shirt when he went to church. Victoria grinned. He and Mary would see eye-to-eye on the serviceability and comfort of a good set of clothing.

Victoria leaned on the counter and watched the men. For a while, she listened with disinterest to the friendly conversation, but a thought suddenly focused her attention. John always treated Sam with respect. He never made any snide comments about him in public or private, which now seemed bizarre to her in light of his recent comments about Tony and Maybell Rannaker. She watched the men enter the backroom. Why did John treat Sam with such respect? What could he have done to have earned this? The question boggled her imagination. The townsfolk joked about Sam's inability to hold a job, get a wife, or grow crops, but not John. John, and Mary, for that matter, remained remarkably silent on the subject.

After Sam paid for the peaches, she walked to the door and sat on the bench on the boardwalk with him. He opened the jar and speared a quarter with his well-used pocketknife.

"Want one?" He pointed the dripping peach out to her.

"No, thanks." She grinned as he swallowed the peach quarter in one gulp then speared another.

"Tastes just like my ma's. She had a way with fresh peaches too." His sigh indicated pure pleasure. He propped his boots on the hitch-rail at the edge of the walk and slumped to the end of his spine.

They sat in the shade in comfortable silence and watched the townspeople go about their business. The ranchers trickled in either by horseback or in buckboards. Sometimes their wives sat next to them on the hard seat, but they all came to do business.

"Sure busy doin' somethin', ain't they?" Sam shook his head and speared another peach quarter. "They seem to get in a sweat and bother about nothin' important. They ought to find themselves a nice bench, or maybe a good fishin' hole and contemplate for a while."

"I guess they think what they're doing is important. Sitting by a fishing hole doesn't pay their bills."

"No, but they can't take money with them when they go, neither, so what good is it? To my way of thinkin', money only causes problems. Some of those people twist a gut tryin' to get all they can, whilst others watch like buzzards tryin' to take their money away from them. Mighty silly, if you ask me."

As usual, Victoria had no answer to Sam's argument. Sometimes his reasoning made sense. She decided to change the subject instead. "Sam?"

"Hmm?"

"How long have you known John?"

He turned and looked at her with his sleepy blue eyes. "Well, I figure we've known each other close on to twenty years now. Why?"

"Oh, I just wondered. He seems to respect you more than anyone else in town, and I wondered why. Seems unusual. I mean, he doesn't talk about you the way he does other people."

Sam let out a bark of laughter. "Is that right? Well, Missy, maybe he's jealous of my lifestyle and wishes he could just sit back and while the time away with a pretty girl."

"I don't think you're right, Sam. I know John too well." Victoria couldn't think of a person who seemed busier trying to accumulate wealth than John. The man had no patience with people who wasted their time at fishing holes.

She stood to go back into the store but stopped when she heard bullying, all-too-familiar boys' voices coming from around the side of the building. *Oh, no. Not again.*

"Come on, Dummy. Let's play Cowboys. We'll be the cowboys, and you be our steer. Round-up time."

She lunged around the building, Sam close on her heels, in time to see Billy Jameson and two of the town's older boys swinging lassos over their heads and whooping. Their intended victim was a tall, stooped, gangly man of forty. He glanced from Victoria, to the boys, and back again, his smile timid.

"Stop." She ordered and planted herself in front of the older man and faced the three boys who stood only a few feet away. She glared at them. "Don't you *dare* rope Arnie, you little weasels."

"Aw, Miss. We were only funnin', weren't we, Arnie?" Billy asked.

The boys snickered.

Arnie stood beside Sam and watched the boys, uncertainty filling his eyes.

Victoria stepped closer to Billy. She was so close to him now she could feel his body heat. She widened her eyes, so he could see the intent in them.

"At whose expense?" She smiled and turned her tone from hard to silky-smooth and soft. Her eyelids drooped. "Perhaps I should have a little fun with you, hmm?"

Billy stepped back and dropped the rope. He couldn't possibly know what she intended, but their past interactions probably suggested to him he wouldn't like whatever she decided to do. She looked at the other boys who hastily backed up two steps. She heard one whisper "witch" to the other, and then all three watched as she and Sam escorted Arnie to the boardwalk. Arnie looked over his shoulder at the boys.

"Did they really want to play, Miss Vicky?" Arnie turned to her with innocent eyes.

"No, they didn't."

"Were they trying to be mean to me again, Sam?"

"I'm afraid so, Arn."

"But why do they want to be that way? I ain't done nothin' to them." He hung his head.

Victoria patted his shoulder and put her arm around his waist. She glared at John, who had watched the whole incident from the walk, broom in hand, making no attempt to stop the boys. "Some people don't feel like they're worth anything, Arnie, until they can hurt other people or make them feel bad."

John dropped his eyes and went into the store just as Tony returned, driving an empty buckboard pulled by one of the ranch horses. Hercules trotted behind on a lead. Victoria watched him stop near the hitching rail then hop down. John, Sam, and Arnie helped him load the fencing material, and Victoria counted the items going out against her inventory list, signed the bill, and handed Tony the receipt.

"One moment, señorita. My mother has sent you a gift. I am sure you will appreciate her sense of humor."

Tony reached across the buckboard seat to the passenger side and handed Victoria a lumpy gunnysack. The others watched as she peeked inside then pulled out a black, wriggling kitten. The kitten's eyes were as green as hers. She sighed. If any of the townsfolk saw this gift, they'd have more fodder for gossip.

Victoria held the kitten close to her face and turned his head so they both looked at the men with unblinking stares. Everyone but John laughed. She guessed two pairs of such eyes unnerved him. Victoria didn't hide her grin when she looked at him, though her grin turned into a frown as she lowered the kitten.

Why do I always respond to John in such a manner? I don't like the way my actions make me feel, yet I seem helpless to stop.

Lately, they'd gotten under each other's skin on a regular basis, and she really didn't know how this had happened. Had she said something? Had he? She could barely tolerate being in the same room with him now, and she knew the lack of peace between them disturbed Mary. Perhaps Mary was right, and she needed to consider her future. Victoria's heart pounded. Where would she go? What would she do? The stable ground of her life suddenly shifted uncomfortably, and a seed of panic grew in the disturbed soil

TWO

Abby's lilting Irish voice returned Victoria's thoughts to the present. "I'm so excited. Thank you for invitin' me, Vicky."

"Thank you for coming. I won't be so nervous." Victoria smiled at the petite, sandy-haired, blue-eyed girl. Up until two days ago, she'd worked as a maid in one of the Amarillo hotels. They hadn't known each other for long, but Abby already seemed like a lifelong friend.

"Me mum's been pumpin' me full of good advice. I hope I remember most of what she said."

Victoria waved at Mrs. O'Brien and the rest of Abby's siblings just as the train pulled into the station. They were bundled up to keep warm on the gray, late November day as they all watched the train screech and hiss to a stop.

Abby's jaw dropped and her lips formed an *O* when Victoria pointed at the private Pullman Mark Silverthorne had sent.

Miguel nodded his approval. "Your uncle is a wise man, *hija*. Elizabeth and I now have one less thing to worry about. Is this not so, my love?" He smiled at his wife.

Elizabeth nodded and placed her hand in his brown one. Her light brown hair coiled atop her head under a warm hat. Her pale skin and unwrinkled face belied her forty-odd years, and her blue eyes shone with love as she gazed at Miguel.

Victoria watched the two, an ache of longing flaring in her belly. She loved Elizabeth and Miguel Morales almost as much as her mother and father, and tears pooled in her eyes when Elizabeth hugged her.

"Go with God, love," she said and kissed Victoria's cheek.

Victoria hugged her. "I'm already missing you, Beth." Over the years, Elizabeth had been her confidant, counselor, and friend. When needed, this dear woman had administered discipline in a firm but just way, and she'd been there to kiss the skinned knees and soothe the hurt feelings.

She'd acted as the mediator between Tony and her during their childish squabbles, and Elizabeth had tried to teach her the ways of an educated and cultured young lady.

"Yes, I'm thankful you can travel in more comfort." Elizabeth slanted a glance at her son, and Victoria's eyes followed.

Tony stood apart, the collar on his sheepskin-lined denim jacket turned up for warmth. Victoria walked to him. As the group watched the other passengers board, she touched his cheek with her ungloved hand and whispered, "I'm sorry I've upset you, but this is something I must do."

He brought her fingers to his lips and kissed them. "Will you come back?"

"Yes." She looked in his eyes then turned to leave.

"¡*Vaya con díos, hermosa mía!*" he whispered.

Victoria remained a moment longer before she turned and walked toward Abby.

Tony stood next to Miguel and watched a muscular, dark-skinned man load the girls' steamer trunks. If Victoria stepped into the car and headed away from her home and him, she would change forever. He did not know if this change would be for good or ill, and he could not envision their relationship in the future. He feared nothing good would come from this trip. This realization churned the acid in his stomach.

"Is this the end of everything I have dreamed, *Papá*?" Tony spoke so only his father could hear.

"No, Antonio, this is the beginning of bigger dreams."

"Are you certain?"

"*Sí, sin duda*. Without a doubt." Miguel put a comforting hand on his son's shoulder. "Have you spoken of your love for her, *hijo*? Does she know?"

Tony considered for several moments. "No, Papá, but how could she not understand what I feel for her after all these years?"

Miguel spoke, amusement permeating every word, "Women are intuitive, my son, but they do not read minds. Have not many of the problems you and Victoria experienced in the past been caused because you expected her to understand your actions, though you did not explain your reasoning or motives behind them? Have you not been frustrated on multiple occasions because she did not respond the way you expected her to?"

"Sí, you are right. She does not think as I do, Papá. I hope when my hair begins to silver at the temples, I am as wise as you."

Miguel laughed. "We are cut from the same cloth, hijo."

They turned to watch as the "all aboard" was called.

As he listened to the goodbyes, Tony gritted his teeth to prevent himself from begging Victoria to stay.

His father spoke as Victoria stepped near. "Vaya con díos, *mijita.*—Go with God, my daughter. May your journey be filled with valuable and enduring lessons."

"I'll write when I can, Miguel."

"Where is your pistol?" he whispered near her ear, but Tony heard.

"In my bag. I'll keep the gun close wherever I go," she returned his whisper and hugged him. "I'll remember what you taught me."

"See you do so, little one."

"I won't forget, Miguel. My wrists ache even now as I remember the first lessons."

Victoria turned toward the train.

Look back at me, Victoria. Give me hope you will return. Tony waited, his fists balled in his pockets. He sighed when she looked over her shoulder and smiled at him.

Victoria stared as a well-dressed, dark-skinned man stepped out of the Pullman and looked around. He noticed her attention and walked to her. He introduced himself as George Spearman, servant to Mark and Bella Silverthorne. His eyes widened when he glanced in her eyes, and Victoria waited to see if the surprise turned into fear or suspicion.

She introduced him to Abby and the people who'd come to see them off.

Tony stepped up next to her and appeared to give George the once-over. "Give me your carpetbag, Victoria. I will accompany you to the car."

Victoria waved to her people one last time before she turned and followed George to the steps of the Pullman. The servant took Abby's carpetbag and helped her into the railway car and waited for Tony to do the same for her.

The plushness inside the Pullman surprised her. The car came equipped with all the comforts a wealthy businessman expected. This included a kitchen, dining facilities, china and silver services, upholstered lounge chairs, beds, wood paneling, draperies and Venetian blinds, cut-glass lamps, plush carpets, a shiny mahogany desk, a wash area and toilet, a heating stove. She noticed Tony's jaw had hardened at the sight of the luxurious accommodations. Did he react this way to be contrary?

The whistle blew in warning just as Tony sat down her carpetbag. He touched her cheek and stepped to the ground, the pain in his eyes piercing her. If she correctly interpreted the look he gave her as love, why hadn't he said anything after all these years? He'd had plenty of opportunities. What hindered his declaration? Did he intend to move the relationship forward, or was he content to remain her best friend?

Victoria watched her loved ones grow smaller as the train pulled away from the station. She leaned her head against the cool glass and smoothed away a furtive tear.

"Are you okay, Vicky?" Abby asked, brushing at her own tears.

"Yes. Just a little nervous."

"I heard you mention *lessons* just before we boarded. Will we be takin' classes then?"

Victoria turned toward her friend. "No. The lessons Miguel taught me followed shortly after my announcement to travel to Denver. When I finally felt I could control my emotions after the big reveal at the church picnic, I went to the ranch to talk to Miguel and Elizabeth at a time when I knew Tony wouldn't be there."

"Ah. What happened?"

Victoria sighed and leaned back. "Get comfortable, Abby. We'll be awhile." She began to relate the story.

"My dear, you've lost weight," Elizabeth hugged her.

"I know. I haven't felt much like eating. I'm better, though."

Miguel seated her, brought her tea and an apple turnover, and asked what plans she'd made for her trip.

"Uncle Mark said he'd provide my rail line tickets from Amarillo to Denver. He said I would be a guest at his home. Apparently, his elder sister lives with him. Imagine that. I have an aunt I never knew existed."

The question of why she'd been brought to Texas instead of being sent to her blood relatives again surfaced. Soon, she hoped she would have answers.

"What do you know of this man, Victoria?" Miguel's clipped tones indicated his concern.

"From what I've found out by asking around and studying newspapers, he's invested heavily in the railroads and land. He's quite wealthy. From what little I've heard, he's a shrewd businessman."

"Shrewd businessmen may also be dishonest. Have you planned for this eventuality, little Victoria?"

"Yes. I'll not remain long with him if he's dishonest or ungentlemanly. I have the names and addresses of several hotels and boarding houses with the reputation of being clean, well run, and safe, as well as the price each charges. A lady I met in Amarillo gave me a lot of the information. She travels back and forth to Denver with her husband for business. Because of her, I know how much a ticket home costs. I'll keep money in reserve for an emergency. I've been frugal with the salary Mary and John pay me for working in the store. I've saved for five years, so money shouldn't be an issue if I'm careful." Victoria studied Miguel from across the table. "I must say, your calm acceptance of my plans has surprised me. I thought you'd try to stop me."

Victoria had seen the way Miguel operated in other dealings—formidable. If he'd caught wind of the plans forming in her mind after she'd discovered she had an uncle in Denver, he might have taken an active role in stopping her. The extreme caution and tact needed to deal with him had almost been beyond her twenty years' experience with people, and she wasn't certain her efforts had been entirely successful. She suspected Miguel knew she was up to something.

He seemed to consider his words before speaking, "Originally, those were my intentions, hija, when I listened to your conversations with merchants and others while we visited in Amarillo, but I have since decided against taking action. You are twenty. There comes a time in every man and woman's life when he or she is tried by the fires of hardship. I think you will soon experience this. How you respond will show your true character. No, my little one, I will not stop you, but neither will I help you."

Elizabeth stared at her husband with lifted eyebrows. "What do you mean, *querido*?"

"If Victoria runs into difficulties, she must determine what she needs to do to get herself out of them. Others should not be expected to solve her problems, nor must she cast blame. She must be willing to accept the consequences of her own actions." He looked in Victoria's eyes, one dark eyebrow lifted in question. "Are you prepared to do this?"

Victoria thought about his words for several moments and then nodded slowly. "I think so. I've been doing a lot of soul-searching since I got my uncle's telegrams, and I've realized some things about myself. I don't know if they're good or bad, but they just *are*."

"Like what?" Elizabeth wondered.

She tried to put words to her thoughts. "Maybe I'm more like John than I thought. I remember the comment you made when I came to the ranch to thank you for the kitten. I hoped you'd give me ideas where I should start in my quest for answers. Remember?"

"Not really. Remind me of our conversation."

"You asked me if I'd asked John these questions."

"And you said …?"

"I told you John and I talk very little because we have nothing in common other than work. He wouldn't go against Mary, in any case. Besides, I don't think he knows much."

"Ah, yes, then I asked you about talking to Sam or Arnie."

"Yes, and I told you I'd tried to talk to Sam, but he wasn't very helpful. You know how he is. Sam isn't all that interested in the past because he's a here-and-now creature. I couldn't imagine how you thought I could get any helpful information out of Arnie."

Elizabeth laughed. "Arnie surprises me sometimes. I thought you should try."

Victoria continued, "Then I wondered if I could find some record of my parents. Did they have a marriage license? Would there be a newspaper clipping relating the news of the accident or of their deaths? That's when

I determined to visit the newspaper office and search through past issues. You asked me why the answers were so important."

"I remember that part of our conversation. You said, 'I don't feel like I know my parents at all, and I want to. Who were they? What were they? What traits did I inherit from them? Who were my father's relatives? Where did he come from?'"

Victoria stirred uncomfortably. "Beth, I'm still restless knowing I can't account for large pieces of my early life. This feeling has increased. Too many loose ends and unanswered questions remain."

Elizabeth chuckled. "I know how disturbing this must be to someone with your personality."

"What do you mean?"

"My dear, you've always disliked loose ends of any kind. You demand that your environment is ordered and efficient." She smiled, softening her next words. "Just look at the painful cleanliness of your room and the order to be found in the store. As much as you probably dislike the idea, you and John share similar characteristics."

"What a truly revolting and frightening thought, Beth."

"Well, John doesn't have your eye for beauty, if this is any consolation. His is a sense of orderliness for the sake of utility, while yours is a sense of orderliness for the sakes of both efficiency and artistic feel."

Victoria mulled over Elizabeth's words. "You're right. I like order. I like the security and comfort a well-ordered life provides. If I could find the answers I need here, I'm not sure I'd go to all this trouble. Knowing I can't plan for or control all of the situations that may arise makes me terribly nervous."

"That's when you agreed to come to Amarillo with us."

Victoria glanced at Miguel, who studied her as she spoke. "I know I'll have to accept the consequences of my actions, Miguel, but I'm trying to think of ways to lessen or avoid difficulties if I can. I'm not a risk-taker to the extent Tony is."

Miguel's smile hinted at secret thoughts. "Antonio is not willing to risk certain things, mi'jita."

Victoria waited for an explanation, but Miguel didn't elaborate. Instead, he changed the subject. "Do you know how to fire a gun?

"No, but I've thought I should learn. I've heard certain parts of Denver are rife with corruption and gangster activity. If I had a small pistol or revolver I could keep with me, I'd feel more comfortable, especially if I knew how to use the weapon."

Miguel stood, strode to the gun cabinet, and pulled out a nickel-tinted revolver with walnut grips. "This will work. Come here, Victoria. You will have your first lesson."

She stood beside him and looked at the revolver in his hand as he pointed to the parts and talked about them.

"This is a Colt Single Action Army. The gun has often been called a 'Peacemaker,' because many law officers have carried them. The Colt is a single action, which means you must pull the hammer back before you pull the trigger. Just remember, little one, you cannot recall the shot once you pull the trigger. You cannot return a life once you have taken it."

She nodded at the seriousness of his tone, and he led her outside. "Come. You will learn to load and fire at a target before you return home today."

By the time she returned home, the wrist and fingers of her right hand ached from trying to control the recoil of the revolver, and her right arm felt leaden. Her ears rang from the percussion of the shots, but she was pleased. She could now point and fire without flinching or aiming, and she had begun to hit the target several times by the end of the lesson. Miguel had shown her how to load, clean, and care for the revolver. She planned to return the next day for more practice.

"So, you learned to shoot? Do you have the gun with you?" Abby's tone hinted at admiration.

"Yes. In my carpetbag."

"Good. 'Tis a comfort to know we have protection."

She and Abby stepped to the windows and waved a last goodbye as the train began to move. When they could no longer see their loved-ones, they looked at their surroundings and then at George, who said, "Please make yourselves comfortable. I will prepare lunch soon. If you need anything at all, let me know. I'm here to serve you."

Victoria glanced at Abby and recognized the same expression she probably wore on her own face. Being served by someone else was a new experience. Victoria had worked from a young age, and Abby had usually been on the serving end of things. What were they to do with a servant?

She paused and looked into the man's chocolate brown eyes. "Abby and I aren't accustomed to others waiting on us, and we're a little uncomfortable with the idea."

Abby nodded and stared at the big man.

George remained silent for several moments before he spoke, "I understand. However, if you are to survive Denver society, ladies, you must learn how the people within this circle think. All of the wealthy have servants, and Mr. Silverthorne moves in the elite circles." George's face, tone, and posture indicated his loyalty to the Silverthornes.

Victoria glanced at Abby before speaking. "I'm afraid we'll need instruction. Are you willing to give this to us? We don't want to make any grotesque social faux pas, but I can assure you Abby and I are fast learners."

He didn't speak for several moments. The girls waited. Finally, he nodded. "This shall be done."

"So, what's next, Mr. Spearman?" Abby's eyes shone.

George shook his head and returned her smile. "First, you must call me George, Miss Abby. In a while, after the train reaches a steady speed, I will prepare your lunch."

"Miss Abby," she repeated and grinned at them both. "I could get used to hearin' that."

For a while, Victoria and Abby watched the landscape pass. Victoria had ridden fast horses but had no memories of riding a train. Abby said she and her parents had ridden many trains as they journeyed to the United States from Ireland, but she'd never traveled in such comfort.

"George, will you tell us about yourself?" Victoria asked.

He hesitated. Perhaps he gauged her sincerity before replying.

"I grew up in the northeast as a grandson of freed slaves. Through the work of different organizations, I received a limited education before I had to work to help support my mother and brothers."

"If your education is so limited, how do you speak so well?" Victoria couldn't resist the question.

George continued preparing lunch as he answered, "Thank you, miss. I was young when I realized people who don't speak in a manner as educated as others are often looked down upon or judged unfairly because of their speech. I determined to change this in my life. I've been fortunate enough to work for wealthy and educated people. I listened and learned to mimic their speech patterns. When I could, I listened in on the lessons when the children worked with their tutors."

Victoria marveled at his confession. She didn't know of anyone else who'd done such a thing. She watched the man for another moment and then turned and studied a large wall map. "George, how fast do you think we're moving?"

"Between fifty and sixty miles per hour." He didn't look up from his task.

"And how many miles from Amarillo to Denver?" Victoria kept her eyes on the map.

"About four hundred and forty miles."

She traced the route they would take. They'd travel northwest to the Texas–Oklahoma–New Mexico border and would then cross into southeastern Colorado at Trinidad. From there, they'd travel north to Pueblo, Colorado Springs, and then Denver. Victoria calculated quickly. "So, theoretically, we should arrive in Denver in about nine hours?"

George brought lunch to the table. "Realistically, the trip will take us a day, Miss Victoria. We must take on fuel, water, and passengers. You will be in Denver on Friday afternoon, barring snowstorms or other unforeseen happenings."

Panic threatened to choke Victoria. "That doesn't give us much time to learn what we need to know. Perhaps you should begin our instruction after lunch."

After lunch, the three talked for hours. George provided necessary information about Denver, Mark and Bella Silverthorne, and the people with whom they associated. He seemed to choose his words carefully when describing his employers, and Victoria understood. He didn't know her or Abby well, and he didn't want any thoughtless words of his to come back to haunt him. She suspected Mark Silverthorne was a powerful man who could make this man's life very difficult.

Each time the train stopped during the day, both girls felt grateful to leave the Pullman for a breath of fresh air, even though the frigid air caused them to shiver under their clothing. They watched as passengers with white, black, brown, and yellow skins—people from all walks of life—boarded. Poor and not-so-poor men, women, and children traveled together. Businessmen sat with frontiersmen, Indians with immigrants, and inhabitants of every region of the country encountered one another when traveling by rail.

Abby identified immigrants from Ireland, Sweden, and Germany. She'd traveled with many such on her way from Ireland to America. All were strangers to one another, and many of their behaviors, clothing, and habits seemed strange to Victoria.

She asked Abby about her experiences traveling by train, and Abby said, "If you travel by rail, you can expect to spend much time in the company o' others. Often, you start to identify these people by their personal habits. You should not expect to have any privacy. Everyone in your car can observe you talk, read, eat, and sleep. You breathe the smoke of others, as well as listen to the arguing, complaining, and fighting o' people from all over the world."

"Your words echo the comments I heard from others when I planned my trip. I made several trips into Amarillo and spoke to many I knew who traveled by train. One merchant's wife said, 'You either freeze or bake depending on where you're sitting.' Another said, 'If the wooden cars don't catch on fire from the stoves and cause your death, then you may well think you're dying from the cigar smoke that's so thick in the car you can cut the air with a knife. Sometimes the men can be convinced to put down a window, but then the icy air rushes in and makes the babies cry.'"

Abby nodded. "Yes, and with everyone huddled around the stove, you can smell the unwashed bodies of your traveling companions. Some of them haven't washed in months. The odor is enough to make a person sick for days." Abby blushed. "What I can't get used to is having to do personal things like eating, washing, and sleeping in such a public setting. Good thing we have our own car. We won't experience such hardships."

"I know. I plan to express my gratitude to Uncle Mark when I see him. I'm not sure why he sent his Pullman instead of the promised tickets, but I intended to enjoy the comfort of the luxurious car."

After dinner, Victoria found the stories of two authors in a small cabinet serving as a bookcase. She thought she might entertain George and Abby by reading parts of them aloud. *Home as Found*, by James Fenimore Cooper, was published in 1838, and *The Celestial Road*, by Nathaniel Hawthorne, was published in 1843.

Victoria read aloud into the night and throughout the morning of the next day. Cooper seemed to have written his novel to denigrate the values of a society in which greed and vanity born of new wealth had replaced moral values, compassion, and loyalty. Abby gave her opinion of, and agreement with, many of the points, while George listened in silence.

Hawthorne compared the experience of the railroad passenger to that of the religious seeker named Christian depicted in John Bunyan's *Pilgrim's Progress*. He managed to find parallels between almost all of Christian's trials of faith and the experiences of the average railroad passenger of the 1840s.

Victoria grinned as she read the cleverly written tale. Hawthorne believed internal improvements, poor service in stations, unsafe tracks, dangerous locomotives, crowds, and even the cities protecting themselves from the hazards of the rail all had a part in the plight of this fictional railroad passenger.

"I thank the good Lord things have changed over the last fifty years." Abby looked at the plushness of the car.

"Yes, perhaps my uncle took the writings of Cooper and Hawthorne to heart when he became involved in the railroad." Victoria replaced the books in the cabinet and sat down to the lunch George had prepared.

"How much longer?" Abby looked toward the map.

"About two-and-one-half hours, Miss Abby."

"Then what will happen?" Victoria had a difficult time getting the question around the tightening of her throat.

"A closed carriage will await us at the station. I will drive you and Miss Abby to the main house where your aunt, and maybe your uncle, will be waiting."

At Victoria's questioning look, George continued, "Mr. Silverthorne is often away from home. Business demands much of his time."

Victoria hoped Uncle Mark could find enough time in his schedule to answer some of her questions, and that he and Aunt Bella would become real family.

THREE

Denver, Colorado
Late November 1894

Mark Silverthorne looked over the rim of his coffee cup at his eldest and only living sister as she sat across from him at the breakfast table. She was fifty to his thirty-three years, but had aged gracefully, as their mother had. Gray streaked her dark brown hair, which she wore atop her head in a conservative but stylish manner. Middle-aged spread had only minimally thickened her waist, but corsets and the elegant day gown of rich brown wool hid any minor problems.

"Are you sure you're doing the right thing, Mark?" Her soft, cultured voice matched her outward elegance.

Emerald eyes met emerald eyes. Mark shrugged, sipped his coffee, and cradled the cup in his hands. "This seemed to be the most efficient solution to me. We know James and Maggie had a girl-child who would now be about twenty."

Bella shook her head and sadness entered her voice. "How did we lose track of time? We sent little Victoria cards and gifts on her birthday, but she was too young to remember. So many years passed, and we lost touch. I suspect she never knew who we were, and the burdens and business of life seemed to get in the way. I lost track of her." She looked at her brother. "I'm glad she's coming, but I wonder why she wants to come?"

Mark couldn't stop his sarcastic smile or tone. "We'll soon see. I have a hard time believing she's coming just to make our acquaintance. Based on my vast experience with people, I expect she wants something."

"You're so skeptical."

He shrugged. "I learned my lessons at an early age, dear sister."

Bella changed the subject. "She's bringing a companion?"

"Yes. Victoria met a friend in Amarillo who will accompany her. I thought this would be the easiest for us both. I have no experience looking after young women, nor do you, so I'm hoping they will look after each other. Hopefully, they won't disturb our lives too much. We'll take them to some parties and show them the sights. Beyond that …"

"But you know they're coming from the plains of Texas. I don't want to sound like a snob or that I am disparaging them, but they probably don't have suitable attire for the parties we attend. They're most likely little country mice. Can you see them socializing or conversing with the businessmen, politicians, and their wives and daughters who move in our circle?"

Mark frowned. "You're probably right. I'm counting on you to take care of such matters, Bella, because I don't have the time or patience to deal with them. Let Sebastian know how much you'll need to rig them out. I'll let him know to plan for extra expenses through the holidays."

She nodded. "You found a gem, when you hired Sebastian. Though he's in his early twenties, he handles our money with a great deal of care and thoughtfulness. Such a quiet, trustworthy young man who is surprisingly skilled for his years."

"Which is why I pay him so well."

Bella changed the subject. "When will they arrive?"

"This Friday. Initially, I planned to send her a ticket, but then I had second thoughts about allowing James's and Maggie's daughter to travel in the regular cars. I decided to send my Pullman for her. I hope she will be pleasantly surprised. George will attend to the girls' needs while they travel by rail, as well as when they arrive."

The metropolis of Denver, now being touted as "The Queen City of the Plains," silenced Victoria's words for a time and created discomfort in her middle. From what she could see in the fading light, unimaginable numbers of people lived and breathed together at the eastern base of the towering Rocky Mountains. She felt small and again questioned her judgment.

"Abby," Victoria whispered, "have you seen anything like this?"

"Yes. Bristol. London. New York. Chicago."

The girls gazed at the lighted, busy streets and tall buildings in awe as they drove toward Capitol Hill. The Silverthorne estate nestled between others owned by many of Denver's wealthiest. Some of these structures stood at the height of three to five stories, and dwarfed the nearby, smaller buildings.

"What will be the hardest thing for you, Abby?"

She chuckled. "Pretendin' to belong to these exalted circles. Though I have an education and have worked hard for my wages, I canna' claim to have friends who can afford their own Pullman, though I saw many wealthy people as we traveled through Europe on our way to America. Money brings different expectations." Abby squeezed Victoria's hand and whispered, "A word to the wise, Vicky. Don't let these people know how overwhelmed you are. Act as if you see this every day o' your life."

"Why?" Victoria tried to make out her friend's face in the dark.

"Because they'll judge you the moment you step foot in their homes. Trust me. They'll be sizin' you up to see if you're worthy enough to belong to them, and part of what they value is the appearance of culture."

"Do you think I did the right thing in coming?" Victoria continued the whispered conversation. "I'm not so sure anymore."

"Only you can answer your question. I'm just grateful you wanted me along. This adventure has the feel o' bein' a life-changin' experience for me."

Snow had begun to fall by the time George drove them down the drive to the main doors. Before he could jump down from the carriage, two other young men servants came out of the house to help with the unloading. George gave the men instructions as he escorted Victoria and Abby through the main door to the large foyer where an older woman with graying hair awaited them.

George bowed and said, "Miss Silverthorne, I have brought you Miss Victoria Silverthorne and her friend, Miss Abigail O'Brien."

Bella looked in Victoria's eyes and cried, "Oh, my dear. You look so much like your sweet mother I would know you anywhere." She clasped Victoria to her. "Please, come in and be warm." Bella turned to Abby. "You're welcome here as well, Abigail."

Abby curtsied. "Thank you, mum. Please call me Abby."

"Let me show you to your rooms, my dears. I'm sure you'll want to rest and freshen up before dinner. Mark will join us soon. Oh, I'm so glad you've finally arrived. I wish to know so much."

Bella led them up a flight of stairs to two large, adjoining bedrooms. The rooms were clean, expensively decorated, and comfortably arranged. A fire and down comforter beds welcomed each girl to her room.

"You'll share the water closet located between your rooms. I hope you'll be comfortable. Please rest. I'll send one of the servants to fetch you to dinner in an hour."

After Bella closed the door, Abby motioned for Victoria to join her at the water closet.

Abby opened the door. "Oh, my. Would you look at that bathtub? The thing is big enough to hold two people. And the water is piped in, and the privy is … is …" Descriptive words failed Abby at the sight of the shining enamel toilet, and she shook her head. "If only me dear mum could see this."

"Well, I don't know about you, but I'm going to use that big tub before dinner." Victoria pointed to the shining tub and offered her friend a warm smile.

"Aye. I'll run your bath and then use the water when you're finished."

"No, you won't, Abby," Victoria's words stopped her. "I'll run my own water. You're my friend, not a maid. Remember?"

Abby blinked. "Well, then, I'll rest on me huge bed until you're finished, then I'll try the tub. Do you think there may be any nice-smellin' bath salts?"

"There." Victoria pointed. "On a stand next to the tub."

The luxurious white towels laid out ready for use were soft, clean, and abundant.

Abby sighed and lifted one of the towels to her face. "'Tis truly as close to a heavenly experience as I'll find on earth, Vicky."

Victoria agreed before shewing her friend from the room so she could enjoy her bath. Victoria soaked in the hot, bubbly, scented water for thirty minutes before surrendering the tub to her friend.

"Don't drown in there, Abby," she joked as her friend turned on the hot water faucet and slipped into the water.

Victoria dressed in the emerald green dress Mary and John had given her for her seventeenth birthday. She hadn't had much opportunity to wear their gift, and she hoped the lovely dress would meet with Aunt Bella's approval. She added the gold nugget necklace Arnie and Sam had given her for the same birthday.

While she waited for Abby, Victoria sat in front of the elegant vanity mirror and combed her long, black hair. Though she looked in the mirror, her thoughts focused on that special birthday three years ago.

Orville Sebastian, a classmate, thought she should have a kiss for her birthday. She'd rather admired Orville at the time. He could do complicated mental calculations at incredible speeds. Even though he was a little pudgy and had spots on his face, his wavy blond hair and honest blue eyes attracted her. Being two years older, he had graduated the year before. He and his family recently sold their ranch and planned to leave at the end of the week.

She and Orville stood under a shade tree behind the store when Victoria agreed to the kiss. She watched with interest as he gulped a few times then put his hands on her shoulders. She felt how damp his hands were through the thin cotton of her blouse. What would he do next?

He shut his eyes, puckered, and planted a kiss on her mouth. The kiss felt warm, wet, and soft—rather like the slobbering of an excited puppy—and Victoria wanted to wipe the kiss away immediately. She was too polite to do so while he stood in front of her, though.

At that moment, Tony stepped from behind the trees. He smiled, but one corner of his mouth curled as he looked at Orville.

"Where did you come from?" she demanded and wiped her mouth.

He brushed an untamable lock of dark hair away from his chocolate-brown eyes and shrugged.

"*Mamá* looks forward to your birthday celebration this evening, Victoria. She has prepared your favorite meal. She expects you and the Keesons at five o'clock *en punto*."

Victoria nodded and Orville said goodbye. Tony walked her home, but had said nothing about the kiss, if he'd seen, and she hoped he wouldn't. She preferred to forget the experience.

That evening, Victoria rode with the Keesons to the Morales ranch. She wore the new emerald-green dress, as well as the gold nugget necklace Sam and Arnie had presented to her. She'd twisted her hair into a French roll, which made her feel grown up and ready to celebrate.

When she entered the Morales home, she smiled her appreciation. Elizabeth had filled the rooms with wildflowers and had brought out her best china. Miguel wore his dress suit in honor of the occasion, and looked the charming *caballero* in his short, embroidered black jacket, close-fitting cream-colored pants, white shirt, and string tie.

They sat down to a delicious, candle-lit dinner. John had promised Mary and Victoria, somewhat grudgingly, he would be on his best behavior. As a result, the evening filled with comfortable small talk. As the meal progressed, however, Victoria's anticipation and impatience grew. She struggled to keep her hands and feet still as the others finished their meal.

"And now, my little Victoria, I have a gift for you." Miguel stood and brought a large wrapped package to her.

She unwrapped the brown wrapping paper and fingered a soft wool blanket. The intricate and elegant designs along the edges spoke of skilled craftsmanship. Miguel must have sent to Mexico for her gift. "Oh, this is beautiful. *¡Muchísimas gracias!* Thank you so much, Miguel." She hugged him.

"Sí. I often use mine for a saddle blanket." He winked at Tony.

Elizabeth gave her a bottle of expensive perfume and said, "Happy birthday, darling." She, too, smiled and looked at her son.

Miguel stood and led Victoria to Tony. "And now, little one, if you will accompany Antonio to the barn, you will see the rest of your gift."

With great formality, Tony offered his arm. "Come with me, señorita."

As the two friends walked across the yard, the barn doors stood open, and Victoria tried to peek inside.

"No, no. You must close your eyes and allow me to lead you."

She did so, and Tony took her by the hand and led her forward. When they seemed to be a few paces inside the barn, Tony let go of her hand and told her to wait while he lit a lantern.

She heard the match strike and the hiss of the candle taking flame and then Tony said, "You may open your eyes."

There, standing before her in golden glory was the palomino gelding Tony had been training for the past months. The horse wore a new leather bridle and shining bits. Tony had obviously brushed him as the pony's coat shone and his mane had been braided with emerald-green ribbons. The horse nickered when he saw them.

In awe, she approached the gelding and rubbed his soft nose.

"Tony, you're really giving Dorado to me?"

"Truly." Tony's smile could be seen in the dimness. He stepped closer and ran his hand over the horse's shoulder. "You may keep him here if you like."

"I don't know what to say. Dorado's the best gift I've ever had. Thank you."

Tony's smile tilted at one corner. She knew that mischievous look well. "Perhaps you should give me a kiss in return for such a lovely gift, no?"

"You *were* watching me today." The fire rose up her neck and into her cheeks. "Tony, how could you?"

"Easily. I wanted to see the skill level of your friend." Tony's expression saddened, and he shook his head. "He does not understand the fundamentals."

"And I suppose you do?" Victoria couldn't keep the scorn out of her voice.

His smile crinkled the corners of his eyes. "Most assuredly."

"Antonio? Will you remain in the barn all night?" Miguel called from the house. "The Keesons wish to leave *al rato*. Please bring their wagon."

Tony grimaced and said something in rapid Spanish under his breath. The tone didn't sound appreciative, but the words came too soft and fast for Victoria to hear and understand. "Sí, Papá. We are coming," he said in a louder voice.

"Why are you smilin' like that, Vicky?" Abby toweled her wet hair as she stepped into the bedroom.

The heat rose in Victoria's face as she turned back to the mirror. "Nothing I'm willing to repeat."

"Uh-huh. That look had Antonio Morales's name written all over it."

"Really?"

Abby nodded. "He had the same look on his face when you walked down the stairs of the hotel in your new, blue velvet dress. I'll never forget that day. You and Tony provided hours of entertainin' talk for me and me hard workin' mum."

Victoria grimaced. "I'm glad you were amused. I don't remember the situation being so enjoyable. In fact, breathing and controlling my shaking hands were the only things I could think about at the time. Everyone in the restaurant stared at me, Abby. They made me so nervous, I wondered if I'd trip or drop food on my new gown."

Abby tossed the towel onto the bed and plopped down in a comfortable chair. She grinned. "Yes. I watched from the stairs. All conversation in the dining room stopped as Tony led you to the table and seated you." Abby laughed. "One o' those rich old cattlemen dropped his spoon in his soup when you walked into the room like the Queen of Sheba. The other men looked like they intended to catch flies, their jaws dropped so far, and their mouths opened so wide. I've never laughed so much."

Victoria turned and looked at Abby. "I don't know how I survived that dinner. I'm sure whatever we ate was delicious, but all those stares took away my appetite."

"And then to see how Tony changed before me eyes." Abby laughed so hard she clutched her middle.

"What do you mean?" Victoria's hand stilled.

"Didn't you notice his posture and expression?"

"No."

"When he saw the reaction of the men in the dining room, he stood straighter and squared his shoulders. Like this," she said and modeled. "I could've sworn he grew an inch. The attitude leakin' from his skin could be seen at a distance. 'You men who think to approach my woman had best think again.' Every male in the place understood each word he didn't say."

Victoria shook her head. "Tony's always been protective even when I didn't need protecting."

"What did he say in Spanish when you reached him at the bottom of the stairs? After he spoke the first words, he said, 'Well done. Without a doubt, I will have to fight off the wolves tonight.'" Again, Abby modeled Tony's tone and posture that Friday night when he'd met her and his parents at the Amarillo hotel for dinner.

Victoria blushed and shook her head again. "I don't remember. He says many things to me in Spanish."

"The words sounded like *air-moh-sah-mee-ah*."

¡Hermosa mía! My beautiful one. Color rose in Victoria's cheeks as she translated.

Abby nodded and poked a finger in her direction. "He loves you."

"I hope so, Abby, but he hasn't said anything. From the time we were children, he's always spoken to me in such a manner, so I don't know how much he speaks from habit and how much is from his heart. He doesn't appear to want to move the relationship further than friendship."

"Well, I'll never forget that night in Amarillo." Abby began braiding her damp hair.

"I won't either, even though those rude stares bothered me. I do remember Tony relaxed after the other diners returned to their meals. I sensed the stress leaving him and wondered why he was so uptight. I was the one wearing the dress."

"Oh, I can tell you why. I watched from the stairs and enjoyed every minute of the drama. When Tony noticed all the attention you got from the men in the room, he seemed ready to fight. Those men gave him measurin', speculative looks, before they turned their eyes back to you. Tony lifted his chin, and his muscles tightened. He met their eyes, look-for-look. A blind man could've sensed the challenge he offered."

"At least something good came out of that evening." Victoria smiled. "You became my friend, and I learned more about my uncle from overhearing a conversation at the next table."

"Tell me again how you heard about your uncle. Seems a remarkable coincidence to my way o' thinkin'—almost like a miracle." Abby leaned back and sighed in expectation of a good tale. "I never get tired o' hearin' your stories, Vicky. Your life seems much more interestin' than mine, though I've nothin' to complain about."

"I doubt this is the case, but I'll humor you even though you were there. You know what happened."

"Yes, but I want you to fill in the details for me—they're the most entertainin' part."

Victoria rolled her eyes. "Okay. Get comfortable."

"I am. Now tell."

COLORADO TREASURE

Victoria glanced around the dining room after she'd taken her seat, and her heartbeat returned to a normal rate. The other diners finally began to focus on their food and tablemates instead of her. Miguel and Elizabeth started a conversation about the mundane things of home. This conversation soon led to one of Miguel's stories about his travels, which somehow led to the topic of the New Mexico land grant battles. A comment he made about the early Spaniards in the area caught Victoria's attention and refocused them away from her discomfort. She remembered the books and manuscripts she'd found in the attic after she'd decided to search more thoroughly for information about her parents. Some of the papers included entries about this very same topic. Again, she wondered about her parents. Why would such topics interest them?

She tried to concentrate on the conversation, wondering how much helpful information Miguel had. Would he be willing to share this information even if he suspected she was up to something? She studied him as he spoke. He loved her, but this fact would not stop him from telling her the truth or checkmating what he might perceive as her possibly dangerous activities. After she'd read the newspaper article, ideas and possibilities percolated, and she suspected he wouldn't approve of any of them. Regardless, she intended to find answers.

The words from the paper were burned into her memory.

August 23, 1879

Two of our prominent citizens, John and Mary Keeson, are now caring for an orphaned cousin, Victoria Silverthorne.

Five-year-old Victoria lost both of her parents in a mining accident near Silverton, in the rugged mountains of Southwestern Colorado. James and Margaret Silverthorne had been living in Denver City, Colorado. Sam Johnson and Arnie Gilford, local residents returning from a trip to Colorado, accompanied the Silverthornes at the time of their deaths.

"Watching the face of the mountain fall, and then to see the valley buried in tons of red dirt was terrible to behold. Arnie and me feared for our lives," Mr. Johnson stated.

Memorial services were held at the Cherry Creek Chapel in Denver City. Mark Silverthorne, James's brother, requested donations be made to the history department of the University of Denver.

The article created new questions. Did she have paternal aunts and cousins as well? What about grandparents? Was Mark Silverthorne still alive? Why had she been sent to Mary and John instead of her paternal uncle? Denver was much closer than the Texas Panhandle. How did Sam know her parents? What, exactly, was Sam and Arnie's purpose in being with the Silverthornes? Neither Sam nor Arnie were miners.

As they finished their meal, she glanced around. Diners had turned their attention to other things. The noise level had risen to a comfortable level, but a conversation she overheard at the next table stunned her. Three men spoke about how the railroads' investors had actively promoted the growth of towns and farming along their lines. They spoke of how they'd pioneered the control of wind erosion by furnishing trees and tree seedlings for windbreaks, and how they had urged the introduction of cotton to the Texas plains to help the farmers diversify. These investors also promoted the use of winter wheat as food for cattle and became involved with experimental farms.

"... and," one of the men spoke, admiration in his tone, "that Mark Silverthorne is one busy man. He has his fingers in several of these pies and is settin' up in his Denver office makin' money hand-over-fist."

The man's words created a tornado of thoughts. Could there possibly be two people with such an uncommon last name living in Denver? She had to know.

While Miguel paid the ticket and Tony and Beth conversed, she made a show of gathering her things, and then turned so she could look at the three men without being obvious.

"Excuse me, sirs," she spoke softly. She had their immediate attention. "I couldn't help but overhear your conversation. Did you say Mark Silverthorne?"

They nodded.

"Where would a person find Mr. Silverthorne in Denver?"

"Hard to say, ma'am. He travels a great deal, but a person could get a message to him at the Union Railroad office."

"Thank you," she whispered, and then allowed Tony to escort her from the room.

The theater had been packed that evening, but Victoria couldn't have told anyone the name of the play or the plot had they asked. As she watched the actors move their lips, she heard only the thoughts in her head. Her uncle was alive and in Denver. She was sure of this. The pieces fit. He was involved with the railroad and traveled often, and she didn't know if he'd want to hear from her, but she had every intention of contacting him. The only questions were how and when she could do this without raising a lot of dust.

Victoria was exhausted as the play ended, and she gladly returned to her room. Abby waited for her there and helped her undress, then began brushing her hair. Victoria shared the startling news and, though interested, Abby seemed disappointed she didn't want to talk about the grand entrance she'd made earlier in the evening.

"Wait, I know how to do this." Victoria looked at Abby's reflection in the mirror.

"Do what?" Abby continued to brush Victoria's hair.

"Get a message to my uncle." Victoria spun around on the vanity stool and clasped Abby's hand. "Abby, if I give you the money for a telegram, would you send the message on Monday?"

"Aye. I think I can slip away at lunch time."

The dream didn't haunt Victoria that evening, and when the Morales's were ready to return home the next day, she felt rested and ready to go. She walked and talked with an air of subdued excitement. She observed the questioning looks Miguel and Tony exchanged, and smiled when Beth said, "Going home is always the best, right, darling?"

Victoria nodded and wondered how her life and idea of home might change soon.

⚬⚬⚬⚬

"So, what did you do after you left the hotel and returned home?"

"I started asking questions. I figured if I asked the right questions, the answers might lead me to more important clues."

"What did you ask?"

"How well did I truly know Sam? Would I get straight answers from him and Mary if I asked them point-blank questions? I thought not, because this strategy hadn't been successful in the past. Then I decided to interview Arnie."

Abby chuckled. "How did that go?"

"As you might expect, though I did learn something."

Victoria sat on the bench next to Arnie and watched him carve a miniature horse. She shifted to catch more shade. "Arnie," she asked after several moments of comfortable silence. "Do you remember much about my parents?"

Arnie stopped whittling and scratched his head as if he were thinking. "Don't reckon I do, Miss Vicky. I only met them when we picked up supplies in Silverton."

"Silverton? Where's Silverton?"

"Colorado. Only a day or two away from where they—" He looked at her with sad eyes and squirmed on the bench. "I better not talk about this. Sam told me not to because you might cry."

"I'm not going to cry, Arnie. The accident happened a long time ago, but I do feel a little sad because I don't know much about my folks. Can you help me? Can you tell me what my parents were like?"

Arnie frowned as he tried to focus on his memories. "Your pa was tall and skinny, kinda like me. I think his hair was dark, but not as dark as your ma's."

Victoria leaned forward. "Arnie, do I look most like Mama or Dad?"

He tilted his head and studied her face. "I'd say you look more like your ma, but you have your pa's eyes."

"Do you know why they were at that place?"

"No, I don't reckon I do. Sam didn't tell me."

Disappointment filled Victoria. Talking to Arnie seemed almost as difficult as talking to a fence post. "Can you tell me anything about them? I'd like to understand what kind of people they were."

He pulled on his bottom lip and thought for several moments. "Your pa did a might of readin'. He always had some kind of journals and books with him. He used big words—words only Sam and your ma understood."

"What about Mom? What was she like?"

Arnie looked up from his carving and studied her. "Well, she was your size and coloring—except for the eyes. I think hers were blue. She had a lot of energy and would still be going when we were half dead. Every night by the campfire, she'd write things in a book."

Victoria touched Arnie's arm. "What kind of book?"

"A thin, dark green one. Weren't as big as the Bible she had."

A sliver of excitement slipped up Victoria's spine. The Bible. She remembered the Bible. For a small moment, she caught a fleeting impression of her mother's hand turning the paper-thin pages. Victoria had admired the graceful movement of her hand and had liked the soft rustlings of the pages as her mother turned them. She remembered the melodic tones of her mother's voice as she read the Scriptures aloud. Victoria had been fascinated with the small picture or flourishing letter at the beginning of each book, and the first word she'd ever read, *God*, had come from that Bible.

"Arnie, what happened to the Bible? To the books?" Victoria grasped his hands. "Think carefully. The information is important. Do you remember what happened to them?"

Arnie squinted his eyes closed. "No, I don't remember, but I know we brought most of them back with us when we came here." He opened his eyes and smiled. "Maybe Sam would know."

Victoria had an idea. She kissed Arnie's cheek before standing. "Thanks. You've been helpful."

Her search led her to the Keesons' attic to an old, dusty trunk. Though she found a daguerreotype of her parents and their papers and manuscripts inside, she hadn't found the green journal or Bible.

However, not long after her visit to the local newspaper office, the Bible had shown up unexpectedly and under suspicious circumstances. Soon after, Victoria began making plans to leave. Why, after all these years, had someone decided to send her the missing Bible? Where had this treasure been, who had kept it, and why did they decide to send the Bible to her via the bank's messenger boy?

Abby frowned and sat up in the chair. "Just when you'd told everyone you were leavin', the Bible showed up? Not an accident, if you ask me.

Someone you know had this and sent the book to you through a messenger boy to avoid suspicion."

Victoria nodded. "But who?"

"You found no note?"

"No. Whoever wrapped the Bible in brown paper and printed my name in block letters on the outside didn't want to be known."

Abby thought for a moment. "Could Mary be the sender?"

Victoria stood and climbed onto the bed. "No. Mary was furious when the Bible showed up. She muttered the whole afternoon about busybodies and trouble makers then huffed off to complain to John when he came in for dinner."

Abby moved from the chair to sit on the end of the bed. "John? Do you think he'd had it?"

"I don't know how or why he would've had my mother's Bible, do you? I've never seen him show more than a passing interest in anything other than his ledgers and business magazines." Victoria stared at Abby as if her friend might understand something she didn't.

"What about Sam or Arnie?"

"Arnie has no idea what happened to the books and papers after we left the mountains."

Abby shrugged. "Then that leaves Sam."

"But why would he do such a thing, Abby? I can't come up with a single reason that will hold water. Keeping such a thing and not telling me isn't in his nature."

Abby frowned. "I don't know him enough to know his nature, but he brought you out of the mountains fifteen years ago. He's not getting any younger, so maybe he forgot until he heard you were looking for the Bible and was too embarrassed to say anything. Maybe Arnie told him about your conversation."

Victoria considered her friend's suggestion. "Hmm. Maybe." Her stomach growled. "I don't know about you, Abby, but I'm ready for dinner. I hope we don't have to linger, because I'm tired."

"I agree. Shall I do your hair first, or will you do mine?"

Victoria hopped off the bed and walked to the vanity. She lifted the comb and pointed to the stool. "I'll do yours. Sit."

FOUR

Abby had dressed for dinner in a warm, earthy brown dress cuffed and collared in a creamy linen. Victoria stood next to her in a midnight blue dress that brought out the bluish highlights in her black hair. She studied their reflections in the glass of a tall cheval mirror. "How lovely, Abby. The color causes the golden highlights of your hair to glow."

"Aye," Abby said with a pat to her pinned up hair. "'Tis the product of me mum's clever needle."

A serving girl led them to an ornate dining room the likes of which neither of them had seen before outside of hotels. Bella chatted with an athletic-looking man who stirred the fire as he listened to her words. His dark brown dinner jacket emphasized the man's muscular back. When George announced the women, both Bella and the man turned. Three pairs of emerald eyes met.

Shock coursed through Victoria. The man looked like a younger version of her father. She knew without a doubt this was her uncle, though he looked much younger than she'd expected. He might be only fifteen years her senior—which, she suddenly realized, might explain why she was not sent to live with him at the time of her parents' death. But what about Aunt Bella? She seemed obviously older than her uncle. Why hadn't she sent for Victoria to live with her?

"Victoria." The man strode across the expensive Persian rug to meet her.

"Uncle Mark?" Victoria greeted him in a soft voice and held out her hand. "You look like my father."

"And you are a replica of your mother, except," he smiled, "you inherited the Silverthorne eyes. Welcome to my home, niece."

COLORADO TREASURE

From the Silverthorne Mansion, Capitol Hill

December 3, 1894

Dearest Mum,

We arrived safely. I wish you and the boys could be here. In some ways, Denver reminds me o' Europe. The Denverites have taken to buildin' their buildin's after the romantic style o' some of the mansions I've seen in London and Ireland.

Miss Vicky and I saw the Windsor Hotel at Eighteenth and Larimer. Mum, you should see this *buildin'! 'Tis* five stories high an' has a bathroom on every floor. No more luggin' water up and down the stairs. Think on it. There are Brussels carpets on the floor, English china, French mirrors, and private baths. But the moneyed gentry wants bigger and better. Two years ago, Mr. Henry Brown built a ten-story buildin' called the Brown Palace. The place has a skylight lobby atrium the full height of the building, mind you. You wouldna' believe, but inside, there is a bowlin' alley, a library, and a women's dinin' room.

We saw the Tabor Block too. 'Tis a five-story development at the corner of Sixteenth and Larimer. After this, Mr. Tabor ups and builds the Tabor Grand Opera House at Sixteenth and Curtis. The buildin' has a red brick outside with white limestone trim. Inside there's an elevator and a saloon with a glistenin' bar, tropical plants, and a ladies' orchestra. People come just to ride the elevator, though I doubt I'd be brave enough to step foot in the thing.

We live on Capitol Hill, Mum. 'Tis where many o' the gentry live. Mr. Silverthorne says a body can reach this area without crossin' either the South Platte River to the east or the bottomlands full of tracks and shacks. This area is much like any other you'd find in other large cities o' the world that are growin' faster than planned. Not all of the Denverites are rich, and some barely manage to stay alive. They come from all o'er the world to make their fortunes, but fortunes aren't to be had for the likes o' them. We've seen these shantytowns before, Mum. The people are much the same when they're poor and tryin' to keep body an' soul together any way they can.

The rooms they've given us are fit for princesses, and our bathtub could easily hold you, me, and the boys. Mum, when I make me fortune, I'm buyin' you a porcelain privy like the one they've got here. The thing is shiny and clean and a real pleasure to use.

You shouldna' worry I will have me head turned by all o' this. I'm takin' your advice. I know this is just a brief journey into fantasy, but 'tis fun while the trip lasts.

Kiss the boys for me.

Love, Abby

Abby sealed the letter and placed the envelope on a stand outside her door. A maid or one of George's underlings would take the letter to the post office that day. She then walked into Victoria's room to find her friend seated in the middle of the bed with pages of aged manuscripts strewn around her. The girls never closed the dividing door between them. The overpowering size of the house seemed a little friendlier when their bedroom doors remained opened.

"You'll be wearin' glasses before your time, me lass, if you keep squintin' in such a manner," Abby teased.

Victoria marked her place with a finger and smiled. George came in to stir up the fire and add more logs as Victoria spoke.

"These are some of the documents I found in my parents' trunk in Mary and John's attic. They had these papers with them in camp when they died. I'm trying to figure out what they were looking for when they went into that mine or cave."

"How do you know that's where they were?"

Victoria picked up another piece of paper and handed her the script. "After I decided to find answers to some questions, I went to the newspaper office and found this."

Abby read the notice of Victoria's parents' deaths.

"I copied each word from the announcement when I'd visited Lawrence Lucky's newspaper office. The strangeness of that visit still concerns me, Abby."

"Why?" She looked up from the notice.

"Mr. Lucky asked me some questions, and I gave him vague answers. I didn't want to give him the real reason I came, because I'm not sure I trust him. Gossip starts easily in a small town, you know. I didn't realize how evasive my answers must have sounded until I saw his suspicious expression."

"Tell me what happened."

The morning after she'd discovered the trunk, Victoria volunteered to do the errands Mary commonly did on Tuesdays. Tuesdays were usually slow, so she asked Mary for a few hours to do a little personal shopping. Mary had nodded without commenting.

The errands took only half an hour to complete, which gave Victoria a couple of hours to accomplish her private task. She walked to the town's only newspaper office and smiled at Lawrence, who busied himself preparing to set type for the weekly printing. Victoria noticed his sandy hair and freckles made him look younger than he probably was—she'd guess between twenty and thirty—but his intelligent brown eyes seemed to miss little.

"Well, well. Hello, Miss Silverthorne." His surprise raised his eyebrows. "How may I help you?"

"Hi, Mr. Lucky. I'm interested in doing a little historical research, and I thought you might be able to help me. Do you have any newspapers dating back fourteen or fifteen years?" Victoria knew he'd only been the editor for two years, but hoped he knew what might be available in their historical records.

"Yes. No one has ever requested them, but I do have collections of several newspapers I brought with me when I accepted this job. Previous editors also saved local papers for the past several years. Have a seat. If you give me an idea of what you want to know, perhaps I could save you some time."

Victoria's inner voice prompted her to caution. The small-town rumor mills could start at any time, and for any reason.

She smiled. "I'm not quite sure yet, but I'd be interested in anything you have on the Spanish presence in New Mexico territory, or about Silverton, Colorado."

Her answer made him blink. "You do know the Spanish presence in New Mexico territory occurred a few hundred years ago, not fourteen or fifteen?"

"What? Oh, yes. Sorry. I didn't mean to imply the two pieces of information I wanted were related." She tried to keep her hands from fidgeting, but she noticed her words appeared to have sparked his investigative reporter demeanor.

He provided her with a stack of newspapers, and she reached for pencil and paper. She jotted down anything she could find about Denver, mining in the area, or anything that might help her in her search.

Occasionally, she'd look up to find Lawrence Lucky watching her. He'd always turn away and busy himself with other things if he caught her eyes.

Victoria was about to give up after three hours, but her eyes landed on the word Silverthorne, and she sat up. At last. She read the article notifying the public of her parents' deaths and the existence of an uncle and aunt then copied the information with care

Later in the week, as she traveled with Beth and Miguel into Amarillo, the editor's suspicious look had stuck with her. In Amarillo, she spotted two newspaper offices—the *Amarillo Weekly News* and the *Amarillo Northwest*—as they toured the town and decided to search for more information there as well.

As she made her requests for newspapers, she had the strangest notion the editors knew she'd been coming. They handed her stacks of newspapers from the right years without having to search for them and didn't seem at all surprised by her requests. They showed her where she could sit and read, and then sat down at their own desks and began to work without further comment. Could Lawrence Lucky have been behind the responses she received?

How did they find the papers so quickly? She eyed the clerks, her suspicions raised, for another moment before taking out her notebook and pencil and noting anything she could find about Silverton, Colorado, mining, and railroad information in that area, or anything to do with Denver City.

She found no information about her parents, though she didn't expect to. She glanced up occasionally to find the eyes of the editor or one of his staff members on her but then they'd look away.

Later, she'd discovered Lawrence Lucky was staying at the same hotel as she and the Morales, which seemed too much of a coincidence to be believable. He'd even offered to escort her to her room. "Well, this may be a surprise to you, Miss Silverthorne, but it isn't to me," he'd said. "I've been planning this trip for several weeks. I must meet with editors from the local newspapers. I'm investigating some leads for an article I intend to write, and I'd hoped for an exchange of information."

His explanations seemed plausible, but were they? Had he followed her to Amarillo? And if he had, for what purpose?

"Ah, so that's how you found out about your uncle," Abby said as she handed Victoria back the newspaper article.

"That's when I knew I *had* an uncle. I didn't know how to find him until that night in Amarillo. Did I ever thank you for agreeing to send my telegram, Abby?"

Abby rolled her eyes. "Only fifty times."

Victoria frowned and looked at the yellowed pages on her lap. "The script is small and written in old Spanish on these documents, and I have a hard time understanding some of the words. I should let Miguel see these. He knows so much about everything." She sighed. "Much of the information is about a Spaniard named Don Diego de Vargas who was appointed captain-general and governor of New Mexico in 1691. He was charged with the territorial reconquest after the Pueblo revolts several years before. Apparently, the Indians had organized under the Tewa religious leader Popé to drive out the Spaniards. By the time Vargas took command, few Christian colonists remained in the area. Seems Vargas also worried about designs the French had on these northern provinces of Spain." Victoria rubbed her eyes. "Abby, I've read through several of these pages, and I still don't understand why my folks would carry this information with them over hundreds of miles, even to their deaths."

"'Tis my thought the manuscripts hold the key to what they searched for." Abby looked toward the wardrobe. "Do you remember we are to dine with the Silverthornes and some o' their guests this evenin'?"

Victoria nodded, but frustration touched her words as she answered. "I hoped I would have time to talk to Uncle Mark and Aunt Bella about my parents, but we've done nothing but see the sights for the last week. I haven't been able to find the right opportunity to ask the questions I need to ask. Uncle Mark comes home late and wants only his dinner and bed, and Aunt Bella is involved with so many things. The Christmas season approaches, and I still have no answers."

The girls chatted for a while longer before Abby took herself off to soak in the tub. Victoria gathered the papers while a chambermaid dusted the room. Victoria watched her for a moment and then said, "Charlotte, do the people around here ever request a pot of pinto beans cooked with onions, garlic, salt, pepper, and green chilies for lunch or dinner?"

The maid's horrified look tickled Victoria's sense of humor.

"Never, Miss Victoria. Beans grow between the toes of cows!"

Victoria laughed. "That's a line I'll have to remember. You don't know how delicious a scoop of hot *frijoles* can be on a warm, homemade tortilla, especially when the weather is cold and unpleasant. I miss the green chilies most of all. Green chilies made almost everything taste better."

The maid nodded but looked doubtful.

Within a few days of her arrival, Victoria had realized the rich foods and sweets available to the Silverthornes and their class on a daily basis upset her stomach. Though she liked to eat, she was used to simpler, more wholesome food. Aunt Bella had told both girls they could ask the cook to prepare for them whatever they wanted for breakfast or lunch since dinner was the only meal they ate together. Still, Victoria tended to avoid much of what they offered, and was able to do this in such a way Aunt Bella didn't notice.

At first, she and Abby had eaten breakfast and lunch together in the large dining room but didn't like the feeling of being dwarfed by the grandeur. Soon, they began eating in the warm, cozy kitchen instead, chatting with the cook as she prepared Bella and Mark's breakfasts. Cooky's thirteen-year-old deaf son, Tim, often sat at breakfast with them since he was on Christmas break and wouldn't return to his studies with a private tutor until the middle of January. His light, curly brown hair touched his collar, and his dark brown eyes sparkled with intelligence. He seemed shy in the beginning, but soon taught Victoria and Abby the rudiments of sign language. Victoria caught on quickly because some of the syntax of the language was similar to that of Spanish. She loved to play with the hand signs and hear Tim's gurgling laugh when she tried to sign a joke or tell of funny experiences back home. When she asked about his studies, he shrugged and told her of his love for mathematics but his dislike of Tutor Archibald. He'd worked with the same teacher since his first year of schooling.

Cooky scolded Tim when he complained and told him he should be grateful. "Mr. Archibald is a scholar and gentleman. We're lucky to find someone who also signs."

Tim shrugged and quickly turned the conversation back toward his new interest. He begged for stories of Texas and Dorado, of ranch life and Tony, which made Victoria homesick. Soon, she, Abby, and Tim became best friends.

Initially, Cooky acted horrified at the presence of the girls in her kitchen, but soon they convinced her that no matter how hard they tried, they could not break the habit of rising early, and they didn't like eating alone.

During their morning chats, Victoria found out about the guests they would have for their first official dinner party. Most of them were neighbors who lived on the Hill, and a few were businessmen and their wives.

"I doubt you'll enjoy yourselves much tonight," Cooky said. "There won't be any younger ones your age here until some of the Christmas parties begin in the next few weeks."

Victoria shrugged. "I didn't come here for parties, but for information."

Abby agreed. "And I came because Victoria asked."

"Don't worry, Cooky, we've entertained ourselves just fine during the last week. Haven't we, Abby?"

Her friend nodded and reached for one of the warm, chocolate chip cookies.

Later, after Victoria bathed, she stood in front of the wardrobe trying to decide what she should wear, while Abby lounged on the bed and told stories of her family.

Abby had piled her clean, sandy hair on top of her head and ringlets fell behind her ears and down her back. Victoria didn't know any girl as charming as Abby. Her friend snuggled into her long, cream-colored dressing robe and prepared to begin another story when Bella knocked on the door.

"Come in, Aunt Bella. I was trying to decide what to wear to dinner tonight. Perhaps you can help."

Bella examined the dresses Victoria had pulled from the wardrobe and selected a deep rose silk with short, puffed sleeves and a scooped neckline. The black satin waistband tied in a bow at the back and flowed over the long skirt. She handed the dress to Victoria and then chose a lacy, cream-colored gown for Abby.

"Your clothes are very stylish, and you look well in them. Your dressmakers are highly skilled." Bella held the garment closer to the lamp.

They both returned her smile, though Victoria knew Abby probably thought "*if you only knew me Mum and I are the dressmakers—*"

"I wondered if ..." Bella's words trailed off as she seemed to rethink what she wanted to say.

"What, Aunt Bella?"

The words rushed out then, "Well, I'm hoping you will allow me to give you both a Christmas gift of a shopping expedition. You would make me happy if you said yes."

The two looked at each other before Victoria spoke. "Aunt Bella, I'd like you to be totally honest with us. We won't be offended, and we need to know the truth. Are you saying this because you think what we have is lacking in some way?"

Bella met Victoria's eyes and must have recognized only honesty would be accepted. "Originally, my dears, I had concerns about this when I first heard you were coming. We have certain social responsibilities to fulfill. I didn't know if you would be prepared for them." She fingered the fabric on Victoria's dress. "When I saw the quality of what you had, I knew I had nothing to fear. You both wear your clothing with such grace. No, I cannot find fault. I just hoped—" She turned her head quickly to hide sudden tears.

"What?" Victoria touched her aunt's shoulder.

Bella blinked a tear away, turned, and clasped Victoria's hand. "You look so much like your mother, and though she was several years younger than I, we had such fun times together. Her energy seemed endless. I rather hoped to go back in time. Forgive me for being such a sentimental old lady."

Victoria looked at Abby, a question in her eyes. Abby simply shrugged and nodded.

"Aunt Bella, Abby and I would enjoy shopping with you. We'll trust you to give us good advice, and I hope to hear much more about my mother and father soon."

"You have made me very happy, my dears. I'll leave you now to get ready. I hope you won't be too bored tonight." She hugged each of them before leaving.

"Whew. What do you think o' that?" Abby asked after Bella had left the room. "'Tis truly a marvel."

"I don't yet know what to think, Abby, but I wish she would've told me more about my mother." Victoria couldn't help but notice that Bella had not agreed to speak more about her parents.

Victoria pulled on long white gloves Bella had lent her and tried to turn her thoughts back to the dinner at hand. "I wonder what we'll be expected to do or say?"

"I'm not certain, but me best course o' action will be to listen and say little. The upper-crusts won't be interested in the most efficient ways to kill chickens or the best remedy for a sore throat."

Laughter shook Victoria. "You're a girl of many talents."

Abby grinned, and they both turned when George came to announce that Mark and Bella awaited them downstairs to receive their guests.

"Well, here we go, George. Our first true test in company. Wish us luck."

George smiled and nodded.

As the two descended the stairs, Victoria noticed Bella and Mark were not alone. They talked with a tall young man with wavy blonde hair whose back was to Victoria. His stance and coloring seemed familiar to her, and when he turned, she knew him. Orville Sebastian's face was no longer covered in spots, and his trim, muscular build and elegant attire hinted at drastic changes in the few years since she'd last seen him. Surprise edged her words. "Orville?"

"Hello, Victoria."

Shock widened her eyes as she immediately flashed back to the day of her seventeenth birthday. He blushed, and his lopsided grin indicated he had read her thoughts.

When had he rid himself of his pudgy waist and the spots on his face? His eyes were the same honest blue, but his expression had matured.

Mark and Bella watched them. Mark's left eyebrow rose. "Obviously, the two of you have already met."

Orville nodded. "Yes, sir. Victoria and I lived in the same town and attended the same school for a while."

Mark looked at Abby. "Well, then, Miss Abby, I would like to introduce you to my accountant, Orville Sebastian. Sebastian, this is Victoria's friend, Abby O'Brien."

Abby curtsied and blushed at the introduction. "Pleased to meet you, Mr. Sebastian."

During the conversation, as they remembered the people from home, Orville apologized.

"Why?" Victoria asked, and Abby tilted her head to look at the man.

"For burdening you with a kiss on your birthday. I was bound and determined you should have one, and I'm sure I acted without finesse or skill."

Victoria laughed. "I forgive you." Relief lightened her to know he was willing to forget the kiss as much as she'd wanted to.

That night, both girls wrote home about the dinner party. They shared what they wrote before they sealed the envelopes and laughed to see how differently they'd viewed the evening.

From the Silverthorne Mansion, Capitol Hill

December 10, 1894

Dear Elizabeth, Miguel, and Tony,

Tonight, Abby and I survived our first official dinner party. We knew we would have to endure these get-togethers, so were somewhat prepared. Both George and Cooky were helpful in giving us background information, so we didn't make any obvious social blunders. From their body language, I think both Uncle Mark and Aunt Bella were pleased with us. Our plan was to say as little as possible and let the guests seated next to us do most of the talking. The strategy worked well, and we intend to use this as much as possible.

Though there weren't any young people present, the dinner wasn't as bad as I had feared. Friends and business associates of Uncle Mark and Aunt Bella's attended, and some of the conversation interested me. I find I tire quickly of the "latest fashions" conversations, though I did hear women have taken to riding bicycles and have changed their dress to fit. They have an adaptable costume that allows the wearer to buckle the skirt around her legs for complete coverage of her ankles. Then she can unbuckle the skirt for a more lady-like, traditional look. You should have seen how scandalized some of the men were with the idea of women riding bicycles. I tried not to laugh. Apparently, a wealthy woman named Mrs. George D. Johnston began riding a bicycle. She has shed her petticoats (forgive me, Miguel and Tony) for a design that lets her ride safely. I think I would like to ride a bicycle, though I don't think this could ever compare to being on the back of Dorado and racing Tony to the cottonwood tree.

The only other interesting thing I heard the women talking about was Margaret Tobin Brown. Sometimes she's called Maggie. She is the daughter of an Irish immigrant who married a mining engineer named J.J. Brown. He developed a method of shoring up the walls of mines with bales of straw. This discovery allowed the miners to dig deeper. Well, last year, because of Mr. Brown's technique, miners made the biggest strike in history, which of course, made the Browns millionaires. They and their children have moved into a house called "The House of Lions" on Pennsylvania Street. Many of the women spoke with censure in their voices when they spoke of Mrs. Brown, but others applauded her. She not only bought a nice house and fancy clothes, but she has hired tutors and is learning to speak five languages. She also plans to travel to other countries to practice her skills. Some of the women said Maggie was the one to call on if you wanted someone to head up charitable fund-raisers. She sounds like a person I'd like to meet.

I was able to listen to some of Uncle Mark's conversation and found his to be more interesting. Miguel, you would probably know all about last year's Depression, but many of the well-heeled

Denverites suffered financial losses. The silver tycoon, Horace Tabor, lost his opera house, his Capitol Hill mansion, his office block, and other possessions. Uncle Mark said the people of Denver began to diversify to survive. The city had relied on supplying and smelting for the mining industry but then shifted to other businesses to weather the Depression. Things are still bad for many families.

Well, I'd best close. Abby and I will shop with Aunt Bella tomorrow. She wants to give this expedition to us as a Christmas gift. I hope we can chat about Mom and Dad soon.

Love, Victoria

P.S.: I was shocked to see Orville Sebastian here. He's Uncle Mark's accountant. He dined with us. He's changed. Orville no longer has a pudgy middle or spotty face. He gave us more background on the topics of discussion when we needed to know. We'll be seeing a great deal of him while we're here.

Abby's letter was stark in its contrast to Victoria's.

From the Silverthorne Mansion, Capitol Hill

December 10, 1894

Dearest Mum,

Tonight was our first official dinner party at the Silverthorne mansion, and you would have been proud o' me. No one knew me dress was homemade, and I didn't give myself away by jumpin' up and clearin' the table. I asked a few questions o' the people sittin' next to me and got them talkin' about themselves. I didna' have to say much.

One o' Vicky's friends from home is Mr. Silverthorne's accountant. He sat next to us and was a great help. He's friendly, real, and good-lookin'.

Mum, I must say I prefer our cozy family dinners in the warm kitchen where laughter and love lives than these stiff, formal affairs where you always have to worry about which fork you're usin' and if you're entertainin' the person next to you with witty talk.

Well, I'm fallin' asleep over me letter. Goodnight, Mum. Sweet dreams.

Love, Abby

FIVE

"Aunt Bella, I'd like to chat with you about my parents. Other than meeting family, this is the main reason I traveled to Denver."

Victoria and Bella sat in a booth and waited for their lunch order. After the morning's shopping, Abby told Victoria she wanted to return to the mansion so Bella and Victoria could talk. Victoria guessed she really wanted to handle and admire some of her new acquisitions.

Bella raised her brows. "What do you want to know?"

"Why was I sent to Texas after my parents died when you and Uncle Mark were in Denver?"

Bella's expression saddened. "Mark had just turned eighteen, so he was not able to care for a young girl. I had lost my younger sister in a carriage accident only a week earlier. When I got word of your parents' deaths two days after her funeral, the news was more than I could bear. I didn't recover for years."

"I'm sorry." Victoria touched her aunt's hand.

Bella brushed tears from her eyes and smiled. "You are so much like your mother. You bring back good memories."

Victoria's own eyes moistened. "Tell me what you remember most about Mama and Dad."

Bella's eyes softened with memories. "Your mother had so much energy, and she spent what she had loving people. Everyone called her Maggie. Her personality won her many friends. She worked long hours on behalf of the underprivileged and loved your father more than her own life. He called her his 'dear treasure.' They were perfectly suited. They had faith in each other, and in God, and their faith translated itself into action. When they suffered, they took solace from each other and from the words found in a Bible your mother had received from her mother. They were such giving people."

Victoria remained quiet for several moments as she tried to reconcile what she had just learned with the pieces of knowledge she had.

Finally, she looked up at her aunt and said, "What did Dad do?"

"He taught in the history department at the University of Denver. He loved old manuscripts and old books, and he had a drive to learn. He wanted to know what motivated people to move. He studied their interactions and believed we all could learn from the past to make the future better."

"Were they interested in mining?"

"I don't know. Your folks were interested in many things."

"What were they looking for in a mine in southwestern Colorado?"

Bella shook her head. "I'm sorry, but I don't know, Victoria. You might ask Mark. He might know, though I doubt it. He was young and involved in his own interests when the tragedy happened." She glanced at her niece. "I'm sorry we lost contact over the years. At first, when we knew you existed, we sent little gifts to you for your birthday and Christmas. Do you remember getting them?"

Victoria shook her head.

Bella sighed. "For the first few years, we got notes from Mary. She told us how you were doing, and then the letters became few and far between and then stopped altogether. We knew you were being taken care of, and as we began to heal from our sorrows, life continued, and we lost touch." She paused and fiddled with her napkin. "For your dear mother's sake, I wish we could have gotten to know each other."

Their waiter brought their lunch then, which resulted in a lull in the conversation. The break provided Victoria with time to think. While they sipped their after-lunch hot chocolate, Victoria asked, "Aunt Bella, do you know how I ended up with Mary and John Keeson? I know that Mama and Mary were first cousins, but …"

Bella furrowed her brow. "I believe your parents made contact with the Keesons because they intended to travel to the area. I don't know why. Mary's brother, Sam—"

"What?" Victoria choked. "What did you say?"

Bella looked at her niece in alarm and reached toward her. "Are you all right?"

Victoria stared at her aunt with shock. "Did you say Mary's brother is Sam?"

"Yes. You didn't know?"

Victoria shook her head, her mind whirling. What other things did the Keesons know they had not told her? Anger welled. Why would they withhold this information, especially since they knew how she struggled to find out about her parents? Had they withheld this knowledge intentionally? And Sam … Her whole mental image of him blurred and changed for a second. He didn't seem to be the kind of person who could practice subterfuge. Were there layers to him she had never seen? Did this relationship explain John's tongue-off treatment as well? She felt as if the solid ground under her feet had suddenly shifted.

As she thought about Mary and Sam, their personalities and attitudes, little things begin to fit together to indicate they were closely related. They both wore articles of clothing until the material grew so thin they had to discard them for modesty's sake. Sam was partial to Mary's peaches because they were "just like Ma's." Their coloring and gestures were similar as were certain phrases they used when they were surprised. Why hadn't she put the clues together before this?

The new information made her feel less secure in her knowledge of the people who had influenced her life to this point. What about Elizabeth, Miguel, and Tony? Had she taken certain things for granted? Had she made incorrect assumptions? What if what she knew about the people in her life, or believed she knew about them, wasn't accurate?

The questions came by the dozens to disturb her. Her hand shook as she set her cup on the table.

Bella watched Victoria during this time with concern etched on her face. Finally, she said, "Are you feeling well, my dear? Would you like to return home now?"

Victoria nodded and placed her napkin on the table. "Yes. If you please, Aunt Bella, I need to think about what you've told me. Some things don't make sense yet."

———— ⦿⦿⦿ ————

As Victoria entered the room, Abby looked up from her sewing. "What's wrong, Vicky?"

Victoria told her what she'd discovered and what questions came as a result. "What do we truly know about the people we come into contact with every day, Abby? Have you ever thought about this?"

As they spoke, George entered the room to tend the fire. Though he came in softly, Victoria sensed his presence and his actions sharpened her attention. He seemed in no hurry to leave.

Abby seemed not to notice George and shrugged. "Aye. 'Tis a puzzle, but I've learned from servin' that you canna' know everythin' about everybody. You'll not always be right in your thinkin' about people, so you live life the best you can and accept the consequences of wrong decisions."

Victoria smiled. "Miguel said something very similar to me before I left."

"You learn from mistakes, my friend, and you understand that others are not perfect either."

Victoria agreed and watched George add more logs to their fire. She suddenly realized he always seemed to be present when she read aloud or talked to Abby about the manuscripts, and she had sudden insight as to why.

"George?" He turned to look at her. "What is one thing you wish you had that would make your life easier or better?"

Abby's needle stilled and she looked up.

George turned back to the fire and began to poke at the logs with a wrought-iron poker. Finally, he spoke. "I would wish to read as you do."

Victoria's eyebrows rose. "What do you mean? I thought you said you could read."

"I can read simple words, but reading is painful for me. You open a book, and the words come easily to you. When you read aloud, they flow from your mouth like, like …" George shrugged.

Victoria thought for several moments. "Is this why you're almost always in the room when I'm reading?"

George looked up and a smile tugged at his lips. "You are observant, Miss Victoria. I like to hear the ideas that come out of the books you read. They make me think."

Victoria glanced at Abby, and then back at George. "Would you like me to teach you?"

His eyes widened, and then he lowered them to look at his hands. "I don't know."

"You always find the time to be in our room after lunch when Aunt Bella is resting. We could work then. Abby and I don't take naps, so we'd have at least two hours. What do you think?"

George continued his concentration on his hands, obviously wrestling with the idea of having his dream fulfilled. Finally, he looked up and said, "I could never repay you for such a gift."

"A gift is a *gift*. I don't offer one, and then expect payment."

After several moments of silence, George searched her face. "Then I thank you, Miss Victoria." His rare smile stretched from one side of his dark face to the other.

Abby clapped. "Good for you, George. 'Twill be so interestin'. May I sit in on some o' the lessons?"

George smiled and Victoria nodded. "Let's start tomorrow then. I'll ask Uncle Mark if I can use his library." When she saw the concern on George's face, she said, "I won't mention your name at all."

Although the interaction with George pleased Victoria, the information she had learned earlier continued to upset her. When Abby and George left her room, she began to do what she always did when she needed to think—she cleaned and reorganized her room. The physical act of cleaning and ordering allowed her to make space in her mind so she could focus more completely.

Then she sat down at the writing desk, took out her journal and pencil, and began to jot down more questions. She re-read the earlier entries, and then made a notation and added a new question.

Why does John treat Sam differently than he does anyone else in town? They're brothers-in-law!

What do I truly know about the people who have been in my life for the last fifteen years? Sam? Arnie?—Arnie is simple-minded and not capable of scheming. He wouldn't keep information from me if he knew something. Sam and Arnie have been friends for years. John? Mary? Elizabeth?—Beth loves me like a mother, and she's my best friend. I don't think she would ever hide anything from me. Beth has had a lot of heartache in her life because she went against societal norms and chose Miguel. Miguel? What you see is what you get with him. He's charming, shrewd, intelligent, and honest. I know he loves me like my Dad would. Tony?

COLORADO TREASURE

Victoria paused when she thought of Tony. Her feelings for him were complicated, and she was too tired to continue with that line of thought. Instead, she penned a short note to Elizabeth.

———— ⟨✺⟩ ————

Tony listened as his mother read Victoria's letter.

From the Silverthorne Mansion

Capitol Hill

December 15, 1894

Dear Elizabeth, Miguel, and Tony,

I got your letter yesterday and hope your Christmas will be beautiful. I'm already missing you all so much. I hope you receive your gifts in the next day or two, and that they please you. No number of dinner parties, theater engagements, concerts, and shopping expeditions can take your place, and I can't imagine spending Christmas away from home. Being away from you saddens me.

Abby is sorely missing her family right now, but Orville will be here soon to lift our spirits. You know, he can still do mental calculations at incredible speeds? He makes us laugh.

Tony hoped Victoria's homesickness would bring her back to Texas soon, so he felt encouraged as his mother read the first paragraph aloud. But when she got to the second, his insides froze. He wanted to leave the room and race across the fields on his fastest horse but forced himself to listen.

Mary's letter came at the same time, which reminds me of what I wanted to ask. Did you know Sam and Mary were brother and sister? Why didn't I know this? Do you think there's a plot to keep me from knowing things? If so, why?

Did you also know Lawrence Lucky is in town? I saw an article in the paper written by him. He condemned the corruption and crime in the city. What's going on? Did he close the newspaper office, or is there someone else running the business? Do you know why he came to Denver?

I miss you all so very much, and look forward to seeing you in the spring. We have another dinner party tonight, which I dread because Mr. Jonathan Hightower will be present. He's got to be the most opinionated, obnoxious, self-righteous man I've ever met, and I don't know how Uncle Mark endures him. When he's around, Beth, I have the most uncharitable desire to hit him with anything handy. I now understand why God commanded us to love each other—we don't love people like Mr. Hightower naturally—and I know Jesus told us to do good to those who despitefully use us, but to do this is so HARD.

I love you. Victoria

Orville stood at the bottom of the staircase as Victoria and Abby descended. He looked up at them and smiled, but Victoria noted an especially soft look in his eyes when he looked at Abby. They'd been drawn to each other from the first moment they'd met.

Abby returned his smile and blushed as he offered her his arm.

Victoria smiled in happiness for her friend and thought she and Orville made a good couple. Their personalities seemed well suited. She stepped back a step to let them go ahead of her and could hear the hum of voices and the clink of crystal. She noticed several guests had already arrived and were enjoying conversations and appetizers.

Just as she was about to enter the dining room, Tim signaled to her from behind a potted plant. "What's wrong?" she asked him.

A frown creased his forehead. "Friends say three"—he made the sign for thieves—"wait. Want rob fat man with large gold watch."

She looked in the direction of Tim's pointing finger. Jonathan Hightower.

"You know how? Certain that man?"

He shrugged and then signed, "Certain. Friends know everything."

She believed him. Cooky told her many of Tim's young friends, both hearing and deaf, worked at any job they could get, day or night, to help their parents keep the family from starving and to keep clothing on their backs so they wouldn't freeze. Because these children were ragged and always around, no one paid attention to them, but they were observant and heard much.

"Where hide they?" she signed.

Tim indicated the locations and Victoria nodded.

"Thank you." She turned to go, but Tim stopped her. He still looked worried.

"Want no trouble for friends."

"No need worry. I not tell. Your friends safe."

Tim smiled and left, and Victoria returned to the dining room. The other guests had waited for her, and as soon as she sat, the servants served the meal. All through dinner, she tried to determine if she should say anything and, if so, how best to share the message. Part of her didn't want to say anything because the man irritated her so much. He needed to be humbled. In her opinion, a robbery might be beneficial enough to take him down a notch or two.

But her conscience poked her. *Who are you to judge?* She hung her head.

Jonathan Hightower sat across the table from Victoria, but she could still hear his opinionated conversation and the condescending tone of voice he used when he spoke to women. Her hackles rose. As the meal progressed, she had a strong desire to say nothing at all, but verses from her mother's Bible pounded through her head.

> "Therefore to him that knoweth to do good, and doeth it not, to him it is sin." "If I regard iniquity in my heart, the Lord will not hear me."

Victoria knew what the right thing to do was, and she did want the Lord to hear her, so she resolved to be obedient.

As the women left the table to retire to Aunt Bella's sitting room so the men could enjoy their cigars and after-dinner drinks, Victoria approached Jonathan Hightower, who conversed with her uncle. They both looked at her as she approached.

"Mr. Hightower, I received information tonight that thieves plan to rob you when you leave here."

Both men snapped upright and stared at her.

"What?" he roared. Every man in the room turned to look in their direction.

"Victoria, how do you know this?" Mark spoke, his voice intense.

"Someone overheard plans being made and reported this to a friend. This friend told me, and now I have shared this with you. Three masked men wait at the bottom of the drive to stop your carriage and rob you as you leave."

All the men gathered around Victoria. She gave them the details and waited as they muttered and exclaimed. Jonathan Hightower reddened, and she noted his hand shook as he placed his glass on the table. He fumed and sputtered for several minutes, but Victoria got the idea this bluster was a front to hide his fear.

Victoria watched as the men made immediate plans to foil the robbery attempt, and most of the men volunteered to help.

"You are my guest, Hightower. I will take care of this problem," Mark said. He went upstairs, changed his clothes, and brought down shotguns and pistols. Then he tossed dark cloaks and gloves to Orville and George, who had also volunteered their help, and handed them scarves to wrap around their faces to hide their identities. She admired her uncle's quick action.

Mark spoke to her, "I have enough knowledge of the criminal mind to know how they work to fleece citizens, Victoria. I am certain someone else is behind this attempt. The men sent to do the dirty work will report to this someone, so I don't want to give these thieves any more information than I have to."

Jonathan would call for Hightower's carriage to be brought around and Mark, Orville, and George, would hide inside. Jonathan would also accompany them and be given either a pistol or a shotgun as well.

Victoria remembered how Miguel described shotguns as "up close and personal," and was certain her uncle knew the strengths of each weapon. Even if the thugs were brave enough to face down a pistol, they probably weren't stupid enough to look in the barrel of shotguns at close range.

Victoria smiled as she imagined the shock on the thieves' faces when a force they didn't expect met them.

Mark spoke to her softly, "Victoria, go to the women, but don't tell them anything about this yet. We don't need to upset them if we don't have to."

She agreed and left the room, though her mind followed the men. Tim stood near the potted plant and watched them go. He looked at Victoria, a question in his eyes. She signed, "Secret safe. Friends safe."

Tim smiled and left once more.

Victoria couldn't concentrate on the women's chitchat, so she sat in a wing chair near the fireplace and listened for any sounds of the returning men. Abby must have sensed something was wrong and came to sit near her. She met Victoria's eyes and raised her eyebrows in question. Victoria shook her head and signed, "Later."

The men who remained waited until Mark, Orville, and George returned a half hour later and listened to the story before they called for their wives and carriages and returned to their own homes. The men left in good spirits and Victoria assumed they felt as much pleasure in the foiled robbery attempt as she. She would've liked to see the shocked look on the thieves' faces.

Larry "The Fixer" Blunting was not in such good spirits when he heard the report of the failed robbery. He sat at his desk in the office of his Larimer Street saloon and fumed.

"Can't you idiots do anything right?" The balding, light-skinned man paced the room and swore at them. His bulbous nose glowed red with anger as he pounded his meaty fist on the desk. The three men stared sullenly at each other and then at the man who had, along with his older brother, Saul, become leaders in Denver's organized crime.

"Boss, someone leaked our plans," Eddie, the spokesman for the group, complained. "They had us dead to rights. We stopped the rig just as planned, but when we demanded Hightower step out, the door opened, and at least three shotguns met us. Hightower covered with a pistol."

"Did you see who held the shotguns?" Blunting demanded.

"No, Boss. They all wore dark clothing and dark masks. We assume they were also guests at the mansion."

"Assume nothing," he barked. "Then what did you do?"

"We ran." The tone of the larger man became defensive. "You would've done the same had you been covered by three or four shotguns."

Larry didn't want to push these men too far. They'd proven valuable to him in jobs needing brute strength and intimidation, so he nodded his head and said in a calmer voice, "You're right, Jack. I probably would've."

The men visibly relaxed and some looked at each other with slight smiles.

"Now what, Boss?" The third man, Red, spoke.

"We need to find out who warned Hightower. Get this information to me by the end of the week."

The men nodded and left, and Blunting leaned back in his chair and looked at the ceiling. His jaw clenched as he made plans to punish whoever had leaked information. He would not tolerate snitches in his organization.

At the Silverthorne mansion a day later, Victoria sat in the library and chatted with Mark and Bella. Orville had taken Abby to the theater and they were expected back soon. Mark stood in front of the fireplace warming his hands, while Bella sat in a comfortable chair near him.

"I have a Christmas gift for you, Victoria, but the gift won't fit in a box." Mark grinned and looked at Bella. She nodded as if to urge him on. "I've made arrangements for you to meet with the Chancellor of the University of Denver where your father worked. Chancellor McDowell knew your parents and may be able to tell you more about them. Would you like this?"

Sudden tears flooded Victoria's eyes as she jumped up from her chair and raced to embrace her uncle and aunt. "Oh, Uncle Mark, this is the best Christmas present ever. When can I speak with him?"

Mark laughed and returned her hug. "He can meet with you tomorrow. Because only three days remain until Christmas, the campus is closed until January, but he agreed to meet with you tomorrow morning. Is this agreeable to you?"

"Yes." She hugged him once more and then bent to kiss Bella. Just then, she heard Abby and Orville returning from the theater. "Please excuse me. I want to tell Abby the good news."

"Before you go upstairs, a letter came for you from Texas. Look on the table."

She hugged and kissed Mark and Bella once more before bouncing out of the room.

Orville helped Abby out of her coat just as Victoria entered the hall. She shared her news, and both smiled and hoped her meeting would be productive. Abby looked particularly lovely and seemed to have matured in the few weeks they'd been in Denver. Victoria suspected Abby's happiness was totally due to her growing love for Orville.

Victoria then grabbed the letter and raced up the stairs, opening the envelope as she went.

December 19, 1894

Dearest Victoria, everyone in town knows Mary and Sam are siblings. We just assumed you knew too. Their relationship has never been a topic of importance or interest in our day-to-day lives, so I guess no one mentioned their relationship. I don't think anyone's deliberately trying to keep you from information, though.

Shortly after you left, Lawrence had the opportunity to work for the Denver Post, so Jack Lynd runs the newspaper now. He bought the little spread for his bride-to-be, and they'll be married this spring.

Tony quit his job to work for Miguel. Miguel finally decided Tony has proven his ability to be his own man, and they're now working together on some big building project on the ranch. They drilled a water well, and I think they're fencing an area near the little stream that runs out of the grove of trees—you remember, the one in the hidden valley where you and Tony used to swing from the rope swing hanging from the gigantic cottonwood tree? Tony's running a few head of cows and his horses there now.

My son has changed since you left, love. He's much quieter and goes about his business without saying a lot. I haven't seen him smile or sing as much as he used to, but that could be because he works from before sunup to after sundown, and the only things he wants to do are eat and sleep when he gets home. I heard him and Miguel discussing the advisability of using adobe bricks or lumber, but I don't know what they're building. Tony will take me to the site tomorrow.

He rides Dorado regularly to keep the horse from getting fat and to make sure he remembers his lessons and his manners. To me, Tony seems more thoughtful—I don't know how to describe what I'm seeing exactly, but I think he misses you more than you can imagine.

Christmas just doesn't feel the same without you. I get a little lonesome when my men are gone all day, and I miss our chats.

I hope you find the information you seek, and that you return to us quickly.

I love you, darling.

—Elizabeth

Victoria brushed away a tear and put the letter away. Her homesickness felt acute at the moment. If she had what she needed, she would've hopped on the first train back home right then. But she couldn't. Not yet. Her spirits raised a little as she thought of the meeting tomorrow.

"Vicky?" Abby peeked around the door. "'Tis bad news you've received?"

"No, Abby. I'm just homesick." She dabbed at her eyes and sat up.

"Aye. 'Tis the first time I've been away from Mum and the boys during Christmas and the sadness squeezin' me heart at the thought near kills me."

Both girls turned when they heard George clear his throat. He stood at the open bedroom door.

"Excuse me, Miss Victoria, but your uncle wishes to see you in his study."

"Now?"

"Yes, if you please."

Victoria slid to her feet and hugged Abby. "I'll be back to hear about your evening."

When she entered the study, Mark stood conversing with Jonathan Hightower, who rose to his feet when she stepped through the doors. Victoria looked at Hightower and then at Mark, her brow raised.

"Victoria, Jonathan would like to reward you for the service you provided him recently."

Victoria turned to Jonathan. "A reward is unnecessary, Mr. Hightower. I did what I thought was my Christian duty."

Jonathan shook his head. "I do not agree, and I feel such care for others should be rewarded." He handed her an envelope. "Please consider this a small token of my gratitude to you. Now if you will excuse me, my wife and daughters are waiting."

George handed him his coat and hat as Victoria watched him leave, then she opened the envelope. To her horror, he'd enclosed a check for ten thousand dollars.

Shocked, Victoria gaped at Mark. "I can't accept this." She spun on her heels to follow the man. "Wait, Mr. Hightower."

Mark grabbed her elbow and said, "No, Victoria, let him go. Jonathan doesn't often let down his mask enough to do something like this, so let him leave with his dignity intact."

"But, Uncle Mark, I can't—"

"Victoria. I hope you will accept his offering of gratitude and begin to think kindlier of him."

Victoria felt the heat climb into her cheeks, and misery tightened her throat. "Was my dislike so evident?"

"Not really, but now and then I've seen your expression when he talked, and I knew your thoughts. My advice is to 'not judge a book by its cover.' I'm sure your father and mother would agree with me if they'd been here."

Her head dropped and her cheeks continued to burn. Mark, as cynical as he was, appeared to recognize the values and kindheartedness of her parents and now compared her actions to their standards. She knew these were God's standards too and she'd come up short.

She nodded. "I'm sorry, Uncle Mark. I'll try to do better, but not because he gave me a reward for my actions."

"Thank you, niece."

Victoria's steps dragged as she returned to her room, and she prayed for forgiveness with each step.

Lord Jesus, please forgive me for my hard thoughts and my lack of compassion and love for Mr. Hightower. I know you've forgiven me my trespasses and have commanded your people to love. I know you sent Christians into the world to show your love, and I'm sorry I fail so miserably sometimes. Aunt Bella told me

Mother loved people, and I ask to be more like her. I know doing this is going to be hard, because I have a difficult time loving unlovable people.

Oh, and will you please show me what you want me to do with this money?

When she entered her room, Abby waited. Victoria showed her the check, and her friend's eyes widened. "What will you do with so much?"

"I don't know, Abby. I'll leave that decision up to God to show me what he wants. I'll cash some of the money in case he has a plan for its immediate use."

Victoria sat at her writing desk and penned a note of gratitude to Jonathan. She felt better after she did this, and then she listened to Abby tell of her evening.

When Abby spoke of Orville, her face glowed with such love Victoria felt a pang and another overwhelming feeling of homesickness.

Before she got into bed, she wrote another letter home.

> Beth, I just wanted to send you a short note before I lie down to tell you I love you. I miss you and Tony and Miguel so much. I guess seeing Abby and Orville's happiness—did I tell you they'll most likely become a couple?—makes my homesickness worse.

> Also, God humbled me tonight and made me realize just how far short I fall on my own merits. Good thing I'm resting in his righteousness and not my own or my goose would be cooked. I've asked him to make me more like my mother, whom Aunt Bella told me loved people very much. Why is this so hard for me, Beth, when loving seemed so easy for Mom?

Tomorrow, Uncle Mark will take me to the University of Denver to meet with the current chancellor who knew Mama and Dad he can answer some of my more pressing questions.

Love, Victoria.

Tony sat across the breakfast table and sipped his coffee as his mother opened Victoria's letter. A stream of sunlight danced through the window pane and over the damask tablecloth and then bounced off the silverware handles.

Tony remained still as he watched his mother open the letter. The letters often distressed him, and he wondered briefly if he should leave the table, but then sat rooted to the spot as his mother read. With just a few words from Victoria, the ice dam encircling his heart since he'd watched her step on the train suddenly burst. He could not contain his joy, so he jumped up and leaned over the table to kiss Elizabeth's cheek.

"Your smile is like seeing the sun after weeks of clouds and rain, son." She caressed his cheek.

"So at least one fear is laid to rest, is it not, *mi'jo?*" Miguel smiled.

"Sí, Papá. You were right."

"Antonito, we must trust *Nuestro Señor* knows what he is doing."

SIX

Christmas Eve morning dawned bright and beautiful. Several inches of snow had fallen during the night and softened the hard edges of the city. Snow crystals, like diamonds, sparkled as the sunlight touched them, and Victoria didn't think she'd ever seen anything as beautiful in her entire life. If she looked carefully enough, the snow appeared to be multicolored where the shadows met sunlight. When she stepped out of the house into the fresh air to enter Mark's closed carriage, she could see her breath.

"Be careful, Victoria. The servants shoveled the path, but you will still find slick places," Mark warned before handing her into the carriage.

Inside, she tucked her hands into the fluffy belly of her muff, snuggled into her warm coat, and smiled at her uncle. She hadn't stopped smiling since she awakened.

"I'm glad to see you're in such spirits, my dear."

"This is one of the best days of my life. Maybe I can finally get some answers to questions that have haunted me for months."

As they traveled, she told him of the recurring nightmares, and how they left her with a sense of uneasiness, of something undone.

"Well, we shall soon see if you'll get the answers you seek. If you look to your right, you can see the University's roof line."

The grand spires and arches of a Romanesque stone building appeared as their carriage edged closer. She asked about the domed roof to the south side of the building.

"That is the Chamberlin Observatory. The building houses a large telescope astronomers use to study the universe."

The carriage slowed and stopped in front of a shoveled walk. Mark handed her out of the carriage and offered his arm.

As Victoria entered the building, she noted the vast marble-tiled room and the elegant furnishings. More noticeable was the coolness of the room and the way sound seemed to be swallowed in the space. Did this quietness disappear with the return of the scholars, or was the silence a permanent characteristic that eked from the walls of warm brown stone?

Mark drew close to her, touching her elbow, and spoke in a low voice which felt appropriate for the space. "We'll meet Chancellor McDowell in the library."

Victoria entered the library and gaped openly at the number of books on the shelves surrounding her. She stood frozen, awed by the books' splendor, until Mark urged her forward. A solemn-looking man of indeterminate age stood as she approached one of the tables where he sat. He rose and shook hands with each of them and then indicated they should sit in a couple of comfortable chairs.

"How delightful to meet the daughter of one of this university's esteemed faculty. Your mother and father were some of the most interesting people I've ever known, and I do offer my condolences for your loss."

Victoria teared at the warmth and sincerity in his voice. She smoothed out her skirt before responding. "Thank you, sir, and I want to thank you for taking time out of your holiday to meet with me."

"My pleasure, Miss Silverthorne." The older gentleman sat back into his own comfortable chair and smiled. "Your uncle said you wanted to ask me questions about your parents. I will be happy to tell you what I know. I was not Chancellor when your father worked here, but I knew him because of his reputation for Christian kindness, and because of his reputation for scholarly work. Our institution benefited from having him here."

Victoria sat forward on her chair. "Sir, do you know why my father and mother traveled to Southwestern Colorado?" She held her breath, hoping for an answer to one of her most disturbing questions.

The chancellor frowned. "I'm sorry, but I don't. I do know before your parents traveled west, your father was fascinated with antiquities and spent hours in this very library researching old documents."

"Do you know what antiquities fascinated him the most?"

"Not exactly, but I know he researched the Spanish presence in New Mexico territory from the time of Juan de Oñate's expedition to the Colorado River in 1605. You understand that the New Mexico territory incorporated vast areas of lands in Colorado and Arizona?"

She nodded and the chancellor continued. "He also conducted a detailed study of the Spanish Inquisition when it was established in New

Mexico in 1626, and then of Don Diego de Vargas when he recolonized Santa Fe in 1692 and 1693, after the Pueblo Revolt.

"We discussed the possible route the Franciscan friars Dominguez and Escalante used to explore the New Mexico territory to California in 1776. He wondered what types of things these people might have carried with them."

Mark nodded. "Even though I was only eighteen at the time, I remember how James and Maggie could talk of little else at the dinner table. I failed to see what excited them so."

Victoria frowned. "Yes, I found some old Spanish documents in a trunk belonging to my parents. I've poured over them for hours, but I still don't know what they were looking for." She spent several seconds in thought, and then said, "Sir, do you think the antiquities my parents looked for could have been Spanish gold?

The chancellor seemed to contemplate her question for a moment and then said, "Possible, I guess. They did speak of lost Spanish gold people may have hidden as they fled before the Pueblo religious leader, and later when the expeditions began anew." He shook his head. "Somehow, I just can't reconcile the picture of your parents looking for gold with what I know of them, though. These actions seem so out of character."

"Chancellor, in my experience, gold often produces powerful changes in people's actions and thoughts." Victoria noticed a hardened note to Mark's words.

Chancellor McDowell sighed and nodded. "Sadly, you are right, but I would not have thought this of the Silverthornes. Did you know your older brother well?"

"Not really. James was several years my senior, though I do remember some good times with him when I was younger. He had been teaching for many years by the time I reached my majority, and I had been living and studying away from home at a boarding school."

While the men began to converse about Mark's times as a teacher, Victoria asked for permission to look around the library. She needed space to think. She began to make her way slowly around the room, stopping occasionally to ponder the spine of one of the books. Could her parents have been searching for Spanish gold? Hadn't her father made an adequate salary? She could almost hear her uncle's answer to the question. *Just because a person has money doesn't mean he doesn't want more.*

As she neared the entrance to the library, she caught movement out of the corner of her eye. Startled, she paused and then peeked around the thick door. She thought she heard soft footsteps retreating down the hall and it seemed as if the temperature had dropped several degrees since she'd first entered.

The hair on the back of her neck raised as she realized the door now stood open, but she was certain Uncle Mark had closed it behind them when they entered. She shivered and looked back at the two men.

Mark stood to take leave of the chancellor, so she walked over and offered her gloved hand.

"Sir, thank you for meeting with me." She smiled and looked around. "Has everyone left the campus, or does someone stay as caretaker while the students are gone?"

"We do have a caretaker, but he has been given a holiday also. Merry Christmas, and may God bless your time together."

"Thank you," Victoria whispered. A chill ran up her back again, and she stuck closely to Mark's side as they walked toward the carriage. Was someone watching them? She glanced around furtively but saw no one. *Quit being silly. You're imagining things.*

More snow clouds had rolled in and hidden the sun while they'd been inside.

"We'd better hurry, Victoria. The weather doesn't look good." Mark grasped her arm.

Victoria hurried as quickly as she could given the condition of the path and her heavy skirts. George waited for them and opened the door to hand them both in. As the carriage lurched forward, Victoria studied the building one last time. Startled, she noted footprints near the entrance to the door and under one of the arched windows. The prints were larger than her own but smaller than George's. She knew they hadn't been there when she and Mark had entered. Besides, they had stayed on the path and not trekked across the newly fallen snow. Fear shot through her. Could the same thugs who planned to rob Jonathan be after Mark?

Later that day, before she began George's reading lesson, she asked, "George, did you see anyone enter the building after Uncle Mark and me?"

"No, miss. Why?"

"Oh, I was just wondering. I thought I saw someone else in the building."

"I got down to remove the snow from the horses' hooves and the wheels of the carriage and to stay warm, but I did not see anyone either enter or exit."

"Oh, George," Victoria exclaimed. "I'm so sorry you had to wait outside in the cold. The sun shone when we arrived."

"Don't fret, miss. I'm fine." He smiled at her and then applied himself to his lessons. Now that Abby had other distractions, she didn't always attend the reading lessons, but today she sat in the wing chair by the fireplace and watched, listened, and waited for Victoria to finish.

When George left the room, Abby bounced out of the chair and hugged Victoria. "I'm so happy, Vicky. Do you want to see me early Christmas gift?"

"Yes, I can tell you're about to burst."

Abby's eyes sparkled as much as the gold and diamond engagement ring she held up for Victoria's inspection. "Didna' I tell you this trip had the feelin' o' bein' a life changin' event for me?"

The ring shocked the words out of Victoria's mouth, and Abby's happiness pierced Victoria's soul with longing. She swallowed and managed to say, "Congratulations, Abby. The ring is beautiful, and so are you. You're glowing." She hugged her friend and sat down with her on the sofa. "You and Orville are well-suited. Tell me everything."

"'Tis hard for me to believe I could have fallen in love so quickly, but I have no doubt Orville is the right man for me. 'Tis certain I am. I know he is the man I want to spend the rest of my life with. He will make a good father to our children."

"Does your mother know?"

Abby nodded, her soft, sandy curls bouncing with the motion. "Aye. Orville sent Mum a telegram askin' if he had her permission to ask me to marry him. I doubt if Mum was surprised after receiving the letters I've sent home from the beginnin'."

"When is the wedding?"

Joy shone from Abby's face. "In April. We saw no sense in waitin' longer. Orville is lookin' to buy us a home large enough to house us, me mum, and the boys. They will travel to Denver before the weddin', help set up the house, and then after the weddin', we'll move in." She paused and smoothed her skirt. When she spoke again, her voice had lowered a notch. "I never thought to be so happy, and I have you to thank, Vicky. If you hadna' asked me to come, I would never have met my love. Thank you from the bottom of my heart, my friend."

Victoria held her tears in check. She'd let them fall when she was alone in her room. "I wish you every joy, Abby. May God bless your union."

When Abby left the room, Victoria closed the door and flung herself onto her bed. She wept for something she couldn't put into words. After a while, she got up and washed her face. She'd go down to the warm, friendly kitchen—her sanctuary in the Silverthorne mansion.

When she arrived in the kitchen, Tim, Abby, and George stood around the table sampling treats and helping with the cooking. Tim did most of the sampling, and Cooky threatened to whack his hand with the wooden stirring spoon if he reached for anything else.

Oh, what marvelous smells issued from the ovens. Cooky prepared a variety of sumptuous treats to be consumed by guests to the Silverthorne mansion over the next few days.

Victoria's spirits lightened as Cooky described the usual Christmas festivities at the Silverthorne mansion. "Your Aunt Bella's friends will stop by for tea and conversation tomorrow in the late morning after they finish their last-minute Christmas shopping, and Mr. Silverthorne will entertain some of his valuable railroad contacts and business associates. Welcome to the Christmas Eve traditions at the Silverthorne home, Vicky."

Victoria experienced a momentary pang of homesickness. The preparations reminded her of Christmases spent with Mary, John, Sam, Arnie, Miguel, Beth, and Tony. Though she didn't remember one special Christmas, she did remember the sense of laughter, celebration, and family. Before they exchanged gifts, Miguel would always read the Christmas story from the Gospel of Matthew. His deep, pleasantly accented voice always filled with emotion when he realized the magnitude of what God had done for him. He would ask, "Is this not truly incomprehensible to think that the Creator of the things both visible and invisible humbled himself to be born as a babe in a manger? Think of this. Have you not seen the multitude of stars at night and felt the warmth of the great sun that shines on our Texas plains by day?

"Yet he loved us enough to become mortal—to live as an example to us and to show us the character and expectations of Almighty God. He died for our sins on the cross of Calvary and rose from the dead to make intercession for us in the presence of the Father. He provided the way for us to live with him forever."

Then Miguel would read of the Magi from the east who had seen the Christ child's star in the sky, and who had traveled hundreds of miles to offer their gifts to the newborn King. Miguel always asked, "What gifts do you bring him?"

Victoria never knew how to answer this question. She didn't know of anything she had of value the Lord could use.

Her thoughts returned to the events of today. Fortunately, she wouldn't be expected to attend either one of these little get-togethers with her aunt and uncle, but she hoped for a cozy Christmas Eve with Aunt Bella, Uncle Mark, Abby, Orville, George, and Tim. Maybe Aunt Bella would tell her more stories of her parents, though she said she'd told her all she remembered.

Orville joined them in the kitchen a few minutes later, and Cooky handed him a soup ladle and gave him instructions. His face reflected his joy, and soon the talk centered on Abby and Orville's plans to wed and move her family to Denver. They spoke of house-hunting, and they signed the conversation so Tim could participate.

The comfort and conversation in the kitchen warmed Victoria's heart and engaged her interest. Soon, she forgot her earlier fears and gave no thought to anything except being with her friends.

In the office of his Larimer Street Saloon, "The Fixer" had not forgotten anything as he listened impatiently to Eddie's report.

"Boss, we don't know who gave the information to Miss Victoria Silverthorne, Silverthorne's niece, but we discovered she shared what she knew with Hightower and her uncle. Said a friend told her."

Larry Blunting sat in silence for several minutes. None of the women of his establishments would ever get within a mile of the nobs on the Hill, especially the women, but what about the men who visited his women on a regular basis? He tried to remember if any of the men who moved in Jonathan Hightower's and Mark Silverthorne's circles were regulars. He'd have to check this out.

COLORADO TREASURE

Mark Silverthorne was shrewd, hard, dangerous, and not a man to cross. He had too many friends in high places who could make Blunting's life miserable, and he could interfere with the smooth functioning of his businesses. The man would not take kindly to anyone who threatened to harm to a family member. Blunting would have to work with extreme care.

"What do you know about this niece?"

"Nothin' much, Boss."

"Well, find out. I want someone to follow her. I want to know who her friends are, where she goes, and what she does. I want to know her habits—I don't have to tell you. You know what I want."

The men nodded and left.

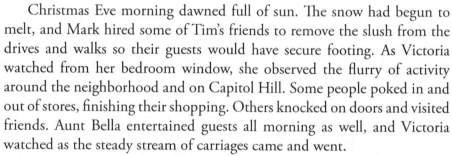

Christmas Eve morning dawned full of sun. The snow had begun to melt, and Mark hired some of Tim's friends to remove the slush from the drives and walks so their guests would have secure footing. As Victoria watched from her bedroom window, she observed the flurry of activity around the neighborhood and on Capitol Hill. Some people poked in and out of stores, finishing their shopping. Others knocked on doors and visited friends. Aunt Bella entertained guests all morning as well, and Victoria watched as the steady stream of carriages came and went.

Bella had invited Abby and Victoria to join her, but they asked to be excused to attend to their plans instead. They didn't tell her their plans consisted only of drinking hot chocolate in front of a warm fire, chatting, sewing, reading, and then exchanging little gifts between themselves.

When they'd finished their relaxed morning, George came in for a demonstration of his reading skills. Victoria had assigned him the task of memorizing and reciting the same passage Miguel always read from the Gospel of Matthew. Victoria handed him her mother's Bible. The book had become precious to her over these past weeks as she sought for clues to her mother's personality.

Sometimes her great-grandmother, grandmother, and mother had underlined passages with meaning to them and had written notes in the margins. Victoria could almost hear the voices of her people. She viewed these handwritten notes as treasures beyond price.

Tim joined them at the beginning of the performance, so Victoria signed the passages. He watched and began to sign with her. His movements made Victoria think she watched a well-choreographed ballet. Each body, arm, hand and finger movement and quirk of his eyebrow added to the telling. The beauty of Tim's signs in conjunction with George's deep voice soon brought tears to her eyes.

She hadn't realized just how expressive and complex sign language could be until Tim signed the story of the Magi as they went to Herod's palace in Jerusalem asking, "Where is He who is born King of the Jews?" Tim's body movements changed to match the character of the evil king, and the nuances he could convey with the flick of his fingers and facial expressions made her marvel.

"Well done, George," Victoria applauded. "You did an excellent job."

George gave her one of his rare smiles, and she could see the thanks in his eyes. He clasped Tim's shoulder and nodded. The four friends chatted and told stories until Tim and George had to begin preparing for the evening guests.

Orville stopped by for a visit, and he, Abby, and Victoria talked about plans. He'd been looking at several different house and wanted to know if she and Abby wanted to see them after Christmas to give their opinions as to their suitability. They both agreed with enthusiasm. As they chatted, Orville pulled out a pad and pencil, and he and Abby made lists of what they wanted or needed in their new home.

Victoria listened and offered suggestions every now and then. She loved working with wood, fabrics, and colors, and she had a secret longing to be planning for her own home. She already had an idea of furnishings and colors. Homesickness suddenly welled inside of her, and she almost choked.

Alone in her room later that evening, she sat up in bed and drew the home of her dreams. She had to get her thoughts on paper. When the plans were laid out to her satisfaction, she wrote another letter to Beth. She wrote of how she had spent Christmas Eve, and how beautifully George had read, and Tim had signed the Christmas story. She told of her visit to the University of Denver and the results of her chat with the chancellor, and then of the plans to visit houses with Abby and Orville the day after Christmas.

> Of course, we'll probably be able to look at only one or two during each week because of Orville's work schedule and our social obligations, but this will fill some of our down time.

> The idea of searching for just the right home caught my fancy after Orville left so—don't laugh at me, Beth—I drew a floor plan. Really. I couldn't sleep. I like the openness, flow, and the way the eastern sun would shine into the kitchen and front bedroom even in winter. I love to wake up to lots of sunshine, because I think God is smiling on me. Sunshine in the morning is a wonderful way to start the day, don't you think?

Beth laughed as she read the letter out loud to Tony and his father. "See how God answers your prayers, son?" she smiled.

Tony nodded as Beth continued to read.

> I will probably stay until April because Abby and Orville asked me to be in their wedding. I'll help them with the planning and whatever else I can. Aunt Bella and Uncle Mark have extended an invitation for me to stay with them, and I heard genuine sincerity in their voices when they offered. I'm glad they don't feel I'm a burden.

Tony's smile disappeared at this news. He sighed his frustration and looked at his father.

Miguel shrugged. "Perhaps this is for the best, Antonio. These extra days will buy us more time, no?"

> Well, I'd best close. I feel as if I can sleep now. We don't have much planned for tomorrow. Aunt Bella expects us to sleep in, and then we'll meet her and Uncle Mark for a meal between breakfast and lunch. We'll exchange our gifts at this time.

Abby and I have never been able to sleep in, so we'll probably get up early and make several fast circuits up and down the stairs for exercise, since walking outside is too treacherous. We have to do this quietly, and before Aunt Bella wakes up, or she'd be horrified and wonder where we learned our manners. Abby and I have a competition to see who can improve her time the most. I won last week, but she won the week before.

The Morales family all belly-laughed at this description. Tony could well imagine how crazy Victoria would be by now if she were not able to exercise as she normally did. In the summer, she would walk each day to blow the mental cobwebs away after working in the store. She also walked to get away from John's irritating presence.

Then we'll slip down to the warm, cozy kitchen and beg for a cup of hot chocolate and a bite to eat from Cooky. We'll probably fill the huge bathtub with hot, bubbly water and take long, luxurious baths. Maybe we'll try new hairstyles, or maybe we'll just read. I'm still trying to figure out the importance of these old manuscripts I found at the bottom of Mama and Dad's trunk. Some of the Spanish is so old I'm going to have to ask Miguel for help. I think I'll send the documents to him with this letter. He can look at them and keep them safe for me. Ha. Can't you tell I'm not suited for a sedentary lifestyle? Oh, I can hardly wait to get on Dorado's back again and feel the wind in my hair as I race Tony and Hercules.

Well, goodnight, dear Beth. Write soon. Love, Victoria.

Tony's smile returned, but his mind wrestled as he tried to remove the image of Victoria soaking in a large porcelain bathtub with bubbles frothing over her from his thoughts. He could almost smell the hot, steamy fragrance as the scent rose from the bathwater. He remembered the intoxicating feel of her hair and could easily remember the scent of meadow flowers clinging to her.

SEVEN

"Well, what did you find out?" The Fixer asked Eddie.

"Victoria Silverthorne is visiting Mark and Bella Silverthorne for an indefinite period. Her father was the older brother. The report is both he and his wife died in a mining accident on the western slope of the Rockies. She traveled here from Texas in Silverthorne's private Pullman."

"Alone?"

"No, another young Irish woman came with her."

"Have you discovered any of her habits or patterns?"

The large man shook his head. "Not yet, Boss. We put a follower on her on Christmas Day, but she didn't move out of the house until the day after Christmas. Then she left with the Irish girl and Silverthorne's accountant. We've followed her for the last week now."

"Well, where does she go?" Blunting snapped.

Eddie frowned. "She, the Irish girl, and the accountant travel around and go inside empty houses and look around."

Blunting stared at the unkempt man in front of him. "What are they looking for?"

"We don't know, Boss. Seems mighty strange." Eddie seemed hesitant to speak.

"Anything else?"

Eddie wrung his hands and shifted his feet. "Yeah, Boss. Someone else is following her."

"What?" Blunting roared and sat up in his swivel chair. "Details."

"I knew you'd want to know, so I had the guy followed, but I think he's on to us. He's slippery and knows the city well. He's connected in some way to a person at the *Denver Post*."

The Fixer's pale eyebrows rose in surprise. "What's going on here, Eddie? Why does the *Denver Post* have an interest in Victoria Silverthorne? Are you sure he followed her and not Mark Silverthorne?"

"I don't know, Boss, but somethin' don't feel right."

Blunting pounded a fist on this desk. "You're right. Keep the watcher on her but stay far away from Mark Silverthorne. He's a knowing one. Pull back enough to see who else may be watching the woman."

Several days later, both Eddie and Jack came to report. The paleness of their faces indicated their concern.

"Boss, you ain't gonna believe this, but two more men are watchin' her besides us, and they don't work for the same people."

Larry Blunting felt the shock to his toes. Too many people seemed to have fingers in his pie. Of one thing he was now certain—the woman either knew something or had something others wanted, and he intended to find out which. If what she knew or had was worthwhile, he wanted a piece of the action.

On the same day Blunting met with Eddie and Jack, Tim rushed into the kitchen where Abby, George, and Victoria chatted with Cooky as she prepared dinner.

Victoria signed, "What's wrong?"

"People watch you." He pointed at her, his movements exaggerated.

"What?" Victoria paled and her legs began to tremble. "Know how?" Her hands punctuated each word with urgency.

"Friends. Friends watch many days. You leave, men follow."

Victoria staggered to the chair. "Someone watched us at the university? Why?"

George, with wide-eyes, said, "What do you mean, miss?"

The others listened as she told about the eavesdropper at the door, the retreating footsteps, and the footprints in the snow. George couldn't believe he hadn't seen anyone and could only presume the watcher had snuck a peek into the library window when he bent to remove snow and ice from the carriage wheels.

"I'm getting your uncle, Vicky." Cooky wiped her hands on her apron.

Victoria stopped her with a hand on her arm. "No. Not until I have more information. I need to be able to handle my problems without running to Uncle Mark for help. I'll go to him if I feel I'm in danger, but not until then. Promise not to say anything? All of you? Please?"

Abby, Tim, and Cooky nodded, but George remained silent.

"What's wrong, George?" Victoria waited for him to answer.

"I won't go against Mr. Mark's wishes."

"You won't have to. I take full responsibility for my actions. You are free to refuse, but I'll hope you'll consider my request."

He finally nodded after several more moments spent in silence. "But I will do this only with the understanding you won't hide any information from me."

"Agreed." She turned to Abby. "Please don't tell Orville, okay? At least not yet. He'll go right to Uncle Mark because he'll feel this is his duty."

Abby nodded, and Victoria hugged them all. "Thank you, my friends."

"But why do they watch you?" Abby asked.

Victoria clasped her hands together. "I don't know."

"What are we going to do then?"

The "we" heartened her. "I don't know. I need to pray. Will you all pray too?"

They nodded and promised to keep their eyes and ears open.

Victoria expected to spend a sleepless night fretting over the news but was surprised when she didn't. After praying for guidance and assurance, she pulled the comforter up, turned over, and went quickly to sleep.

The next morning, before she opened her mother's Bible and once more prayed for guidance, she stepped to the side of the curtained window and peeked out. Just as she expected, she saw at least three different men she hadn't noticed before engaged in activities within view of the Silverthorne mansion. A couple shoveled the snow off sidewalks. One lounged in the shadows of privacy hedge and smoked a cigarette before picking up his shovel. Their movements were expressly designed to look natural, but each would stop to rest on his snow shovel handle and look toward her window and the other windows of the mansion.

The watchers also kept a distrustful eye on each other but didn't approach or acknowledge they engaged in the same activity.

Victoria's stomach lurched and her throat tightened. She turned then from the window, but could barely breathe as she opened the Bible.

She smiled when the first passage she turned to was Matthew 10:26. God had a sense of humor. "Fear them not therefore: for there is nothing covered, that shall not be revealed; and hid, that shall not be known." Her breathing eased. God was the revealer of secrets and still retained control.

When she found Romans 8:15—For ye have not received the spirit of bondage again to fear, but ye have received the Spirit of adoption, whereby we cry, Abba, Father—and 1 John 4:4—Ye are of God, little children, and have overcome them: because greater is he that is in you, than he that is in the world—her breathing and heartbeat returned to normal.

After she finished her devotions, Victoria piled her hair on top of her head, dressed, and went down to the kitchen where her friends waited for her. At her cheery hello, they smiled, but appeared nervous and unsure of themselves.

Cooky handed her a mug of steaming hot chocolate and signaled for her to sit.

"Would you like to hear the plan?" Victoria grinned when everyone nodded with differing degrees of enthusiasm.

"Well, God reminded me that I have minimal control over this situation, and he expects me to trust. He knows how difficult this is for me because I like the comfort I feel when I can control certain things in my environment."

They all nodded. She imagined they understood perfectly.

"He's leading me to pray and trust, and I'm to wait, watch, and try to get as much information as I can. I intend to confuse these watchers by acting in random ways, but I'm not to fear." She looked at Tim and George. "Much of the information I need must come from you, my friends." She waited for her words to sink in and then said, "Are you willing to help?"

Tim smiled his agreement while George stood without moving, obviously waiting for more information. Victoria understood he couldn't jeopardize his job, nor ignore the responsibilities he had to Mark and Bella Silverthorne.

"George, I'll not ask you to do anything Uncle Mark wouldn't like. You get around the town a lot when Uncle Mark sends you on errands. Would you keep your eyes and ears open?"

He nodded. "Certainly, Miss Vicky. You have done so much for me."

She signed to Tim and spoke at the same time, "You have many friends who go around city. Can they help us?"

He nodded and smiled.

Victoria grinned. What better game could one play than outfox the foxes?

"I will pay for your friends' help. Will you manage money and give fair wages?"

Tim's grin stretched from one side of his face to the other, and he stood a little straighter. Cooky's eyes filled with tears. Victoria understood. Most of the polite society probably didn't have much use for a child with any special condition, unless their usefulness extended to running errands or working in mines or factories. Tim was fortunate enough to have been well-educated and to live in a home with certain advantages, so he didn't have to live the same kind of life.

"Friends must watch and listen only, but not let people see them," Victoria continued. "They can't say name Silverthorne to anyone. Only find information and give to you. You tell me, George, or Abby. I will give you one thousand dollars to pay helpers. Buy them warm clothes, shoes, and food for their families. You make all the decisions. You good at mathematics. I trust you."

Tim nodded his right hand. "Yes." The joy in his beautiful brown eyes melted Victoria's heart.

"Please pay yourself twice what you pay your helpers. Tell me when you need more money for this work."

Tim's eyes widened. "No one ever trust me so much. I start today. Now." He hugged Victoria, Abby, and his mother. George shook his hand and gave him a thumbs-up.

Victoria stopped Tim as he was about to leave. "Wait. Three men watch outside. Don't let men see attitude or action changes, okay?"

Tim put his thumb and pointer finger at the side of his temple and flicked the finger up in the sign for "understood" before he left.

Cooky watched him leave and then turned to Victoria, tears running down her cheeks. "Thank you. You've given him a gift of such value. He'll never forget this gift, or you."

"The money?"

"No. Trust." Cooky brushed at her tears and adjusted her apron before returning back to her work.

Over the following weeks, Victoria and Abby shopped for a trousseau and houses. George always drove them, and sometimes Aunt Bella accompanied them. Orville went when they looked at houses, but whenever they left the Silverthorne mansion, they made certain to go on different days of the week, at different times of the day, and Victoria always watched for The Watchers or for Tim's spies.

She, Tim, Abby, and George had modified some signs to be used to communicate with Tim's network of spies and with each other should the need arise, and Victoria watched the urchins on the streets for any signal they had information for her.

Despite their constantly changing schedule, she knew anytime she walked out the door, The Watchers would signal others who waited at different locations. They followed her on foot, by horseback, or by carriage everywhere she went, and the watching made her as uncomfortable as the experience in the Amarillo hotel when she had made her grand entrance wearing the blue velvet dress.

Often, she had a hard time pushing down the fear and battled daily to give God the control. Some days, she wanted just to hide in the sanctuary of the Silverthorne mansion and not leave. Because she didn't know what to say about The Watchers, her letters to Texas became fewer and far between. She filled them with talk of the wedding and house hunting expeditions instead.

As the days passed, however, her fear changed to anger. How dare these people make her feel as if she were a fish in a fishbowl? Her restlessness and discontent increased as the weeks passed, and she was no closer to discovering why her parents had died such untimely deaths.

Victoria mulled over what she'd learned since coming to Denver and wondered if the trip had been pointless. True, she'd learned much more about her parents from the stories Aunt Bella and Uncle Mark told, and she felt she'd grown closer to her mother because of the daily reading she did in her mother's Bible. Mom's handwritten notes and comments were priceless, but Victoria had hit a dead end. She wondered if she should give up and go home.

Victoria studied The Watchers and their patterns of behaviors and noted how they acted. Once, when she'd accompanied Mark to his office downtown, she noticed how they seemed to melt into the landscape. Obviously, these people didn't want Mark Silverthorne to discover them. Perhaps they feared repercussions from such a powerful man.

One sunny but cool day in the middle of March Victoria, Abby, and Orville had stopped by a restaurant for a bite to eat after revisiting the house Orville had recently purchased for his soon-to-be bride and her family. As they sat waiting for their meal, Abby slid her foot over and tapped Victoria's under the table and then tilted her head toward the small, ragged boy who stood outside the door asking people to buy his newspapers. When he caught Victoria's eye through the plate glass window, he tilted his head and glanced down at the newspapers he carried. The boy looked around as if to see if anyone watched before repeating the motion.

Victoria nodded and held up a finger indicating he should wait.

Abby kept Orville occupied with her chatter and questions, while Victoria strolled toward the door.

Outside, she motioned for the boy to sell her a paper. She drew a coin from her reticule and bent down to give the money to him. He pulled a newspaper from the bottom of the stack and said, "Thank you. Look inside." His raspy tone matched his ragged dress.

Victoria smiled and pressed the folded newspaper close to her chest, curious to know what might be hidden inside, then she turned and waited for Abby and Orville.

Once they're returned to the mansion, Victoria opened the paper in her bedroom and a piece of paper fluttered to the floor. Abby picked it up between two fingers and curled her nose. The note was dirty, misspelled, and unsigned, but Victoria had no trouble understanding the message. She mentally corrected the errors as she read.

Men think you have Spanish gold papers. Some men work for Blunting. CAREFUL.

Victoria's knees buckled and she sat down abruptly on the edge of the bed, trying not to faint. She'd read of a Larry Blunting—called The Fixer—and his cronies in the *Denver Post*. In fact, Lawrence Lucky had written several scathing articles about the riffraff infesting Denver, and both the Blunting brothers and the Soapy Smith gang figured prominently in his articles.

Abby rushed to her side and massaged Victoria's hands before calling for the maid to fetch her a glass of water.

George entered with the water instead and frowned. "You are ill?"

"No, I'm fine." Victoria sat up straighter. "Just a little disconcerted."

"What does the note say?" Abby's asked.

Victoria handed Abby the letter and drank the water as her friend read the note aloud.

"Spanish gold? Why would they think such a thing?"

"I don't know, Abby, unless—" She frowned. "The last thing Uncle Mark and I talked about with the chancellor at the university was the possibility my parents had acquired documents indicating where lost Spanish gold or other antiquities lay hidden. The chancellor thought gold hunting was out of character for my parents, but Uncle Mark was sure the lure of gold could change even them. I'm certain this is the topic we discussed when I thought someone listened. Do you think whoever snooped on us reported to Blunting?"

Abby frowned. "To him, or to someone else, Vicky. He got the information from someone, but however he got this, I know gold has a way of bringing out the worst in people, especially someone like him. But what about the documents? O' what does he speak?"

"The only documents I had were the historic journals and papers I sent to Miguel several weeks ago. They made no reference to Spanish gold, though. *Oro* is not a word easily missed, even when the Spanish is old."

George straightened. "We must notify your uncle."

"No, George, not yet. I still don't feel in danger, but I'll be extra careful. Why hasn't Blunting made a move to try and get this information from me? He's been watching for months. What holds him back?"

———————

Blunting could have told her why he hadn't moved. The other watchers worked for someone and, after all these months, he still couldn't locate the sources with certainty. He didn't feel he could act until he knew what he was up against. He'd traced the one group to that Lucky fellow at the *Post*. He grew tired of the nasty articles the guy produced, despite the fact his henchman had visited Mr. Lucky's apartment and busted things up as a warning. The visit had only antagonized the writer, and his articles had become vituperative.

He didn't recognize the watchers from the next group, though, and they worried him the most. They moved quickly, quietly, and rotated often. Not only did they watch the woman, but they watched his people, making him nervous and irritable. He thought someone had recruited tails from the

Mexican sector of the city, but he wasn't sure. He only knew his boys stayed away from the group, even as tough as they were, because the Mexicans tended to be quick to use knives or pistols before they asked questions. What frustrated Larry the most was the fact Victoria Silverthorne didn't seem to have any established patterns of movement. Predictability of human behavior allowed him to make plans, but she either holed up in the Silverthorne fortress for days at a time or moved in erratic ways. If he didn't know better, he'd say she was wise to him. He shook his head. No, he wouldn't credit any woman with that much intelligence, so he watched and continued to lay his plans.

That evening, Victoria made her decision. After much prayer and soul-searching, she decided to return home. She would leave immediately after Abby and Orville's wedding, but would make a stop at her parents' graves, if she could find them. To do this, she'd need help.

She wrote two letters: one to Sam and Arnie asking them to accompany her, and one to Tony, asking if he would send Dorado with the two men.

EIGHT

The few weeks before the wedding were hectic and full of last-minute things to do. Abby's mother and siblings had traveled to Denver and stayed at a nearby hotel with her until everything at the new house could be made ready. Victoria helped where she could but was often in the way. Instead, she spent most of her time with Aunt Bella and planned for her return home. She hoped once she left town, The Watchers would leave her alone.

The more Victoria observed Abby's joy at the thought of becoming a wife, mother, and mistress of her home, the sadder she became. She didn't know what God intended for her life. She knew what she wanted, but her wishes seemed unlikely to be fulfilled at this point. Victoria dreamed of having her own home—one full of laughter, love, and energy. If she closed her eyes, she could feel the warmth of the space and could see out the window to the rolling Texas plains. So, as she planned, she prayed.

Victoria knew returning home might be difficult. She was not the same woman who had left the Amarillo train station all those weeks ago. Neither was she the same person who had lived with Mary and John for fifteen, relatively contented years, and tended their store in a tiny community full of people who didn't accept her. The thought of returning to face more of the same criticism, judgment, and gossip she'd grown up with filled her with restlessness. *I don't want to tend store for the rest of my life either*. Her options seemed limited, though, in the small ranching town. She thought maybe she'd move to Amarillo and find work there, but this thought also filled her with a sense of restlessness and uncertainty.

"Vicky, dear, do you feel like going into one more store with me before we go home? You'll love this fascinating décor shop just around the corner. I've ordered a couple of end tables for the sitting room, and they've come in. The manager was going to deliver them, but I told him I'd pick them up since we'd be in the area."

"Sure, Auntie. I'd love to." Victoria restrained her sigh. Lately, nothing held her interest.

"We'll be just a few moments, George."

"Yes, Miss Bella."

Victoria smiled at George then walked around the corner into the store.

A lovely aroma tickled her nose as she stepped inside the quaint little shop. The hint of wood polish, scented candles, and new fabric smelled almost as good as the mercantile back in Texas. Someone with excellent taste had arranged the furnishings to appear at their best. Victoria's depression lifted as she walked around the room fingering fabrics and looking at the vibrant colors of wood. She noted the way the dining and living room furniture sets were placed, and how the Persian carpets added to the feeling of style and elegance. A gorgeous bedding set in rich shades of creams, tans, and brown silk drew her attention. She slid her hand over the sheets. They were the softest and silkiest she'd ever felt. The softness of the pillows invited her to touch and, though she didn't know where her next bed would be, Victoria had a sudden yearning to own something this exquisite.

She stood for a moment and fingered the material but then turned as the salesman approached. Within moments, she had purchased the bedding and matching draperies, and the clerk promised they would be delivered to the Silverthorne mansion the same evening.

Bella called for George and, as he walked to the carriage with laden arms, the two followed.

Suddenly, something hard and cold poked Victoria in the ribs. Someone wearing the sour stench of unwashed body hissed near her ear.

"If ya want to live ta see your next birthday, Missy, you'll hand over yer fancy purse."

The blade moved from her ribs to her throat. She stilled and fought panic rising in her chest.

Bella opened her mouth to scream, but the masked robber turned his knife on her and threatened, "Go ahead, lady. Screaming will be the last thing ya ever do."

"Don't worry, Aunt Bella," Victoria spoke with a calmness she didn't feel. "I've been expecting something like this to happen for quite a while now." Her quiet declaration seemed to shock the robber into lowering his knife.

"What?" Bella yelped and then fainted.

"Here. Here's my money," Victoria reached into her reticule, stepped back, and cocked her pistol she drew from the bag, holding the weapon with steady hands.

The man's pupils dilated; his knife hand shook.

"Drop the knife."

The knife clattered to the ground as the thief lifted his hands and stepped back.

"Wait."

The man was thin, as tall as she, and dressed in dark clothing. He'd covered the lower half of his face with a scarf, and a black cap covered most of his head. His eyes widened as he looked in her eyes.

"You listen to me, Mister, and you listen well. Tell your boss I don't have any documents or maps he's interested in. I want him to leave me alone. Do you understand?"

The man nodded.

"You make sure he hears you. He's had me followed for months now, and I'm tired of him."

Sweat dripped down the man's face, and the look in his eye signaled his thoughts.

"Don't try to wrestle this gun out of my hands. I'm coiled as tightly as a snake, and this Peacemaker is a touchy weapon. Besides, I've never missed something as close as you. Now get back to your boss." Victoria took a small step forward. "Go on, get."

The man backed up the alley then turned and ran. Victoria let the hammer down and stuck the gun back in her reticule. Minutes had passed, but their passing felt like hours. She turned to help George with Aunt Bella. "Here, George, let me help you get her into the carriage."

Once inside, Victoria began to tremble and thought she would lose her lunch. She lowered the window and hung her head out the side, breathing in the crisp air and trying to calm her nerves. The nausea left as they pulled into the Silverthorne drive.

"Go get Mr. Silverthorne!" George ordered one of the boys who came to open the door. The fear in George's voice sent the boy up the stairs two at a time.

Mark came immediately and helped his sister out of the carriage. He carried her to her room, laid her on the bed, and called for her maid. George and Victoria followed.

Soon, Bella began to moan and tried to sit up. "Victoria. Is Victoria here?" she cried. Fear sharpened her aunt's voice as she looked around the room, her eyes wild.

"I'm here, Auntie." Victoria stepped from behind Mark so her aunt could see her. "I'm here, Aunt Bella, and I'm okay. You're home, and everything's fine now. Don't be afraid."

Bella moaned again and then flung herself into Mark's arms as he sat on the bed next to her. Her eyes filled with tears when she looked in his. "That thief threatened to slit our throats." She wept uncontrollably, and she could not be consoled for quite some time. Bella's maid brought her tea containing a sleeping draught, but Mark wouldn't leave his sister's side until the tea began to take effect.

When Bella had finally nodded off to sleep, Mark indicated with a sharp tilt of his head that Victoria and George should follow him. By the time they reached Mark's library, his mouth had flattened into a slit and his eyes had hardened into green flint.

"What happened?" He stood in front of the fireplace; his hands fisted at his sides.

George spoke first. "Sir, a man tried to rob Miss Victoria as she and Miss Bella left a shop near Sixteenth and Larimer. He timed his actions so I was not close enough to the women to be of help. Miss Bella had sent me to the carriage with a couple of large boxes, so I was around the corner when he must have snuck up on them from behind. The deed happened in less than two minutes. By the time I got back, Miss Bella was on the ground, and the man had run away."

"Tell me the rest, Victoria. Why did a thug run away from two defenseless women?"

She closed her eyes and prayed for the right words. When she opened them, Mark continued to stare at her, impatience tightening his lips and deepening his frown. "I'm going to tell you some things you won't like, Uncle Mark, but I want you to hear me out before passing judgment. Also, if you must get angry at someone, let this someone be me, and no one else in this household. Do you agree?"

He frowned. "I can't promise anything until I've heard what you have to say, Victoria. Then I will decide."

"Well, in that case, I can tell you only part of the information." Victoria felt unwilling to give him information that might cause him to dismiss George or Cooky. Hard green eyes met hard green eyes as Victoria waited.

"Very well. I will reserve judgment and hear you out. I will try to contain my anger."

His words were the best Victoria could expect from him, so she nodded and then indicated two chairs. "Can we please sit down?"

He agreed, and they sat across from each other. George stood near the door, waiting.

"So, I again ask you to tell me why a robber ran from two defenseless women."

"I wasn't exactly defenseless. I always carry a Colt Single Action Army .45 caliber with me whenever I leave."

He stared at her, amazement and doubt written across his face. "Why would you do so?"

"Because three different groups of men have followed me since Christmas."

"What?" he roared and leaned forward.

"Yes, I think someone spied on us when you and I went to see the chancellor. Someone listened to our conversation."

"How do you know this?"

"I saw movement when I walked by the door. Do you remember closing the door after we entered?"

He nodded.

"Well, the door was open, and I heard retreating footsteps. They echoed down the hall, which is why I asked the chancellor about the caretaker. When we got into the carriage, I saw tracks in the snow. They led from the front door to the windows."

Mark looked at George. "You saw no one?"

"No, sir. While I waited, I removed ice and snow from the horses' hooves and the carriage wheels."

Victoria then told him everything else. She explained how her friends had helped, and how the network of young spies worked. "Uncle Mark, you're not to be upset at George and Cooky for not telling you, because I asked them to promise not to. I told them I'd come to you if I felt threatened."

"That wasn't wise, Victoria."

"I disagree. Before I left home, Miguel Morales, who is like a father to me, told me I was old enough to make my own choices, but I also had to take the consequences for these choices. He told me I should not expect others to solve my problems for me, and I think he was right. Though I've been frightened, irritated, and angry much of this time, I've learned some things about myself I would not otherwise have known if I'd depended on you or someone else to solve my problems. I am a stronger person for this."

Mark sat back in his chair and said nothing for several moments. Finally, he leaned forward once more and said, "Intellectually, I agree with everything you say, Victoria, but I disagree at an emotional level. My job is to protect the women of this family from as many ill winds blowing through life as I can. I seem to have done a poor job."

Victoria shook her head. "No, you haven't."

"Tell me about your spies then. You say the deaf boy in this house organized the network? The deaf boy?"

"The young man's name is Tim, not 'the deaf boy'." Her voice filled with reproof. "And if Tim and his friends hadn't spied for me, I'd never have known someone followed. The attack would have caught me unprepared."

"But how did you communicate with someone who can't hear?"

"Easily enough. Abby, George, and I learned sign language. Much of the syntax is similar to Spanish, so the language was easy for me. We adapted the signs into a code we and his ring of spies all understood."

Mark pushed his hand through his hair and fought back a grin. "I marvel at such creativity, niece."

"Because of the signs, I felt safer. Not only did The Watchers follow me when I went out, but Tim made certain our watchers were close as well. They could've run for help at any time."

"I want to see how this works. George, bring Tim to me."

A few moments later, Tim entered the room like a mouse entering a ring of hungry cats. His guarded eyes moved from Mark to Victoria.

"Uncle wants to ask you questions about our business." She smiled her reassurance. "Tell him anything he wants to know."

Tim signed "yes" and looked at Mark.

Mark asked the questions and seemed to be impressed with the fluidity and complexity of the language. He looked from George to Victoria. "I'm amazed at your ability to share so much information. I would never have believed this to be possible. What you just demonstrated has opened up a wealth of possibilities for me."

Victoria acted as the translator between Mark and Tim, but when Tim signed answers, he looked directly at Mark, not at Victoria. He spoke face-to-face in the only way he could.

"Do you know who attacked Victoria today, and why?" Mark's calm tone reassured Victoria.

"Yes. Man followed after attack. Went to saloon on Larimer Street. He works for crime boss. They think she has maps to lost Spanish gold."

Mark's face hardened and anger tightened his voice. "I know exactly who this crime boss is. Do you know who else watches?"

"One group hired by reporter. He works *Denver Post*. Others we not know. They not so close after attack."

Victoria's eyebrows lifted. The only reporter she knew at the *Denver Post* was Lawrence Lucky. Had he followed her to Denver, or was his presence here just a coincidence? Why would he hire people to watch her? Did he think she knew where gold could be found, or was he trying to protect her because he knew Blunting watched? She'd read Lawrence's blistering editorials aimed at Blunting and others who contributed to Denver's skyrocketing crime rate, and she knew Lawrence would've been concerned. Her mind raced. She didn't have answers, but she determined to find them before she left.

A burden seemed to roll from her shoulders. At least she knew two of the groups who watched, and one of them probably meant her no harm. Tim said the other group had backed off since the attack, and the relief lightened her even though she wondered why they had retreated.

Mark rose from his chair and offered his hand to both Tim and George before saying, "Well done, both of you. I am in your debt for taking such good care of Victoria. We may speak later, but the hour is late, and I must check on Miss Silverthorne before I retire."

Tim and George left, and Victoria jumped up and hugged Mark.

"Thank you for not blaming them. I asked for their promises, and they've been faithful to keep these. I'm glad you won't hold this against them."

Mark returned Victoria's hug. "Though I wish I had known, I'm glad you were wise enough to provide for your safety. No, I won't hold their promises against them."

They walked toward the door together, but Victoria stopped before the threshold and turned to her uncle. "Uncle Mark, I'm leaving in two weeks, immediately after Abby's wedding."

His eyebrows rose.

Victoria rose on tiptoes to kiss his cheek. "Thank you for your hospitality and kindness to Abby and me."

"What is your hurry, Victoria? You are always welcome to stay in my home as long as you like. I know Bella would say the same."

"Thank you, but I still haven't found all the answers I need. I've sent for my horse and asked some friends to return with me. I plan to try and find my parents' graves before I return to Texas. These friends were there when they died, so they can show me the way. I'll tell Aunt Bella tomorrow when she feels a little better."

"Be careful, Victoria. You probably haven't heard the last of Larry Blunting. Please ask Tim and his friends to continue watching until you leave Denver."

"I will."

Larry Blunting's face purpled when his man returned empty-handed. Then he ranted and raved for several minutes while the thief cowered in fear.

Blunting felt certain something as precious as a treasure map would be hidden on her person and not at the mansion where a servant could find the thing during routine cleaning, but he couldn't get anyone into the mansion to search for what he wanted.

"She ... she sent you a message, Boss," the thief finally said.

Larry straightened. "What message?"

"Well, after she pointed the gun in my face and looked at me with those strange, witch-like eyes, she said to tell you she didn't have any maps and she'd expected you to do something like this. She knew you've had her followed since Christmas, and she said she was tired of this. I'm to make sure you got the message."

Larry fell into his chair. "She's known we've watched her since Christmas?"

The thief nodded.

Unbelievable. How could she have known? He slammed his fists onto the desk and glared at the man before him. "We've got a leak somewhere. Get out of here."

The man turned and scurried from the room. Blunting yelled for Eddie and Jack, who spent most of their time hanging out in the attached saloon smoking and gambling. "We've got a weasel," he spoke without preamble. "That Silverthorne woman has known we've followed her almost from the beginning." He swore. "I want to know who's talking. Do you hear me?"

"We've tried, Boss. No one knows how she gets the information," said Eddie.

Blunting stopped ranting. "Wait a minute. If she's known for three months, why didn't she tell Silverthorne?" He slapped his thigh. "I bet she hasn't said anything to him because he has done nothing, and that isn't like him. Hmm. Let me think about this."

<hr />

A few nights later, Blunting returned to his saloon to hear the screams of "Fire! Fire!" Someone had torched three of his other saloons simultaneously, and he could barely muster enough help and water to quench the fires.

He climbed the stairs to his office at midnight, smoke-streaked and raging, to find a handwritten note pinned to the door. The letters were well-formed and educated, and Blunting had no doubt who had written the note.

Next time, I won't play games. If I find you are still following my niece, or if I find any hint you plan another ill-advised robbery, your saloons will not be the only thing you lose. S

NINE

The next day, Victoria sent a message to Lawrence Lucky at the *Denver Post* asking him to come to the mansion after work to chat with her.

He sent a reply and showed up promptly at five o'clock. George ushered him into the library where both Mark and Victoria waited.

Victoria rose to meet the reporter. "Lawrence, thank you for coming."

Mark moved from the fireplace and shook the reporter's hand. "Please be seated." Lawrence sat down in a plush arm chair and Mark sat across from him. "Mr. Lucky, we have information leading us to believe you are paying several people to watch Victoria and have been for several months. We would like an explanation."

Lawrence smiled. "You're a man after my own heart, Mr. Silverthorne. I am pleased to meet you and will be happy to answer your questions, though you probably won't like the answers."

Victoria cleared her throat. "Mr. Lawrence, did you follow me to Denver?"

"Originally, yes. John paid me to come here to keep an eye on you."

"John?" Victoria shook her head as if to clear her hearing. "Why?"

"He thought you would come to Denver, find the information about your parents and what they sought, and then go looking for their treasure. He wanted to know if you would find more gold coins like the one Sam and Arnie brought back with them." Lawrence paused as if to soften the next blow. "He wants a few of the coins for himself."

Victoria's stomach lurched and her head spun. Had she not been sitting, she would've fallen. Why would John would do this? Did Mary know?

Several moments passed before Victoria could force any words between her teeth, and then she could only speak in a whisper. "How did you get involved?"

"The day you told everyone you were coming to Denver to meet your uncle," he glanced at Silverthorne who watched him with a cold expression.

COLORADO TREASURE

"I waited at the buggy when John came to take you and Mary home. From everyone's expression, I saw something big had happened, so I waited and tried to pry the information out of him. His preoccupation made him share with little prompting. I'd guessed the Denver trip was your news, because I'd seen the addresses on the telegrams you sent."

"What?" Victoria straightened.

Mark growled deep in his throat, but Lawrence continued. "I'm an investigative reporter, remember? I was curious and wondered what you were up to ever since you came to my office and asked for fifteen-year-old newspapers, yet in the same breath, you told me you searched for information about the Spanish presence in New Mexico territory. I figured you were either trying to keep me from finding out what you really wanted or that your knowledge of historical events was way off. I couldn't believe the latter."

"Solving mysteries is the life blood of a reporter like me." He shrugged and then grinned. "You know, Miss Victoria, in a way, you have a mind like mine. When you're on a quest for information, you're tenacious, but this means you're also predictable. When you drove to Amarillo with the Morales', I knew you'd probably stop by the newspaper offices for information. So, while you were sightseeing, I prepared the editors for your visit. I asked them to copy any information you found interesting."

"So that's how they knew which papers I wanted before I asked. Very clever. I thought as much."

"Then John asked me to send your mother's Bible to you to get you stirred up even more to come to Denver. He figured at some point in time, you would decide to go to Colorado to visit your parents' graves, especially since your nightmares were so vivid and disturbing, they gave you no peace." Victoria startled, and he answered her unasked question. "Yes, John told me about these nightmares."

Victoria grimaced. "He got someone stirred up, all right. Mary was so mad about me getting the Bible, she marched away buzzing like an angry hornet. I bet John got an earful that day."

"So, you chose to take advantage of my niece, correct?" Mark's voice remained cool and unimpressed.

Lawrence grimaced and squirmed a bit in his chair. "Originally, yes, but things have changed."

"How so?" Mark crossed his arms over his chest.

"Something more important than the quest for elusive gold caught my attention and raised my ire. Crime runs rampant in this beautiful city, and a handful of no-goods are working with police, judges, and crooked politicians to rape this town and her citizens. They scam, cheat, lie, and rob without much fear of repercussions. If the general public remains in ignorance, these actions will continue. I must do my part to try and stop this, and I need all my wits and attention to stay alive to write."

"What does all that mean?" Victoria asked.

"I wrote to John the first week in December and told him I was no longer interested in continuing my investigation."

"So why, then, did you hire people to follow me?"

"At first, I wanted to discover if you searched for anything. One of my men followed you to the University of Denver." Victoria's eyes slid to Mark's and then back to Lawrence. "But soon after, I got the report The Fixer watched you. I knew if he showed interest, you were in danger."

Lawrence frowned and looked at Mark then returned his gaze to Victoria. "I think you're also being watched by someone else, but I can't discover by whom, or why."

Suddenly, Victoria remembered something Lawrence had said. "Did you say Sam and Arnie returned with a gold coin from the site?"

He nodded. "Yes, that's what John told me."

Victoria looked at Mark, who stood to his feet. Lawrence rose with them. "Is there anything else we should know, Mr. Lucky?"

The reporter shook his head.

"Mr. Lucky, did you find out anything about my parents when you investigated? Do you know why they were in Colorado?"

"No, Miss Victoria, I didn't. They looked for some kind of treasure, though I don't know what. I assumed they looked for more of the gold coins."

Mark moved forward and shook Lawrence's hand. "Thank you for coming today, and for not withholding information. I'm sure Victoria appreciates having answers to her questions. As you can see, you no longer need to worry about my niece's safety. You may recall your people."

Lawrence agreed, and they walked with him to the door.

Mark's soft voice halted the party of three before the threshold. "You don't have to worry about Blunting. He will no longer bother Victoria while she is here. I gave the man other things to think about."

Lawrence stared at him a moment and then grinned. "I hope so."

After she and Mark returned to the library, Victoria paced up and down the room and stared at the thoughts behind her eyes. "Uncle Mark, do you really think my parents searched for gold? Really?"

Mark shrugged. "Does the answer to this question matter anymore, Victoria? Perhaps the secret will never be discovered. Maybe this information should stay buried with them. Do you think the answer is important enough to spend more of your time and energy?"

"I don't have an answer, Uncle Mark. What bothers me is gold hunting just doesn't seem to fit with what I've learned about my folks. Even the chancellor said gold-hunting would be out of character for them. In the letters and papers I found, the writer said nothing about gold. Don't you think my parents would have mentioned this if gold is what they sought?" Even to her ears, she heard the pleading in her tone.

"Victoria," Mark used his gentlest voice, "gold does strange things to people." He laughed then without humor. "I spent many years away from James and Maggie, and they may have been different, but I know I face people on a daily basis whose sole purpose in life is to get rich any way they can. Why should your parents be any different? This desire doesn't mean they are better or worse than others for wanting this."

Victoria knew in the deepest part of her being, something was wrong with the picture of gold-hunting parents. *Why should they be any different?* She thought about Mark's question long after he'd left the room. Her inability to give him an answer left her feeling uneasy and restless. She should know the answer, but she didn't, though the response hovered close to the surface of her consciousness, just out of reach. The more she tried to grasp the clue, the more her head throbbed with the effort.

The nightmare troubled Victoria's dreams that night.

───────❧───────

She darted this way and that along the bank of a virgin mountain stream and played tag with a chipmunk. The animal whistled and chirped at her from under the rocks or deadfall.

In moments, she lay on her stomach, her right hand extended. She pushed a lock of black hair away from her face with a grubby hand.

"Come on, little guy, you know you want this bread." She held her breath as the little rodent moved to within a hair's-breadth of her fingers.

"Hey, young'un, what are you up to?" Sam ambled toward her, and the chipmunk vanished under a log.

Victoria sat up, "Nothin', Sam. Just makin' friends."

He winked at her. "Well, don't go wanderin' off, you hear, Vicky? Your ma and pa should be done soon, and then Arnie and me'll find shelter for you all." He looked at the darkening sky. "Looks like we're fixin' to have a real lollapalooza."

"Sure, Sam." Victoria waved at Arnie, who waved back at her from the other side of the creek. Then she looked at the sky. The sun had disappeared, and heavy gray thunderheads filled the narrow space between the steep sides of the red canyon walls. She shivered.

Victoria watched Sam's slow, bow-legged walk for a moment, and then returned her attention to the chipmunk. Gone. She glanced at the hole in the side of the mountain where she'd last seen her mother, and then decided to look for more rocks with people's faces in them. She'd found two keepers yesterday.

She examined each rock carefully before her bare feet touched them, and she chose only those with face-like features to put in her apron pocket. She'd almost filled her pocket when she spotted the shiny gold object caught between two rocks near the stream bank. She examined the round object and smiled. Not only did the rock have a man's face on the front, but the rock shone.

"Sam, look what I found." She held her treasure toward the two men, who stood talking on the other side of the stream.

Victoria hiked up her skirt and petticoat and hopped from rock to rock until she'd crossed the stream and stood next to the two men. She held out her fist. "Look what I found, Arnie."

"Now look at you, Miss Vicky. You got your dress all wet and dirty," Sam scolded. "Your ma is gonna be mad at us both." He tugged at a lock of her hair, but she brushed his hand away and waved her fist in front of his face.

"Okay, little one, let's see your rock with the man's face."

She opened her hand and waited for their admiration.

Sam reacted even better than she'd expected. His eyes popped and he inhaled sharply. "Land sakes alive, Arnie. Will you look at this? I ain't seen anything like this—not in all my born days. Where did you get this, young' un?"

Even at her young age, Victoria recognized urgency when she heard the tone. "Over there," she pointed back toward the stream. "Want me to show you?"

"Yes sir-e-e-e, I do. Maybe Arnie and me can find some for us."

Victoria nodded and started back across the stream.

They were stopped by the voice of her father. "Hello down there," Dad called and waved from the cliff edge.

"Dad," Victoria waved, "Where's—"

Just then, the ground seemed to tremble, and Victoria watched as part of the cliff wall collapsed beneath her father. He disappeared under tons of red earth and pine trees. When the mountain quit roaring, falling, and spitting out red rock fragments, the hole where Victoria had last seen her mother was no longer visible.

"Mama! Daddy!" Victoria screamed and raced toward the rock pile, "Mama! M-a-m-a!" she wailed piteously.

———————— ✺ ————————

"Mama!" Victoria cried and reached toward the jumble of rocks, which disappeared as the mists of sleep left her. She sat up in bed, grasping at thin air, while tears dripped from her eyelashes onto her white cotton nightgown.

She waited for the misery and wisps of dream scenes to pass and realized two things: she'd handed Sam a gold coin, and she had heard her father mention a "treasure far beyond that of rubies" just before he'd climbed toward the cliff above the cave. He seemed to have been speaking to her mother. Mama had smiled and nodded and followed him.

In previous dreams, she'd handed Sam the chipmunk or a gold coin, but now she knew what was real. She tried to rub the headache away, but the ache remained with her as she completed her circuit up and down the stairs and went down to the kitchen.

She told her friends of her plans to leave in two weeks and cringed at the shock on their faces. "I can't live here forever, Cooky. Did you think I would?"

"No, Vicky, but you're a part of the family now. You've brought such joy and sunshine to my life, and to my boy's."

Tim nodded emphatically.

Cooky continued, "With Abby gone, and you talking of leaving, this house is going to be a mighty lonely place."

Victoria hugged the old cook tight and then told them of her plans to visit her parents' graves, and how Sam and Arnie agreed to return with her. They would bring Dorado and other riding and pack animals with them, because they could take the train only part way to the gravesite. From the train station, they'd have to ride several miles by horseback to the mining town of Silverton. Sam said from Silverton, they would ride at least a day south along the Animas River. "I'm acquiring supplies for the journey now, but I'm trying to do this in such a way The Watchers won't know," Victoria told her friends.

Tim asked many questions about the trip, and Cooky smiled as he signed to Victoria. Both of them recognized the signs of longing in his eyes and movements.

"I wonder what will happen to him when you leave?" Cooky spoke to Victoria—not using signs. "He'll be inconsolable."

"I hope not, Cooky."

"What will you do after you visit the graves?" Cooky resumed signing.

Victoria pondered the question for several heartbeats. "I don't know. I'm not comfortable living with John and Mary anymore, and not many opportunities present themselves in our small community. I've thought about moving to Amarillo or staying here in Denver, but the Lord hasn't given me peace about either of those choices. I'd prefer to live with Miguel and Beth …" She thought about Tony. "But I can't. Too many complications associated with that idea."

"They have a ranch?" Tim's eyes sparkled as he signed the question.

"Yes. A very big ranch." She smiled at his fascination with all things to do with ranches, cows, and horses.

After Victoria left the kitchen, she visited with Bella and told her of her plans to leave. Her aunt's unenthusiastic response warmed Victoria's heart.

"Promise you'll write regularly, Vicky. Now that the trains make travel much easier, I'll expect you to come see me. I might even plan a trip to see you if Mark will come with me."

Victoria agreed.

"Please keep your promise, love. I will miss you so much when you are gone. Having you here has been a joy."

Victoria kissed Bella and returned to her room. She thought a hot bath might relieve the headache and ease the tension she felt as she thought about returning home.

As she leaned back against the porcelain tub and let the scented bath oils work, she looked toward the ceiling and began to pray aloud. "Lord, please show me what I'm to do. I'm so confused and uncomfortable when I think of my future. You know how much I hate this feeling of not knowing, but I know you hold my life in the palm of your hand. You know the beginning and ending of my story. Help me to trust your judgment and to remember you love me. Please show me your will."

An hour later, feeling warm and soothed, Victoria descended the carpeted stairs and glanced out the window at the mid-morning sun. As she reached the bottom stair, someone rapped the door knocker and George opened the door.

Astonishment stopped her in her tracks. There stood Tony, twisting his hat between his hands and wearing his special-occasion black cowboy boots, black slacks, black jacket, white shirt, and black string tie. Though his face appeared tranquil, she sensed he was poised to move quickly. He stared at her, and the look in his rich brown eyes could only be described as "hungry." Her heart about exploded at the sight of him. "Tony!" She raced the few feet to the door and flung herself into his arms. "I'm so glad to see you."

He held her close and inhaled. "¡Cariño mío!" he breathed near her ear. "¡Qué hermosa!" He held her for several moments.

Victoria rested her cheek against his chest, closed her eyes, and listened to the rapid beat of his heart. When she remembered where she was, she opened her eyes and slid her palms down Tony's chest until she found his hands. She linked her fingers with his and said, "Come in."

She tugged at him, but as she turned, she caught sight of Hercules and Dorado standing on the side lawn munching on the grass near the drive. Both horses were saddled, and Tony had again woven green ribbons into Dorado's mane.

"You brought Dorado. Oh, Tony, thank you."

Tony smiled and kissed the fingertips of one of her hands. "Sí, he has missed you mightily, cariño. Perhaps you should say hello to him."

Victoria called to the horse as she walked toward him. He lifted his head and pointed his ears at her. The horse stood ground-hitched, as he had been trained, but whinnied and pawed the ground when he heard her voice. She rubbed his velvety nose and scratched around his ears and eyes as she spoke to the gelding. "Hey, big boy, I sure have missed you."

The horse nickered and sniffed her hair and face. She put her arms around the big horse's neck and leaned her cheek against his. Tony stood beside her and watched, stroking the palomino's flank as she talked to Dorado.

"The beauty of your voice soothes my spirit, Victoria. These last four months have been *muy difícil*. Dorado is not the only one who has missed you mightily."

Victoria turned toward him, tears in her eyes. "I know, Tony."

He brushed away the droplets.

When Hercules blew, they looked toward the house. Young Tim approached as if mesmerized and Cooky, George, and Aunt Bella watched from the doorway.

Victoria signed and spoke, "Come and meet Dorado. His name means golden in Spanish."

Tim stopped beside Dorado but did not touch him. His eyes remained glued on the horses, until he finally looked to Victoria for reassurance.

"You can touch him. Hold your hand flat, like this, so he can smell you." Tim's smile caused Victoria's heart to swell as the boy began to softly stroke the horse's neck. Dorado nudged him for more scratching, and Hercules pushed his head into the circle for attention.

"They like to be scratched here and here," Victoria demonstrated and allowed him to copy her motions. Her hands would smell of horse, but she didn't care. "They will be your slaves forever, if you'll stand here and scratch them for a while."

Tim made a soft, gurgling sound indicative of his pleasure. As he petted the horses, his eyes slid to Tony and then to Victoria.

"This is Tony. He came all the way from Texas to bring Dorado to me." She looked at Tony. "Tony, this my friend, Tim. His mother is the cook here."

Tim and Tony sized each other up, then Tony held out his hand to the young man. Tim looked at him intently then shook his hand.

"*Mucho gusto.*" Tony seemed to know instinctively to look at Tim when he spoke and not at Victoria, though she signed Tony's words.

She recognized the touch of hero-worship in Tim's eyes as he gazed at Tony. Tony—the dark, handsome, athletic man who rode horses and lived on the ranch Tim had heard so much about, and now the man of the tales—stood before him in flesh and blood.

"Beautiful horses," Tim signed and pointed, and Victoria translated.

"Yes, and I came to see if the very beautiful lady would like to ride her very beautiful horse."

Victoria laughed. "I'd love to. Give me time to change. I'll let Aunt Bella know our plans."

"Would you stay with the horses, *Amigo*, until we return?" Tony waited for Victoria to interpret.

No one would mistake Tim's enthusiastic answer.

Both Bella and Cooky appeared to be taken with Tony. *Who wouldn't be?* Victoria grinned. He was soft-spoken and charming. His quiet assurance and controlled movements must have convinced the two they need not worry about her safety while she was with him.

"Please return for dinner this evening at seven, Mr. Morales. I'm sure my brother would like to meet you."

"I will be honored. Thank you."

Victoria rushed into her split riding skirt and jacket. She adjusted the lace at her neck and wrists before she slipped on her low-heeled, black leather riding boots. Then she set her wide-brimmed, gray felt hat firmly on her head.

She descended the stairs, riding gloves in one hand and a small set of silver spurs in the other as Tony, Cooky, and Bella watched her. At the bottom of the stairs, she handed Tony her gloves while she bent to buckle on the spurs. "We'll be gone awhile, Auntie. I want to show Tony some of the sights." She observed the concern in both women's eyes. "Don't worry, I'll be okay. I'm safe with him."

Victoria determined to give Tim a ride soon after she saw longing in his eyes as he watched them mount.

The sheer joy of being on the back of a horse and riding in the warm spring sunshine with Tony brought color to her cheeks. She felt like racing Dorado down the streets of Capitol Hill.

Tony easily interpreted her feelings. "Not here. Not yet, señorita. A stretch of ground a few miles away will suit our purposes perfectly. This time, cariño, we will have a fair race, no?"

Victoria's full-throated laugh was contagious.

"I have missed you, *pequeña*." His voice caressed her.

As they approached an open, park-like area a few miles from Capitol Hill, Tony pointed. "When we pass the first tree in that line of trees, we will race for a quarter mile to the end of the grove, agreed?"

"Yes." Victoria laughed once more as they approached the tree.

"Ready? Go." Tony yelled.

They each touched the sides of their horses with the spurs, and both horses laid their ears back, bunched the muscles in their powerful front and hind quarters, and then stretched their necks out to run.

Victoria leaned forward and low over Dorado's neck and used her inner thighs and stirrups to balance.

"Run, Dorado, run." Her breath came in short gasps.

Tony whooped. The pounding of the hooves on hard ground matched the pounding in Victoria's heart.

Her hair came loose from the pins and whirled and danced around her as she and Tony raced neck-and-neck, but she didn't care. She hoped the strands would stay out of her eyes long enough for her to see Dorado's nose pass the finish line.

The tree came into sight, and they remained neck-and-neck. Just before they crossed, Hercules gave a mighty heave and finished a half-nose ahead of Dorado.

They slowed the horses to a lope to cool them off, and then eventually pulled them down to a walk. Both horses breathed hard, but Victoria sensed contentment. They walked in silence for several minutes.

"You can't imagine how much I've longed to do that, Tony."

He chuckled. "Sí, I can well imagine. Running circuits on the stairs would not expend enough energy or create enough of a breeze to tumble the hair from your head."

"You heard, did you?"

"*Claro*. We laughed much."

As they neared Capitol Hill, Victoria turned Dorado toward the west. "I want to show you the house Abby and Orville bought. Orville still lives in his apartment until after the wedding, but Abby, her mom, and her brothers now live in the house. They're planning a small church wedding at a nearby chapel, and then Uncle Mark and Aunt Bella will host their reception at the Windsor Hotel."

When they arrived at the house, Abby smiled widely to see Victoria and when she saw Tony. Victoria thought Abby had never looked more beautiful—she seemed content and fitted for her new home. She gave them a tour of the house and told of the interior painting they'd completed, and of the shopping trips she, Orville, and her family had taken to find just the right pieces of furniture for her home. She explained what they intended to do with the house in the future, and blushed when she talked of plans for a nursery.

As she listened, Victoria could not help but feel wistful. Would she ever have a home of her own? One she could decorate and make beautiful for her loved one? Would she ever have babies to cuddle?

Did the sigh the thoughts generated escape from her heart or her mouth? Had anyone heard? She glanced at Tony from the corner of her eye. He watched her, but his face remained unreadable.

Orville stopped by while Victoria and Tony visited, and Tony offered his congratulations. Orville invited him to the wedding and reception, and Tony accepted.

Abby spoke of the wedding and of new friends she had made. Many of them were long-time friends and family members of Orville's. She spoke of enrolling her brothers in a nearby school in the fall.

Victoria felt herself sigh again.

By the time she and Tony rose to leave, the sun had passed its zenith, and Victoria knew she should get back and wash the horse smell off her hands before dinner.

She dismounted near the front door of the mansion and gave Tony Dorado's reins. "Where are you staying?"

He gave her directions. "We have lodgings near the train station and are boarding the horses close by. Sam and Arnie prepare for our journey."

Tim slipped up beside her. "Fun day?"

Victoria laughed. "Wonderful day."

When Tim looked at Tony, sitting so easily in his saddle, the hero-worship returned to his eyes. Victoria smiled and, while Tim stroked Dorado, asked Tony to take him for a ride around the neighborhood before he returned to the hotel.

Tony hesitated then nodded.

"Thank you," she said, before she tapped Tim's shoulder. "You want ride Dorado?"

Tim's eyes widened and his face paled. He looked from Dorado to Hercules and then at Tony. His intense desire seemed to war with his fear.

Tony nodded at him and dismounted. He showed Tim how to mount and dismount and signaled for him to practice. Tim watched Tony with every bit of attention he had and demonstrated how quickly he could learn.

When Tim sat tall in the saddle, looking as if he had struck pay dirt, Victoria knew Tony would let no harm come to the young man. Before she went into the house, she watched the two ride down the drive side-by-side. Tim mimicked everything his mentor did, and Tony nodded his approval.

As she ran her bathwater, Victoria smiled, and her heart swelled with gratitude. Tony had accepted Tim at face value and had not devalued him because he was deaf. She knew Tony had won a friend for life.

TEN

The next few mornings before the wedding, she and Tony took the horses for a run, and then would cool them down as they rode by some of Denver's famous sites. Tim often accompanied them on the back of Victoria's horse or Tony would let him ride his while he walked a bit. Victoria never tired to see how effortlessly Tim mastered the finer points of riding. He seemed to have an intuitive understanding of the balance needed to turn his mount, or to urge him forward. When she watched him brushing and signing to the horses, she had the uneasy feeling they understood his conversation.

The day before the wedding, while they rested the horses in preparation to return to the mansion, Tim looked at them from atop the back of one of the pack horses, his expression so solemn, Victoria asked what was wrong.

"Want to ask you something. Okay to say no if you don't like."

"What?" She sensed Tim's eagerness, hope, and uncertainty in his movements.

He looked at Tony for a long moment before he signed to Victoria. "I want go with you Texas. Work on ranch. I do all you tell me. I work hard. Not afraid to work hard." He then watched Tony's face and body language as his new hero considered his request.

Tony studied him. "What about your mother?"

"She say she will be sad without me, but also happy for me if I go with you. She trusts you. If she misses me too much, the train will bring her quickly to see me, or me to see her."

"What about your schooling?"

"I learn much from books. Now want learn more from life on ranch." Tim waited, his eyes reflecting eagerness and dread.

Tony continued to look at him. Finally, he nodded. "Before the answer is final, I want to speak with your mother."

Tim pumped a fist in the air and then rode his horse in a circle around Victoria and Tony as they walked the horses to the Silverthorne mansion.

"You won't regret this decision," Victoria told Tony. "Whenever we sit in the kitchen in the mornings, Tim begs for stories of you, the ranch, Miguel and Beth, and the horses. Always the horses." She looked in Tony's eyes. "Here, he's just another deaf boy. On the ranch, he can be a contributing member and feel he has self-worth despite his deafness."

Lucky him. Victoria didn't know how she could be a contributing member of anything. Suddenly, the lack of control and the uncertainty of life welled up to choke her and bring tears. She brushed them away. Her future loomed dark.

"Why do you cry, Victoria?" Tony leaned away from his horse and touched her hand, a frown creasing his brow.

She shook her head and wouldn't look at him. "Nothing. Nothing I can explain right now without weeping uncontrollably and making my eyes puffy for dinner."

Tony straightened in his saddle but kept a concerned eye on her for the rest of their ride.

When they arrived back at the mansion, they dismounted near the carriage house and left the horses ground-hitched as they went to talk to Cooky. She waited for them, a sad but proud look in her eyes as she gazed at Tim. "So, he asked you, did he? I can already tell what your answer is by the glow in his eyes." Tim hugged his mother, and she brushed a lock of curly brown hair from his eyes. "My baby isn't a baby anymore."

"You agree, then? *Timo* may come with us, *Señora*?"

Cooky nodded. "Yes, this has been his dream for a long time. When Victoria came with her stories, he dreamed even more. Then she taught George to read and they discussed books and articles they read. Tim often listened to their signed conversations. He began to think more opportunities awaited him in some other place."

Tony nodded and glanced at Tim. "With your mother's permission, I would like for you to begin work today. Pack what things you will take to Texas. If they are too large or cumbersome, send them by train with Victoria's trunks." Tony looked at Tim's mother and she nodded. He continued, "Then come with me. Sam and Arnie need help with the packs, supplies, horses, and mules, and I know you will be of great assistance. We will leave early in the morning the day after tomorrow."

He turned to Cooky. "If you should change your mind, I will understand." He then told her where he, Sam, and Arnie stayed.

Cooky went to help Tim pack, and Victoria walked with Tony to the horses to wait. "You're coming, Tony?" Her heart sang.

He nodded, a fierce look in his eyes. "Can you doubt this, hermosa mía?"

She took his hand, turned the palm up, and kissed the warm brown skin. "Thank you, Tony. I know how stupid you thought this idea and how nonsensical you thought me to let a dream influence my life to such a degree, so—"

"Shh," he murmured and embraced her. "We will say no more about this."

She laid her head on his chest and closed her eyes. Some of the burden of worry she carried when she thought of the difficulties of the trip eased. "Thank you, querido,"

He lowered his cheek to her hair.

They stood together until they heard stirrings from the house. Before Victoria stepped away, Tony tightened his grip and lowered his lips to hers. He released her quickly.

"Tony—"

He stepped back and took her hand in his. "I will see you tomorrow morning at the wedding."

She watched Tim and Tony mount and ride down the drive. Tony waved to her as he led Dorado away. She returned his wave and watched him go. Her emotions rode a gigantic emotional swing: high one minute and down the next. The feelings bothered her. She'd always been more emotionally stable, so why did she feel this way? Was she coming down with something?

In the kitchen, she asked for a cup of hot herbal tea. She took the cup up to her room and ran a hot bath. She would miss the convenience of being able to bathe every day, whenever she wanted, but the only way she could do this when she returned home would be to find a place in Amarillo with gas. Most people in the surrounding area still used a large wash basin filled with water that had been heated on the stove. As she waited for her hair to dry, she finished packing. Most of her clothing and the bedding set were packed in her steamer trunks waiting to be shipped to Elizabeth tomorrow evening. Victoria had bought another large trunk to contain the gifts, clothing, and other things she'd bought while in Denver. She hoped Elizabeth could find a place to store them until she returned.

Another pile contained several pairs of undergarments, two durable riding skirts, three clean blouses, leather riding gloves, a couple of pairs of riding boots, her wide-brimmed hat, and a fringed leather jacket. The fringes would help to shed rain. These items, if she weren't wearing them, would be placed in a cotton bag in one of the pack animal's panniers.

The saddlebags held her toiletries and essential items she'd need on the trail. She kept checking her lists to see if she'd forgotten anything. Once they were in the Rockies, she couldn't replace anything she'd forgotten.

Victoria fingered the silk of the dark rose dress she'd wear tomorrow. After the wedding and reception, she would change into the cotton gingham dress. Then the rose-colored dress would be packed and sent, but she would take the gingham and petticoats with her in case of need.

"Boss," Eddie reported, "Looks like she's leaving either tomorrow or the next day."

"Where?"

"Well, don't look like she's goin' back to Texas. At least, not yet. Two older men and a young, brown-skinned feller rode in and brought some riding stock and pack mules. Two of the geldings, a large chestnut, and a palomino, look like they have a lot of bottom. The woman rides the palomino, and she rides him well. That young Mexican feller looks like he was born in the saddle, and I bet he's slick with that lariat. Carries himself well but seems mighty cautious. He pays attention to everything that moves. Even when he rides with the woman, he's noticing things.

"The two older men have been buying ropes, tackle, pick axes, and a goodly food supply. They purchased tickets on the Fort Worth-Denver City line, but they're leaving the train at Pueblo and heading west to Canyon City. I heard the heavier-set man ask for distances from Canyon City to Gunnison and then from there to Montrose. They intend to head on down to Silverton."

"Silverton, eh? A lot of things are happening in that area, Eddie. I hear tell millions of dollars in gold have come out of the Gold Prince Mine at

Animas Forks alone, and the silver ore coming out of the mines around the area is rich. Might be a place I'd consider visiting."

"You think she's interested in mining, Boss? Those men with her look more like cowboys than miners."

"Don't be ridiculous. She's going after the gold, but the gold is already coined." He rubbed his chin and smiled. "Get Dan for me. Give him the details and tell him I need him to be packed and ready to leave by tomorrow morning early. He's to take an extra riding horse and pack mule. Tell him to buy a ticket to Ouray and be waiting before they get there. He's to follow them and send me word as often as he can."

The Fixer pulled out a roll of greenbacks. "Here, give this to him and tell him it's an advance. Half now, half when he finds the gold."

Eddie nodded and stuck the bills in his pocket. "Dan Black's the best tracker and rider I know, Boss. He's perfect for this job."

"Yep. Dan's big, morose, and dirty, but he doesn't mind getting wet, cold, or hungry when he's after prey—not like you sissies." Blunting scowled at his hired hand.

"Boss, something else you should know. The young Mexican feller was seen talking to some of that group who watched the woman—the ones we couldn't figure out who they were? Seemed mighty friendly."

"Do they continue to watch?"

"Not since the young feller came to town." Eddie paused and then said, "Boss, the deaf boy from the Silverthorne mansion rides with them."

Blunting evaluated this new piece of information but brushed off the comment. "Well, done, Eddie." He threw the man another wad of bills. "Keep your eyes peeled. I want to know when the group boards the train."

ELEVEN

Abby and Orville exchanged vows in a beautiful little chapel near their new home. From her position at the back of the church where she waited with the bride, Victoria scanned the crowd. Mrs. O'Brien sat in the front row with her children, but often glanced toward the back of the church. When she caught sight of Abby, her face seemed to glow with pride and love.

The ceremony was short and straightforward and brought moisture to Victoria's eyes. Orville and Abby turned and smiled at the crowd as they were presented as man and wife. During the reception, the newly married couple held each other's hands and gazed in each other's faces. They ate cake and drank punch but seemed so engrossed with each other, Victoria wondered if they even noticed as the last few guests departed.

Tony slipped his hand down to Victoria's and linked his fingers with hers as they walked toward the carriages. "*Buenas noches, hermosa mía. I* will fetch you as the sun rises." He raised her fingers to his lips. "*Hasta mañana.*"

Aunt Bella watched from the carriage, and when Victoria entered, she asked, "What does he call you in Spanish? The words sound lovely."

"He calls me many things, Aunt Bella." She paused before continuing, "He has from the time we were young. He's very much like his father, Miguel. Miguel is unpretentious and charming to the bone. He uses the same phrases when he speaks to his wife, Elizabeth."

"But what does he say?"

Victoria blushed. "Hermosa mía means 'my beautiful one.' Often, he calls me pequeña, which means little one, or cariño, which means dearest. When he wants to annoy me, he calls me brujita, which means something like little witch. The *-ita* ending makes the word more affectionate."

"He must love you very much, Victoria, if he uses such endearments."

"I hope so, Aunt Bella. I'm uncertain, though, because Tony's called me those terms since before I was sixteen. We grew up together, and I often wonder if he's just in the habit of saying them. I know he's fond of me, but ..." She bit her lip and looked out the window.

Bella patted her hand. "I have seen the look in his eyes when he gazes at you, dear, and fondness is not the emotion I see."

That night, Victoria stayed up late and visited with her aunt and uncle as she would be leaving early the next morning. She told them of her immediate plans, and what she would do if she found the graves. As the hour grew late, she rose to go upstairs.

Mark and Bella hugged her and told her she would always be welcome in their home whenever she chose to come. Their affection touched Victoria's heart and she thanked them for their sentiments. As she made to leave the room, Mark reminded her, "Don't forget to take the letter Chancellor McDowell sent." Victoria nodded and, when she'd returned to her room, placed the letter in her mother's Bible. She would read the chancellor's words when she had an extra moment.

Early the next morning, she rose before dawn and dressed in her riding gear. She had rested the saddlebags over her left shoulder so she could carry the large bag of clothing with both hands. She tried to walk down the stairs as quietly as she could in boots and spurs and toting her heavy pieces but had only limited success. She soon realized walking down a flight of stairs with all her gear wouldn't win her any prizes for gracefulness.

Her intention was to slip out of the house and wait for Tony under the portico, but Cooky intersected her path and sat her down in the warm kitchen to provide her with breakfast. She had also packed a basket of goodies for all of them to eat on the train.

"Thank you, Cooky. I can't tell you how much I appreciate your kindness."

George sat across the table too and she reached for his hand. "You are a special person, George. I've enjoyed our reading sessions tremendously."

The man nodded and squeezed her hand but said nothing.

When Victoria heard the sound of shod hooves on the pavement and the light creak of leather, she stood. "Pray for us, please."

They nodded.

George carried her saddlebags and clothing bag outside, and Tony buckled them behind Dorado's saddle as Tim hugged his mother. Tony placed her bag on one of the large pack mules.

They would meet Sam and Arnie at the train station with the rest of the stock and supplies. Together, they would unload the animals, and reload them on the train. They would repeat the process when they got off the train at Pueblo and took another to Canyon City. From there, they would pack up, ride the trains or horses, and camp until they reached Silverton. If any other trains were available, they would ride as far as they could to save the wear and tear on the animals. If Victoria's calculations were correct, they would return to the plains of Texas by mid-summer.

As they left the Silverthorne drive, the sun had begun to peek over the horizon and the morning birds began to call to each other. Victoria inhaled the fresh, fragrant air, and smiled at Tim. "You ready for adventure?"

"Yes. Sam and Arnie tell me we ride through mountains," he made the signs for long and deep. "See many new things."

"How did Sam and Arnie tell you this?"

Tim grinned. "Sam and Arnie think, and then make pictures with hands." He mimed the two men. "Sometimes they draw. They funny."

Tony chuckled as Victoria translated. "We must teach them more signs. Yes?"

Tim nodded his fist.

Sam and Arnie waited at the depot with the animals and gear. They greeted her with smiles and questions about her visit, and then got down to the serious business of loading the horses and mules into the stock cars before they loaded the supplies and equipment. They watered the animals again then finally entered the passenger car and sat down on two inward-facing benches. Sam, Arnie, and Tim sat on a long, padded bench and faced Victoria, the picnic basket of food, and Tony.

Victoria gave a passing thought to the luxury and privacy she'd had last time she traveled, but then chuckled as she observed Tim's expression and movements. It seemed obvious he'd never ridden a train before. His eyes darted back and forth, watching everything and everyone. When the train began to move, he glued his nose to the window and gazed at the passing scenery. He turned quickly to her and signed. "We move fast."

COLORADO TREASURE

Victoria nodded and translated for the others as Tim once again plastered his face against the window, his nose smushed and a fog painting the window from his breath.

Sam belly-laughed. "Hope his face doesn't stay that way."

Victoria smiled and then said, "I think you should learn some signs so you can communicate with Tim, and he can talk to you directly without using an interpreter."

They agreed, and by the time they were halfway to Colorado Springs, Victoria had taught them the alphabet, their name signs, numbers, the days of the week, and months of the year. They also learned question words.

Sam's signs were understandable but awkward as he struggled to conform his fingers to the signs, but Tony and Arnie signed with more grace and less effort. Arnie said this was a good game, and quickly became adept with simple, straightforward communication.

By the time they stopped in Colorado Springs to let off or take on new travelers, they knew the signs for a variety of different animals, geographic features, basic colors, and could use a few verbs. Many of the signs made with the hands mirrored the characteristics of the object, so Victoria instructed the new learners to make mental connections between the object and its sign.

Victoria showed how the masculine words like man, boy, father, brother, and uncle were signed from the head and top half of the face, while feminine words like woman, girl, mother, sister, and aunt were signed from the cheek and lower half of the face. She explained the difference in meaning when a signer used straight fingers, as in "see," as opposed to clawed fingers, as in "blind."

"Sign language has its own structure and syntax, so signing words like a, the, and other small words as one would speak them in English is not necessary. These are the movements Tim will make if he wants you to understand the timing of events in past, present, or future tenses." She modeled the signs and the men nodded.

They practiced what they learned, and the lessons kept them occupied and interested for several hours.

Tim had finally turned away from the window and had helped them all sign correctly. Victoria noted his straighter posture and the gleam in his eyes as he did this.

Just before they reached Pueblo, she dug into the basket for the sandwiches, cheese, and apples. She and Tim gave the men the signs for each food item, and they had to form the signs correctly before they could receive their meal.

"Please. Food. Stomach empty," Tony signed. They all laughed. When Victoria gave him his food, he smiled and signed, "Thank you."

When they reached Pueblo, they unloaded the animals and supplies and then loaded them on the cars on the Rio Grande Western. This train would take them to Canyon City, along the banks of the Arkansas River, and through the Royal Gorge to Salida. Before they entered the gorge, the conductor told them how two big railroad companies, the Denver and Rio Grande Western, and the Atchison, Topeka and Santa Fe Railways began fighting over the right to build a system connecting Pueblo to the western mining towns. "Both companies hired gunslingers and bought politicians, and the problem got so out-of-hand, Congress had to settle the dispute."

The motto of the railroad was *Through the Rockies, not around them*, and Victoria soon learned what this phrase meant as the train snaked through the deep, rocky gorge.

Tim's eyes widened as he stood on a small platform at the back of the car with the others. He craned his neck to see the top of the canyon walls. According to the conductor, some of the canyon walls rose to twelve hundred fifty feet.

Victoria had seen the Palo Duro Canyon near her home, but she hadn't seen anything like the Royal Gorge. She marveled at the engineering feat that allowed trains to run on narrow shelves of rock through some of the wildest, most mountainous country in the United States.

The conductor explained the advantages a narrow gauge had in this treacherous terrain over the standard gauge the rest of the railways used. He spoke in admiration of Otto Mears, a man known as "The Pathfinder of the San Juans," because of his railroads and road building projects throughout the San Juan Mountains of Colorado.

When Victoria mentioned Silverton was their destination, the man raised his eyebrows. "Then you will experience one of his major engineering triumphs. You will climb from Ouray over a steep, narrow pass called Red Mountain. This pass is more than eleven thousand feet above sea level and separates the Uncompahgre and the Las Animas River watersheds. You will travel over the Million Dollar Highway." He chuckled. "Some folks say that's how much Mears spent to build the road, but miners say the road got the name because of all the rich ore beneath."

He warned them to be prepared. "That stretch of road may well be the most dangerous in Colorado. From Ouray, the road is steep and winding and, part way up, you'll come to the brink of a precipice. A fall from this will mean almost certain death. Those afraid of heights should not travel the Million Dollar Highway."

Sam and Arnie nodded their agreement, and Victoria attempted to swallow her fear.

She didn't know if the conductor realized she was new to the area and wanted to incite panic, or if he simply liked to dramatize, but by the time he'd mentioned the snow in April, Victoria wondered if she'd made the right decision.

The conductor continued his narrative. "As we travel from Salida over Marshall Pass to Gunnison, we'll pass another deep gorge—the Black Canyon of the Gunnison. The canyon is narrow, and the walls are sheer. The depths are spectacular from the rim. I haven't heard of anyone who has climbed down to the river bottom." He shook his head. "Even the people of The Shining Mountains—the Utes—don't occupy the area."

They looped through the mountains and as they ascended Marshall Pass and crossed the Continental Divide between Gunnison and Salida, the jovial conductor entertained those listening with the story of "The Phantom Train of Marshall Pass," one of the most bizarre railroad ghost stories any of them had ever heard.

Tim's eyes were as round as silver dollars as Victoria signed the tale of Nelson Edwards, an engineer who, along with his crew and passengers aboard the same train, had tried to outrace another train bearing down on them from behind. The crazy, doughy-faced engineer from the other train approached, and everyone involved thought they would die that night.

Word of a defective rail and problem with the suspension bridge hanging across the gorge had come down the track earlier in the day. They would soon cross the bridge. Edwards began to sweat as he barreled through the snow on the tracks, trying frantically to escape the maniac behind him.

The engineer also raced against time. He had to get his westbound train through the switches before eastbound Engine No. 19 switched onto his tracks. If he couldn't get there in time, both trains would be on a collision course.

Edwards decided: better to be hit from behind than to face a head-on. As the wild train behind him almost leaped upon them, the tracks spread, and the engine and cars toppled from the bank and rolled into the dark canyon.

Nelson Edwards shuddered and expected to hear the screams of the dying and to see steam hiss from the broken engine, but nothing but the groan of wind sounded from the canyon depths.

The next morning, Edwards walked toward the locomotive but stopped. In the frost on the cab window, someone or something had scratched a warning. *If you ever make another run on this line, you will be wrecked.*

The conductor stopped his story and the group grew restless for him to continue.

Soon Arnie asked, "What happened?" The conductor shrugged. "Edwards quit the railroad that morning and went to work for the Union Pacific."

"What happened to the passengers of the wrecked train?" Sam wanted to know.

"Though all the passengers on Edwards' train swore the train existed, rescuers never found evidence of a wreck, and no one has seen the ghost train with the mad engineer."

By the time the train reached Salida, Victoria's nerves had been stretched raw by the conductor's stories, and her dread of the future increased. *God be merciful.* Tiredness seeped through her body, and she wanted warm food, even though her stomach twisted with worry. She longed for a hot bath before bed.

She would stay overnight at the Hotel Turret while the men slept in a structure near the horses and supplies. They would continue to Montrose by rail the next day. From there, they would ride south to Ouray, and then ride the horses over the fearsome pass to Silverton. They would continue down the Animas River valley.

Tony ate with Victoria in the hotel's dining room that evening. He'd ordered meals for the others and promised to bring the food with him when he returned.

Even though she had longed for a hot meal, she could taste nothing but worry with each bite.

"What bothers you, querida?" Tony inquired with a frown. "You are pale and quiet."

Tears filled her eyes. "I never realized how dangerous this trip would be, Tony. I don't think I have the right to ask you all to do something for me when your lives may well be at stake."

He put down his fork and waited for her to continue.

"When I first decided to make this trip, I knew the journey would be difficult. I studied maps and calculated routes, distances, and times. In my mind, I knew we'd be traveling through mountains, so I tried to prepare for them as best I could, but ..." She flung out her arm and pointed in the direction of the mountains from which they'd come, and then toward the ones they would soon enter. "I could never, in my wildest dreams, have imagined what mountain travel actually meant. I'm wondering if what I have to do is worth your lives."

"What concerns you the most, pequeña?"

"The pass. The possibility of accidents. The weather ... Tony, did you see the snow? The conductor said the high mountain passes could get snow through May. May! Do we have enough food? Do we have enough warm clothing? Does Tim have enough? What if we get snowed in? What if we get hurt? What if we get sick? Do we have enough medicines?"

Her panic choked off more words.

Tony reached for her hand and spoke, "*Entiendo,* querida. I felt the same fear when you told me you would leave your home and everything you knew to travel far away, beyond my ability to protect you, to stay with someone of whom you knew little."

She stared at him and saw the pain in his face. Victoria kissed his palm. "I'm so sorry. Truly, I didn't understand why you were so upset with the idea. I'd planned so carefully and thoughtfully. Your anger seemed unreasonable to me."

Tony remained silent for several moments before saying, "Perhaps *Jesucristo* may be trying to teach us something, no?"

"What? What are we to learn?" Victoria realized she had not thought to turn her troubles over to God. She'd tried to figure things out in her own strength, and she now understood just how futile this was.

Tony shrugged. "Maybe, *en realidad,* we have little control over anything, and that we should trust him."

"I thought I understood this lesson, Tony, but the lesson doesn't seem to stick in the face of real danger and uncertainty."

"Do you believe the Lord has led you to search?"

"Yes. When I prayed for guidance several weeks ago, this is the idea put into my heart. I'd already decided to go home."

"Then we continue," he spoke matter-of-factly.

"But what about the danger to the others? I can't ask them to—"

"So, you think to do this alone?" His tone indicated his amusement.

Victoria shuddered. "No, but—"

"Sam and Arnie have traveled this road before. They know the dangers." He raised her chin and forced her to look him in the eyes. "Do you truly think I would abandon you at the first sign of danger? Truly?"

"No, Tony, I knew you wouldn't. You've been such a good friend—"

"¡Basta!" Tony stood to his feet, his posture reflecting irritation. "Enough, Victoria. You are tired, and I must take the food to the others."

"Tony, what did I say?" Whenever he called her Victoria in that tone of voice, she knew she'd offended him.

"*¡No importa!*" Tony snapped and bowed over her hand and then signaled for the food. "We leave early, *chica*. You would be wise to get some rest."

"Will you make certain Tim has enough warm clothing before we leave?"

He nodded and left with the food, while she went upstairs and ran a hot bath. She didn't know when she'd next be able to wash her hair, so she took advantage of what may well be the last time for several weeks. She could always heat water over the campfire and wash the rest of her body, but her hair was a different matter. The thick tresses took hours to dry. She tried to accept Tony's words about never leaving her and about God being in charge, but the nagging doubts and Tony's abrupt departure continued to worry her mind.

When she breakfasted the next morning, her hair remained damp, but she'd braided the sides and back in such a way the strands stayed out of her face and hung down her back. She hoped the braids would keep her hair cleaner.

The men had already loaded their gear and the animals onto the train, and they waited for her. She trudged through two inches of snow to hand them her saddlebags and some food she'd ordered for them. They all smiled their appreciation and helped her into the train.

With a subdued spirit, Victoria looked out the window and noted the heavy snow clouds. She felt like a mouse in a giant's castle as they moved toward the towering peaks. The feeling increased with each turn of the locomotive's wheels.

TWELVE

Montrose, Colorado, nestled in the beautiful Uncompahgre Valley. The town felt warm, pleasant, and busy, and Victoria wished this were as far as she needed to travel.

As the men unloaded the animals, she and Tim took them to a nearby watering trough, looking around as the animals drank. To the north, the valley stretched toward the farms and food-producing areas of the Grand Mesa region, while to the south, hazy blue and purple mountains towered.

They let the horses and mules graze a little until they were ready to be loaded onto the Rio Grande Western to Ouray. As they waited, Victoria watched the street vendors hawk their wares to the passengers who de-boarded the train.

One young man approached as she waited, and he showed her pen and ink drawings he'd made of the surrounding area. The artist's skill was remarkable. He'd captured the essence of the countryside she had passed through with utmost skill. She bought two pictures of the Royal Gorge, two of the Black Canyon, and two of Montrose. She intended to give one set to Tim to send home to Cooky.

"Do you have any pictures of Red Mountain Pass?" she asked the man.

"Yes. I have one oil-on-canvas of Silverton and the Pass, but they're more expensive than the ones you just bought."

"I'd like to see them."

"All right. Give me ten minutes and I'll bring them."

The pictures were large, long rectangles intended to be hung vertically. When he removed the protective wrappings, she understood why they had to be so large. Capturing the magnificence of the area she would travel through in the next several days on any canvas smaller than these would seem unfit.

She felt the blood leave her face as she gazed at the eyebrow of a road or trail edging a vast depth. Ore wagons, drays, horseback riders, and mule trains crowded this narrow road. As she understood the immenseness of the towering cliffs in the painting, she felt small and insignificant.

The second painting depicted Silverton in the fall. The town lay nestled in a bowl-like valley surrounded by more towering mountains. Many of the aspen leaves had changed to gold and, as the sun touched the rocks, they glowed with many shades of yellows, oranges, reds, and browns. These colors contrasted with the blue of the sky, the dark greens of the spruces, and the light-green of aspens yet to turn. Once again, she realized how truly talented this artist seemed to be.

In the painting, the Durango-Silverton narrow-gauge train puffed up the Animas River valley toward the town. She could almost hear the sound of wheels turning on the rails and smell the coal smoke in the clear mountain air. The paintings took her breath away, and she wondered what the real sights would do.

"If I buy these, can you send them to me in Texas? We have no room to pack something of this size."

"Certainly. Give me the address." The artist smiled and took out a pad and pencil. Victoria gave Miguel and Elizabeth's address.

"Would you also be interested in a commission to paint the Royal Gorge and the Black Canyon of the Gunnison on the same size canvases?"

He smiled once more and said, "Absolutely."

Victoria negotiated the price and paid him for the two paintings and part of the commission for the others. She would pay him the rest of the money when they were finished and sent to her. She mentioned she might have other work for him if all the paintings he completed for her turned out as beautifully as the ones she'd just bought, and they exchanged contact information.

In addition to her paintings acquisition, she also purchased fresh tamales from one woman, and spring vegetables and lemonade from another.

Soon, Tony and Arnie came to get the horses and mules, and she and Tim followed them back to the train and watched them lead the animals into a stock car. They had already loaded the rest of their gear.

"Forty miles to Ouray." Sam stood beside her and pointed toward the south.

"Yes, I made hotel reservations for the night at the Western Hotel. I'll be glad to get there." She turned slightly to study his face. "Do you know about the hot springs?"

"Sure enough, Miss Vicky. They rise to the surface of the ground from the fiery depths below."

"I hope we have enough time to see them."

As Victoria entered the car, the unpleasant sensation of being stared at returned. Men stopped in the middle of their conversations when she walked down the aisle. The car was filled with men and women of all shapes, sizes, and ages. Miners, prospectors, gamblers, investors, and adventurers all believed they'd make their fortunes in the gold and silver mines blanketing the area. Some of the passengers would leave the train at Ridgeway and take the Denver and Rio Grande Southern line to the Telluride mines, while others like them would continue to Ouray and beyond.

She took a seat by the window, and Tony slid in beside her. He frowned when he looked around, and his muscles tensed. He'd been distant since their conversation at the dining room in Salida. However, when she handed him some of the fresh food she's bought, he gave her a brief smile and signed his thanks. Tim, Arnie, and Sam did likewise.

Victoria couldn't eat much of anything except the vegetables, because her stomach felt tied in knots as she thought about the journey ahead. As the train moved through the valley, men lit pipes, cigars, or cigarettes and the tobacco smoke soon thickened the air.

"Tony," she groaned. "Please put down the window or I'm going to be sick."

He moved quickly, and the fresh spring air blew across her face.

She groaned again, put her head in her hand, and leaned toward the window.

"What is wrong, Victoria?" His soft voice sounded filled with concern. "Your complexion has a greenish tint."

She shook her head and closed her eyes. Talking required too much energy. Besides, her head ached.

The headache worsened when, a few minutes later, some of the men brought out banjos, harmonicas, and violins, and began playing lively tunes. Sam remained in his seat and listened, while Arnie and Tim clustered around the musicians. Arnie pulled out his harmonica and joined in. Tim tapped his foot in time to the vibrations he felt, and the other passengers clapped, stomped, or slapped their thighs or the seat backs in time to the music.

COLORADO TREASURE

My head is about to explode. She covered her eyes, groaned, and leaned toward Tony's shoulder.

He pulled her into the circle of his arms.

Victoria listened to the steady beating of his heart. As he stroked her hair, his heartbeat increased. He spoke to her softly in Spanish, but she couldn't distinguish his words. The tone and stroking motion soothed her enough to reduce some of the tension and she finally fell asleep.

She opened her eyes as the train reached Ridgeway to let off and take on passengers. Tony continued to hold her, and she imagined he was numb from staying in one position so long. She moved, and he lifted his head from hers. She pushed away from his warm chest and looked in his face.

"Thank you," she whispered.

His only response was to lower his face a few inches and kiss her. She locked her arms around his neck and returned his kiss before slowly disengaging to stand and stretch.

Though her attire was rumpled, and the remnants of a headache still clung to her, she felt slightly better. She felt better until she stepped onto the platform for a breath of air and noticed they were at the foot of a range of mighty snow-covered mountains whose tops rose hundreds of feet into the air and touched the impossibly blue sky. They stood as blue-gray sentinels to the abundant minerals resting beneath the surface.

The snow had melted on the lower slopes where clusters of tall, dark, viridian-colored evergreens grew in abundance. Bright meadow flowers and new grass pushed their way through the snow to what little sun reached them in the shady canyon.

"This cold, thin air takes my breath away." She shivered and turned toward Tony. He reached for her gloved hand.

"Come, chica, let us walk for a few minutes before we re-board."

They walked toward the stock cars where Arnie, Tim, and Sam checked the animals. Victoria marveled how Tim and Arnie had become good friends in such a short time. As she watched their rapid signs, she noted Arnie's fluency. He would never be able to understand the complexities of the language, but he had an adequate working knowledge, and she smiled to see how happy both Arnie and Tim were to be in each other's company.

Tim asked many questions about everything around him, especially the horses and mules. Neither Sam nor Arnie could answer him fast enough before he'd asked them another question.

"Let's go back, Tony. My head aches, and I can't get enough air."

Victoria watched in silence from the hard seat as the train began to move up the slope to the south. As they climbed toward Ouray, the cliff walls seemed to close in and limit their travel to a few hundred yards in the bottom of the canyon next to a wide, rushing stream. They climbed higher and higher, and her headache intensified. She thought she would vomit. Her misery increased, and she pinched her lips together and prayed with every passing minute she wouldn't get sick.

They arrived in Ouray in the late afternoon. Victoria dragged herself out of the seat and forced her feet to move. Without Tony's support, she would've fallen.

"Your appearance alarms me, Victoria. I will ask for a doctor when we get to the hotel."

"No, just get me to my room, please."

"The color of your skin and the dull look in your eyes worry me. You appear to move in slow motion which is not like you."

"I just need to sleep, Tony."

He gave the others instructions, and Sam promised to bring Victoria's clothing bags.

The Western Hotel combined the elegance of Victorian Italianate architecture with a western style. The wide, second-floor veranda extended over the sidewalk to the street and made a grand, covered entrance for guests.

As sick as she was, Victoria noted the high, ornately decorated tin-covered ceilings and stained-glass windows.

"Welcome to the Western Hotel." The clerk eyed their approach. He stood behind a heavy, mahogany registration desk and one side of his mouth tipped up when he saw her. Victoria wondered what he thought when he observed how much she leaned on Tony.

"We are five weary travelers with reservations. Our rooms are available?" Tony said, taking matters in hand, for which Victoria felt grateful.

"Yes, we still have a few. One is a suite overlooking the open second-floor verandah. The room has a private bath and hot running water. Two smaller guest rooms are also located on the second floor. The bathroom is at the end of the hall."

"We will take them. The lady will occupy the room with the private bath."

"How many days will you want them?"

He looked at her and said, "Perhaps for two or three." He signed for the rooms and took the keys, but before he helped Victoria upstairs, he asked for directions to the nearest doctor's office.

Victoria protested, and the clerk studied her.

"He's got an office down the street." He pointed. "If you don't mind my saying it, ma'am, looks like you have a case of mountain sickness. Some call this altitude sickness."

She lifted her head which felt unbearably heavy. "What is that?"

"Altitude sickness happens when folks come from the lowlands to high altitudes. The air up here is thin and, for some reason, makes 'em headachy. They often have upset stomachs and can't eat. They feel weak or lazy, and they may not have enough energy to eat, dress, or do anything until they get over the illness."

"My symptoms exactly," she moaned. "How long does this last?"

The man shrugged. "Depends on the person, but as soon as you get used to breathing this rarified air, you'll be okay. Drink a lot of water. Seems to help." He smiled. "You might also try a soak in one of the area's hot springs. Most have private bathing quarters."

Tony guided her to her room and unlocked the door to her suite. Victoria gasped. The spacious room was papered in a two-tone blue and white design. White lace curtains covered the window, and a plush carpet invited her to step further into luxury. The room contained a bureau, closet, a comfortable-looking bed, and a dark wood vanity table with a curved mirror and padded bench. The seating area consisted of a white upholstered sofa and matching chairs. Most important to Victoria was the large, shiny bathtub and marble sink in the corner. A dark blue paneled curtain could be drawn to hide the private bathing area.

Victoria's head spun with dizziness as she took a step into the room. Her knees weakened, and the darkness began to close in from the sides of her eyes. Blindly, she grasped for Tony's arm with both hands.

"Victoria," his voice sharpened with concern.

"Tony, I'm sorry. I have to sit down—right now."

With one smooth movement, he swept her off the ground and into his arms. He carried her to the sofa and laid her on the cushions.

"I will bring the doctor." He touched her forehead.

"Wait, not yet. Let me rest awhile, and maybe I'll feel better."

He appeared to debate within himself before nodding. "You rest. I will give the others the keys to their room, and then will fetch you some water. Do not move while I am gone, pequeña. I will return shortly."

Victoria rested on the sofa with her eyes closed. After several minutes, she opened them and noticed the darkness had disappeared. When she turned her head slowly, the walls and floor stayed in one place. With great caution, she eased herself higher on the pillow. Her stomach didn't revolt, and the dizziness didn't return, so she sat up slowly and swung her legs over the edge of the sofa and walked to the tub. She turned the faucet handles.

Just then Tony knocked on the door.

"Come in, Tony."

"¿Qué haces? What are you doing?" he demanded. "You were not to move, chica."

He handed her a large glass of water and then filled the pitcher on the bureau.

"I had to see if I could walk from here to the tub. But don't worry." She held up her hand, palm toward him, and smiled. "I wasn't going to try by myself without supervision."

"Always so independent, are you not, cariño? Why do you resist help, especially from me?" He spoke softly, but the look in his eyes gave her pause.

She recognized the seriousness of his question, so she didn't minimize her answer. "I don't know, Tony." She paused to find the exact words. "Maybe I fear becoming so dependent on you or others around me that I lose my identity—my self-worth."

His eyes searched her face before he nodded. "Will you join us for dinner?"

She walked him to the door. "No, my stomach doesn't feel up to food yet. I'm going to soak and then go to bed."

"Buenas noches." He kissed her fingertips. "Sam and I share the room next door, so if you need anything, knock on the wall. Arnie and Timo share a room across the hall."

When Victoria awakened feeling anything but refreshed the next morning, she wasn't surprised. She had awakened several times during the night with a throbbing headache. However, moving around seemed to help.

She wondered if her traveling companions noticed the dark circles under her eyes as they breakfasted.

"You better?" Tim's face showed his concern.

"Better than yesterday. Still tired." Even Victoria's hand movements seemed subdued. "What are our plans?" She looked at her men.

"We remain here at least one day more until your energy and health return. More, if necessary." Tony's words brooked no argument.

When he spoke with such firmness, Victoria knew he wouldn't change his mind. "Well, in that case, I'd like to find a laundress before we head over the mountain." She shuddered at the thought of riding over the pass. "And maybe we could visit the hot springs?"

Later, as they wandered about the town, Victoria learned the bustling mining settlement of Ouray had been born in 1875 when miners discovered silver, gold, and other precious ores in the surrounding mountains. The miners appeared to like "the best," and dismay filled Victoria when she realized "the best" included not only beautiful hotels but saloons, gambling halls, and houses of prostitution. From the sloping main street, she saw the cribs and brothels of the red-light district on the west side of the Uncompahgre River.

A school, community building, three churches, a hospital, the County Courthouse, the Beaumont Hotel, and the Wright Opera House populated the space on the east side of the river.

"Look, tall houses." Tim stared at the buildings with an open mouth.

Sam agreed. "They have to be tall and pointed so the snow won't collapse the roofs."

Victoria grimaced at the drifts of snow piled on the north sides of the buildings.

The mountains to the east towered above the town, and the ground sloped toward the river and more cliffs on the west. Citizens had built close to these rocky cliffs, in places she would never have imagined.

The road they would soon take climbed suddenly and looped from south to east, and then back to the west until the street disappeared around a rocky wall. Victoria swallowed. She feared visualizing what lay around the corner, so she returned her focus to several places where steam rose from the ground. She drew her jacket closer and sighed. The hot springs and one more day of civilization beckoned to her before she must face the treacherous journey.

That night, as she read the small Bible Elizabeth had given her for Christmas, she contemplated the terribly beautiful surroundings. The words of Isaiah 40:12 gave her a clearer understanding and appreciation of who God was, and his greatness and majesty dwarfed her.

> Who hath measured the waters in the hollow of his hand, and
> meted out heaven with the span, and comprehended the dust of
> the earth in a measure, and weighed the mountains in scales, and
> the hills in the balance?

Who indeed?

THIRTEEN

"I'm counting on you to get me safely over the mountains, boy," Victoria whispered in Dorado's ear. He flicked his ears and leaned in for more scratching. She smiled and patted his neck before swinging into the saddle to wait next to Hercules.

The men checked the cinches and breast collars, the security of the knots, the balance of the loads in the panniers, and the hooves of each animal one last time. Tony insisted they take every care to ensure their comfort and safety, and Victoria, for the hundredth time, lifted a silent prayer of thanks for his presence.

Tim hadn't stopped smiling from the time he'd awakened, and he watched everything with hawk-eyes. His signs were energetic, and he couldn't sit still.

The sun would rise by the time they started up the first hill. Victoria glanced at the sky and then studied the other travelers who prepared to make the same climb.

A large, dark-haired man stood nearby and checked the cinches on his horse and two pack animals. His beard poked out from his face in an unkempt manner and appeared tobacco-stained. Every now and then, he spat onto the cold, hard ground at his feet. Once, his eyes met hers and the cold, hard look she saw in them made her take a small step back. She sensed darkness and evil enveloping his soul. He reminded her of a poised rattlesnake and fear radiated from her center.

Fear not, child, the still small voice of God calmed her heart. *Greater am I who is in you, then he that is in him.*

"Thank you, Lord, for reminding me."

When Tony swung into the saddle, he looked back and signed, "Ready?"

Victoria nodded and grinned. She felt proud that Tony had begun to integrate Tim's signs into his conversation, especially when they got his point across quickly and effortlessly. The others signaled yes, and Tony turned Hercules toward the road out of town.

They rode at a slow pace to help the horses acclimate to the altitude and because so many people now crowded the road to Silverton. A returning miner drove an empty ore wagon immediately in front of them. He whistled, spoke, or sang—though rarely on key—to his mules as he drove.

Ahead of the miner, a dour muleskinner led his train of huge, heavily-packed mules. He hurried his animals and often passed slower travelers when the trail widened slightly. When others got in his way, he swore at them until they moved. These travelers hugged the trail furthest away from the drop off and returned his curses.

"Why is he in such a hurry?" Victoria spoke aloud, though to no one in particular.

Sam answered. "He's got supplies for the miners. The quicker he can get these delivered, the more money he makes. Muleskinners have more patience with their animals than they do with people."

Victoria glanced over her shoulder at Sam. "You seem to know a lot about them."

Sam chuckled "Ought to. Made my living at this for more years than I care to count."

Muleskinning? Sam? Victoria returned her gaze to Tony's back. *How many more surprises will I find out about the people closest to me?*

Behind Victoria and her crew, two horses pulled a dray. The large, dirty man followed the dray, and others came behind him.

Victoria attempted to ignore those around her and inhaled the fresh mountain air instead as she patted Dorado's neck. He tossed his golden head and pranced at her touch. None of their animals seemed to be bothered by the altitude. She turned to see how the others behind her fared and gave Tim a thumbs-up when she saw how easily he sat in the saddle and how eager he seemed to be on the journey. Sam and Arnie nodded at her and smiled too. Victoria faced forward then and watched the natural ease with which Tony sat in his saddle and moved with Hercules. Horse and rider moved as one, wasting not a single movement.

As they climbed the switchbacks out of Ouray and rounded the corner. Though the road narrowed, their way didn't skirt the edge of a cliff like she'd expected. Victoria felt herself relax a bit more. She noticed the creek ran over rocks and boulders to the west side of the road as the water flowed around patches of dense spruce trees. Some of the trees on both sides of the steep canyon walls grew from the cracks and crevices.

She looked at the blue sky and watched the high clouds pass. The sun peeked in and out of the clouds, but the morning had the makings of a warm, pleasant spring day. She relaxed even more.

They continued their slow climb and stopped for a breather whenever the horses needed one. The creek now flowed further down the incline, and the canyon walls had steepened.

More than two miles out of Ouray, they approached a tunnel that had been blasted or dug from a finger of rock projecting from the eastern cliffs to the west. The tunnel provided access for travelers, but also served to shed snow that fell from the cliffs to the creek below. A wide band of striated rock and soil supported the spruce tree and grass growing above the tunnel. The dirt-covered snowfields had not yet melted.

The horses and mules snorted and tossed their heads at the dark hole but walked through without mishap at the urging of their riders.

Higher and higher they rode until they rounded the mountain, reaching the place Victoria feared most. The artist had portrayed the vastness and grandeur of the scene with perfect detail, but the sight of their line of travel to reach the summit sickened her.

The road had been blasted out of the eastern side of the cliffs and seemed to hang over the edge of eternity to the west where miners worked their claims on the slopes. A waterfall cascaded from the cliffs to her left into a large pipe buried under the hard-packed earth of the roadway. The water shot out of the pipe on the other side, roaring and crashing to the creek bottom far below.

Victoria feared to keep her eyes open but feared even more to close them. The altitude sucked every bit of oxygen out of her body and her hands began to tremble. Dorado sensed her unease and tossed his head.

"Victoria." Tony dropped back to ride beside her. "What disturbs you? Are you ill again?"

"Tony, I don't think I can—"

At that moment, a large, tawny brown mountain lion screamed and jumped from the rocks above onto the road in front of the miner ahead of them. Victoria couldn't stem the horror as she watched the miner's panicked mules buck and plunge. The man tried to keep them in control, but the ore wagon slewed back and forth perilously near the cliff's edge. The cat disappeared just as quickly back over the edge of the cliff, but left pandemonium in his wake. Dorado, Hercules, and the rest of their animals began to dance and snort as all the other horses and mules on the road began to whinny and crow-hop. Chaos erupted on Red Mountain Pass.

"¡Basta!" Tony commanded. Their animals quit plunging, though they still shook. The animals looked as if they wanted to bolt in all directions, but when they saw Hercules's and Dorado's subdued demeanor and heard Tony's reassuring voice, they huddled near. Sam and Arnie moved quickly to control the mules and Tim's horse. Tim, with wide eyes, stroked and signed to his mount, and the animal calmed.

Victoria's attention diverted back then to the miner, just as he, his wagon, and mules slipped over the edge, his scream echoing around the canyon. Companion travelers, still trying to calm their plunging, terrified animals, cried out as they heard the wagon splintering on the rocks as it tumbled to the canyon bed below.

Victoria covered her ears, trying to shut out the shrieks of the mules as they fell to their deaths below. *Oh, God. Oh, God. Please be merciful, Lord.*

Then, an eerie silence fell over the group. Death had come so quickly, stunning everyone.

Soon people began to move and talk again, tending to their animals. Once the animals had calmed, the people clustered at the edge of the precipice, peering into the depths below.

"Look," a man yelled and pointed. "I see him. He's on a ledge, and he's moving."

Without a word, Tony unloaded rope from a pack. He tied one end to his saddle pommel and looped the other end into a harness he placed around his waist. Victoria knew Hercules worked cattle regularly and he would know what his master expected of him. As Tony started down the cliff's edge, the horse shifted his weight to his hindquarters and held the rope taut. Sam and Arnie brought their horses near, lassos in their hands.

Victoria peeked over the edge, but vertigo overwhelmed her. She stumbled back to Dorado and rested her face on his shoulder. His soft coat and sweaty scent calmed her for a moment. He arched his neck and sniffed her hair, but stood quietly.

Tim, after watching the rescuers for several moments, led his mount and Sam and Arnie's mules to Dorado. He touched Victoria's shoulder and signed, "Okay?"

She shook her head. Knowing they'd have to return this way was an idea too horrible to contemplate.

"*¡Atrás!*"

Victoria raised her head enough to watch Hercules respond to Tony's command to back up. The horse backed slowly toward the eastern wall keeping the rope taut as he moved. Inch-by-inch, Hercules pulled the man from the canyon where others immediately unharnessed him. Sam then lowered the end of the rope down the cliff face to Tony. With the help of his horse, Tony scaled the cliff in moments. His face seemed paler under his darker skin and, when he saw Victoria's expression, he stripped the leather gloves from his hands and walked to her.

She leaned against him as he placed his arms around her. Now she couldn't control her shaking.

Tony held her without speaking until travelers coming down the mountain from Silverton loaded the injured miner into a wagon, covered him, and hauled him to the doctor in Ouray.

Tony squeezed her. "We must mount, querida. We must reach the summit and set up camp before the sun sets."

Victoria turned in his arms so she could look in his face. "Will he live?"

"*Sí.* The man is scratched and bleeding from the fall and ribs are probably broken, but he will survive. *¡Gracias a Dios!*"

She leaned her head against Tony's chest again and listened to his rapid heartbeat. "This is a terrible place, Tony."

He chuckled. "*Pues*, the sooner we get on our horses, the sooner we can leave, no?"

He released her then and turned toward Dorado. Tony held her stirrup for her and she mounted. The rest did the same, and soon Tony again led them up the mountain. Victoria closed her eyes, trusting Dorado to get her safely to the top. She couldn't look into the void again without being consumed with panic. If she could have, she would've gone around the world to avoid this place.

By the time they topped the summit at a little more than eleven thousand feet, morning had changed to late afternoon. Victoria fought mental and physical exhaustion.

COLORADO TREASURE

Sam pointed ahead. "Only a mile or two from here is a broad, high valley—good place to camp."

They watered the horses from the nearby stream then continued into the lovely valley beyond where other travelers hurried to find campsites before night fell.

Tony led them through the meadow grass toward a relatively flat spot bordering the forest to the west. Victoria noticed signs of past travelers—rocks encircling a fire pit, and stacks of firewood of different sizes, ready for the next traveler's use. Their fellow travelers camped in the valley all around them.

In less than an hour, the men had unsaddled the animals, checked their legs and hooves, picketed them on the meadow grass, and built a fire. Sam filled the coffee pot and set the container on a metal rack over the fire to boil then poured water into tin pans for Victoria to use for washing and cooking. She sighed. For her, the only reward to being the camp cook was to hear the satisfied thanks of those who enjoyed her meal. She liked to eat, and usually she enjoyed cooking, but all the preparation on the trail took time and effort. Victoria was so tired after her emotional upheaval of traversing the pass, she didn't know how much reserve energy she could count on. The men expected food for breakfast, lunch, and dinner tomorrow and breakfast and lunch the next day.

She washed her hands and prepared their supper while the men erected two small tents, brushed the livestock, and gathered firewood to feed the fire through the night. Tim worked as hard as any of the others and, once he'd helped care for the horses, began hauling in firewood without being told. Sam signed for him to get enough to leave for the next travelers to the site.

By the time the men returned and washed in the pans she set out for them, a tasty stew bubbled in the cast iron pot. She ladled the meal into bowls and handed one to each man with a slice from one of the loaves she'd bought in Ouray.

"Good." Tim signed his contentment after he finished his meal. He leaned back against a stump, put his hands behind his head, and looked at the stars glittering in the velvety sky.

As Victoria washed their bowls and utensils and set them to dry, her thoughts turned once more to her parents. "Sam, how did my parents get over the pass fifteen years ago?"

"You don't remember?"

"No."

"We all rode. Your dad put you in front of him when we came up the pass and then switched off with your mother. Sometimes you rode pillion behind me or Arnie."

For an instant, Victoria remembered the safe feel of her father's arms around her and the sound of his deep voice as they ascended the trail. *Oh, Daddy, I miss you.*

As the group began to settle down for the night, Arnie took the harmonica from his pocket and played several songs. The night temperature dropped, and Victoria was thankful for the fire as she snuggled in a blanket next to Tony. From a campsite down the valley, another harmonica player joined in to form a distant duet with Arnie. The tunes spoke of love, loss, sadness, and joy. Soon other musicians joined the serenade.

The music created an overwhelming sense of longing in Victoria. She looked into the night sky then rose and stooped over the fire to lift a pan of hot wash water.

Tony stood. "Give the pan to me, querida. I will carry this to your tent." He walked through the tent opening and set the water on the ground near a pile of blankets Victoria intended to use for bedding and then stepped back outside.

"Do not light a lamp, Victoria, or anyone looking will see your silhouette from a distance." He brushed her cheek with the back of his fingers then left. "Do not worry. You are safe. Sam will guard the horses and camp for the first watch. He will change the pickets so the horses and mules can graze all night. He knows to sit away from the fire so he can see and hear better in the dark." Tony smiled. "He said his trusted twelve-gauge shotgun was all the company he needed. He patted the barrel and said the weapon discouraged predators of the human kind who might get a notion to steal."

Victoria nodded.

"I will take the second watch, and Tim and Arnie the third. They will take the animals to water then bring them close to camp for loading." Tony paused for a moment and then said, "I am impressed with your friend, Tim. He insists that, though he is deaf, he could watch with Arnie. He said he had become skilled at noticing the body language of the horses. They would be his eyes and ears."

"The third watch means the sun will rise during their rotation?"

Tony nodded and threw some more wood on the fire. "Rest well."

Victoria tied the tent flaps closed, undressed in the dark, and washed as best she could by the light shining through the canvas from the nearly full moon. By the time she dressed in her warm undergarments and nightdress, she shook with cold.

She nested into her blankets, curled into a ball, and covered the top of her head to keep any cold air out. Eventually, she warmed enough to sleep and didn't awaken until she heard Tim and Arnie bringing the animals back from the creek.

The cold encouraged her to remain snuggled in the warmth of her blankets, but finally, she sighed and dressed. As the camp cook, she couldn't sleep in. She felt thankful her guards had fed the fire all night. She blew on the hot coals to stoke the flames and then began preparing the buttermilk flapjack mix. As she laid the bacon on the griddle, she watched Tim brush their animals. When he'd finished, Sam, Arnie, and Tony saddled them and laid the panniers over their backs. Then, they dismantled the tents and rolled them compactly so they would fit in each side of the pannier. They balanced the loads with the remaining items.

As they asked for God's blessings and started through the frost-covered grass down the trail to Silverton, the sun had just begun to peek over the eastern mountains. Victoria sighed her relief when Sam told them, though the way would still be winding and steep in some places, they wouldn't have to traverse anything the likes of Red Mountain Pass the rest of their journey.

Others broke camp and began to move, too, so they weren't alone on the road, but now they traveled near the front. Tony intended to ride twelve miles that day, eleven the next, and then they'd stay in Silverton at the Victorian Grand Imperial Hotel before continuing to the graves.

For the most part, the ride now traversed downhill, increasing their speed. They traveled through spruce and aspen groves, and Victoria enjoyed the spring colors and fresh air. When they descended the last miles into Silverton, Victoria recognized her surroundings due to the accuracy of the artist's painting. The depth and variety of the colors amazed her. Iron oxide in the soil had turned the ground red, and the tailings from working mining claims added creams, yellows, and browns for contrast. The spruce trees loomed tall, but compact, and viridian green, while the white trunks of the quaking aspens silvered under the shadows cast by their small, bright green leaves.

They rode two abreast as they turned north onto the main thoroughfare. The town bustled with miners and their strings of pack mules and railroad people. Victoria counted a church, at least two banks, a post office, jewelry store, bakery, hardware store, clothing stores, five laundries, and twenty-nine saloons. The bawdy red-light district off Blair Street appeared to thrive.

"The place has grown." Sam looked around. "Looks like more than two thousand people live here now. Mines must be doin' well."

The hotels and Exchange Livery were some of the fanciest buildings and livery stable she'd ever seen. When they stopped in front of the Victorian Grand Imperial, she noted the ornately decorated façade and the arched, stained glass windows.

As she dismounted, Victoria was surprised to see respectable women and their children strolling the streets, often stopping to chat with neighbors then continuing in their shopping. The influx of families seemed to have kept at least part of Silverton respectable. "Law-abiding, church-going residents on one side of Greene Street, and gamblers, soiled doves, and other unruly types on the other," Victoria whispered and shook her head.

She walked into the hotel lobby with the men and looked around. Victoria yearned to eat a meal she hadn't cooked over a campfire, to bathe in a hot tub of scented water, and to sleep in a comfortable, warm bed, even if these pleasures lasted only one night.

They'd ridden into town early enough that, once checked into the hotel, they could spend a couple of hours shopping for anything they might need for the next several days.

After they'd agreed to meet at a certain restaurant for dinner, Sam, Arnie, and Tim went off in one direction, while Tony accompanied Victoria to a market, bakery, and clothing store.

As they walked, she noted Tony's eyes seemed never to be still. He assessed everyone who passed and, if an unaccompanied male passed and then turned for another look, Tony stiffened.

Victoria smiled. From the time of their youth, Tony had always been her protector and, no matter how vehemently she denied needing one, she knew he would never stop acting the way he did. And she didn't think she wanted him to anymore.

COLORADO TREASURE

They stopped by several stores to see what merchants offered customers and, as they walked by the jewelry store, the salesman signaled them to enter. Business must have been slow for him to stand outside as he did.

"We have the widest selection of gold, silver, and diamond jewelry in the San Juan Mountains. Many of our finest offerings came from local mines. You'll have to see them to believe them."

Before Victoria or Tony could say anything, he had ushered them into the store and opened a glass showcase. He pulled out several dainty, velvet-lined jewel boxes containing rings, earrings, and necklaces in fabulous designs. Victoria couldn't resist reaching for the beautiful items. She touched a sparkling diamond ring set in a silver filigree crown. Four small round cut diamonds rested in the crown, and four other smaller diamonds flanked these.

"This little beauty is entirely handcrafted. Note the detailed engraving of the wheat pattern on all three outward facing sides. Do you see this?" The salesman pointed and they nodded. "You'll not find anything like this in the world."

Victoria held the ring to the light for closer examination. "Beautiful."

"Put the ring on," the salesman urged.

Victoria slid the ring on her finger and held her hand to the light, turning and moving to see how the light interacted on the diamonds. Then she shook her head and made to return the ring. "It's too large."

"No worries, ma'am. We can resize any of the rings in the store."

Still, Victoria removed the ring and returned the piece of jewelry to the salesman. He accepted the ring, but then looked at her with a bit of a twinkle in his eyes. "I'd like to show you something else you may like." He selected a black velvet box and opened the case. Two diamond-encrusted emerald earrings and matching necklace invited her to touch.

"*¡Que magnifico!* The emeralds and your eyes are a perfect match, no?" said Tony.

Victoria smiled and nodded.

They spent a leisurely half hour examining other pieces of jewelry before turning to leave.

The salesman rushed to open the door. "Thank you for coming today. If I can help you with anything, please stop by again."

They returned then to the hotel so Victoria could freshen for dinner. Tony promised to come for her in thirty minutes.

Sam, Arnie, and Tim had also returned for a quick wash, and soon they all walked the short distance to the restaurant.

Tim signed with enthusiasm to Victoria. He commented on everything and everyone he saw.

Victoria grinned. "You should write to your mother soon, my friend, and tell her what you've seen and done. Maybe she won't worry so much if she knows you're safe. I think she'd like to see the pen and ink drawings, don't you?"

"Yes, I write soon." He glanced from her to Tony and back again. "We leave tomorrow morning? We find your parents' graves?"

"Yes."

Tim extended the thumb and small finger in the shape of a Y. He pointed to Arnie with his little finger, and then to himself with his thumb. He moved his arm back and forth and looked in Victoria's eyes. "We make grave markers. Official goodbye. You tell my mother you have bad dreams. No more bad dreams. Search finished, then home to Texas."

Victoria nodded. Search finished. Home to Texas. And then what?

FOURTEEN

They started out early the next morning and headed southeast down the Animas River Valley. Tim rode in front of them, and Sam and Arnie led the pack mules in front of him. The sky shone bright blue and clear, and not a touch of any breeze whispered through the leaves of the quaking aspens. The people of the valley began their daily routines. Axes rang as several chopped wood. Roosters crowed, donkeys brayed, a child laughed, and the miners who worked in the nearby mines greeted each other as they either disembarked from the Silverton Northern or got on the train to go to work.

Contentment spread through Victoria as breathed in the high mountain air and listened to the rhythmic click of Dorado's metal shoes on the rocks as she rode along the trail beside Tony. She guessed worry would soon overshadow this contentment as the future pressed, but she intended to enjoy the feeling while it lasted.

She glanced at Tony as he watched the movement of the animals in front of them and then looked around at others who traveled the same trail. Tony appeared relaxed but watchful.

"What brings such a smile to your face so early in the morning?" he asked.

She shrugged and gestured with her right hand. "The spring freshness, the colors and textures of the landscape, the movement of Dorado beneath me, riding with special people, and," she paused, "the hope that the nightmare won't trouble me soon."

He watched her face. "For what do you hope if we can find the location of your parents' graves?"

"I don't know exactly, but I'm counting on the Lord to reveal what I need to know when I get there. Many questions remain. Though I know I may not find all the answers, I know God put the desire to come in my heart." She grimaced. "Had I known about Red Mountain Pass, though, I would've questioned his leading."

Tony laughed. "Of a certainty. That is not a trail to be ridden by the fainthearted."

"Nor by those afraid of heights. I don't know how I'm going to face going over the pass again."

"Perhaps you should close your eyes, chica, and think of something more pleasant when the time comes."

"Good idea, but I don't know how useful the technique will be, even with my eyes closed. The image of those mules lying broken on the rocks at the foot of the cliff and the screams of that poor man as he went over the edge has been imprinted on my mind forever."

"Sí, and without a doubt, I will remember the scream of the *leon de montañas*. That is a sound one does not forget easily."

The day was warm and pleasant, perfect for riding. They rode all day, though they stopped periodically to let the horses and mules graze and drink from the river. When they pulled off the trail and into the trees to set up camp and get ready for the night, Victoria wondered at the mixed feelings of anticipation and apprehension she experienced. Tomorrow, they would camp in the narrow valley between the red cliffs and the clear stream of her past.

They camped and rotated the guards. Just before the sun went down, Victoria watched Tim brush his horse as Dorado and Hercules grazed nearby. At some noise or smell undetected by the humans in camp, the heads of the horses and mules lifted, and they stared intently toward the east. Their nostrils spread to catch any scent, but they didn't whinny or snort in fear, as they would have had they caught wind of lion or bear. Soon they returned to grazing.

Sam picked up his shotgun and Tony grabbed his rifle. Since coming to Colorado, he'd begun to wear his belt pistol. The two faded into the twilight, while Arnie and Tim brought the horses closer to the fire and tied them to a picket rope.

Victoria cooked the pinto beans she'd bought in Silverton. She'd cleaned and soaked them overnight and all day on the trail. She placed the beans in a cast iron skillet and added water, garlic, onions, green chilies, and a little butter and covered them with the lid.

The clerk at the market had warned her she'd have to cook the beans longer at this altitude to soften them. "The boiling point of water is lower at higher altitudes due to the decreased air pressure," he'd said. "This results in a lower boiling point and an increase in cooking times or temperature."

As the beans cooked, she mixed up the dough for flour tortillas. She added more flour and a little more salt to adjust for the altitude as well.

By the time the men returned to camp and raised the tents, Victoria had patted the dough into flat tortillas. She heated another cast iron skillet, put in a touch of rendered lard, and cooked them until light brown spots speckled both sides.

Tim, who had never eaten the tortilla and beans, watched the others first and then scooped beans from the pot onto his hot tortilla and then rolled it into an easily held wrap as the other had. His eyes widened at the first taste, and he smiled.

The next morning, the group ate the rest of the beans and tortillas for breakfast and then packed and returned to the trail. They rode a couple of hours before Sam turned into a long canyon. An ancient eyebrow of a trail led toward other canyons to the west, and they turned onto this. The path twisted and climbed to higher elevations then dipped down to lower ones. As they climbed, rain or snow clouds formed overhead. Victoria wondered if they would have to stop before they reached the site.

Finally, the trail plunged into a narrow valley surrounded by sheer red cliffs. A clear stream ran through the middle of the valley, and ponderosa pines, aspen, and spruce trees grew near the edges.

Victoria knew this is where she'd been fifteen years ago. "Stop, Sam. This is the place."

"Yes, you're right," Sam agreed and looked at the sky. "We better get the tents raised before we get drenched."

They dismounted and Victoria smiled. "The last time we were here, you said we were going to have a real lollapalooza."

"You remember that? I said that fifteen years ago." Sam shook his head. "You weren't no more than a little pixie with green eyes and grubby hands."

Victoria grimaced. "My hands may still be grubby after two days on the trail, Sam."

COLORADO TREASURE

The clouds built and the temperature cooled as they rushed to set up the tents and prepare a meal. Several aspen trees grew near the cliff walls where they would raise the tents, and the trees grew in such a way the men decided to use the cliff wall and aspen trees to make a large corral to hold the animals at night. They tied dead aspen branches to the living trees and made the corral rails. Aspen trees self-pruned themselves, so as the trees got older and bigger, they dropped their lower branches. These were straight enough to make relatively good rails.

The men unsaddled the animals and let them roll in the meadow grass. The livestock, like humans, were creatures of habit. They would feed for a while and drink from the stream. If nothing bothered them, they would lie down, rest, then get up and continue to graze. All the animals had plenty of food to keep them occupied for several days and seemed content to stay in the narrow valley.

Victoria built a fire and organized the pots and pans as she looked at the sky. She hoped she wouldn't have to prepare a meal in the rain. Soggy food and soggy clothing made for an uncomfortable night.

When the men finished the corral, they built a frame of aspen roughly six feet wide by eight feet long to hold the canvas. They lashed this to the frame and tied one end of the canvas to taller outside posts. These posts held the canvas above the fire pit and allowed any rain to drain off the sides. They could move around under the tent-like structure without getting wet.

As they ate, Victoria looked across the creek to the place where the mountain had fallen on her folks. Boulders and rubble remained at the base of the scarred cliff face, but time had softened the appearance of the site. Trees and grass now grew over the previously disturbed ground.

"I remember Dad standing right over there"—she pointed—"and Mama was in a cave just below him."

She looked to Arnie and Sam for confirmation, and they both nodded.

"Sam, I showed you and Arnie a gold coin, didn't I?"

They nodded again.

"Near took my breath away when you handed the gold piece to me." Sam shook his head. "Never seen anythin' like it to this day."

"What happened to the coin?" she asked.

His eyebrows lifted. "Don't you know? Arnie and me melted the coin and made a necklace for you. Gave you the necklace for your seventeenth birthday."

Victoria pulled the necklace from her bodice and examined the thumb-sized gold nugget. Tiny ridges on one side indicated the marks of a minted coin.

"Did you find any more of them?"

"Nope. The accident happened immediately after, and we had more important things to think about—like keepin' you safe."

She thought for a moment. "Sam, why didn't you tell me you and Mary were brother and sister?"

Both Sam and Arnie stared. "Everybody knows, so I thought you did too."

"Why did you bring me to Mary instead of to the Silverthornes in Denver?"

Sam shrugged. "When we got to Silverton, we sent a message to your aunt and uncle. Some lawyer answered. Said the family had suffered a tragedy and couldn't care for a young child at the time, so I took you to Mary."

Victoria again looked toward the slide. "Why were they here? Why were you and Arnie with them? Had they found lost Spanish gold?"

"Your ma sent a message to me askin' if I'd meet them in Denver and travel with them to this area since I'd been to the Animas River Valley a few years earlier. Arnie wanted to come and see the mountains, so he came with me. Your folks didn't say nothin' about looking for any Spanish gold that I ever heard. Kept talking about some feller named Oñate who'd come through the area quite a while back with some settlers. Seems he made a lot of enemies with both his people and the Utes. When the Utes made life hot for him, some of his people fled to this canyon and hid out until the danger passed. Your pa and ma figured these people left in a might of a hurry and left somethin' valuable behind."

"How did they know this, Sam?"

"Your pa always read old documents and journals. At the university, he came across a diary of one of these settlers. Seems the writer left directions to this place."

Victoria arose and looked at the lowering sky. She placed her dishes in the wash pans and walked out from under the canvas toward the creek. She jumped the creek and walked toward the base of the slide.

"Mama, what was so important?" She bowed her head. The wind arose and Victoria shivered and rubbed her arms. She realized the bones of her loved ones rested nearby and tried to blink back tears when she thought of what could've been.

Tony walked up behind her, dropped a blanket over her shoulders, and then held her for several minutes.

She turned in his arms and looked in his face. "Why did they come here, Tony? Why did I have to be without a mother and father for fifteen years? This isn't fair." Grief and anger shook her as she wept against his chest.

When he spoke, his voice was soft and warm against her cheek. "Life if full of questions with no answers, *mi amor*. Do you wish to hear what I think?"

She raised her head and leaned back so she could look at him more fully. "Yes."

He paused to frame his thoughts and then said, "In life, there is death. According to Scripture, this is the price we pay for our sin, no? Does the Bible not say we will face judgment after death? That each of us will give an account to God of what we did with His Son, *Jesucristo*?"

She nodded. Death had come to Adam and Eve and their sons and daughters because of disobedience. They paid a high price for choosing their own ways.

"And we know all have sinned and come short of God's glory. Is this not true?"

"Yes, those words are found in Paul's letter to the church at Rome. He says that, in God's eyes, our righteousness is as filthy rags." Victoria tried to follow his reasoning.

"John the beloved also tells us in his first letter that if we say we have no sin, we deceive ourselves, and the truth is not in us. So, what must be done for us if our righteousness is unacceptable to God?"

Victoria shook her head. "We can't do anything for ourselves. Jesus Christ, God made flesh, had to pay the price for us. Only His innocent blood redeemed us."

"Did not your *padres* believe this to be true?"

"Based on all the information I've read and heard, yes. Aunt Bella said their lives reflected their faith in the truth of God's word. Even Chancellor McDowell talked about Dad's Christian character.

Tony smiled. "So, what are the promises made to those of us sinners who trust in God's righteousness instead of our own? Need we fear the wrath of almighty God?"

Victoria thought of all the verses she'd studied. "No, we were God's enemies, but are now reconciled to Him. We stand uncondemned." She stared in his face. "Are trying to tell me I'm focused on the wrong things? Are you leading me to think about what they've gained, instead of what I've lost?"

Tony shrugged.

Thunder rumbled through the clouds and electricity crackled from cloud to cloud.

"Come." Tony urged her toward the tents. "We must find shelter *inmediamente.*"

The other men had already penned the animals, and they stood nose to tail with their heads drooping. They didn't like the storm but took comfort from the fire and presence of humans.

In the fading light, Tim and Arnie whittled crosses to place near the grave sites. They each carved the name of one of Victoria's parents then carved the date they met their appointments with the Lord.

Victoria huddled in a blanket and watched in silence, the raindrops tapping the canvas with a steady rhythm soothing her. She sniffed the fragrance of rain on dirt and watched as puddles soon began to form.

Sam and Tony trenched around the tents and the firewood with pickaxes to drain water away from them then returned to the fire for more hot coffee. Sam pulled a rain slicker from his saddlebags. "I'll take first watch."

Victoria fought the drowsiness but finally stood. "Goodnight, I'll see you in the morning."

The singing of the valley birds woke Victoria the next morning. She lay for a moment and listened to them. The stream gurgled. She heard the ring of an ax and the thunk of logs. Arnie spoke to his mule. She stretched and smiled. She'd slept well.

Victoria threw off the blankets and wished for a bath. After last night's rain, everything she touched felt muggy. She dressed and opened the tent flap. Someone had put the coffee pot over the fire to boil, and she hurried to prepare breakfast.

The men led the horses and mules to new grass, and Tony brought a large armful of wood and stacked the logs under the canvas top. "Did you sleep well?"

"Wonderfully well." She made a face. "I only wish I could bathe and wash my hair."

"Come." He held out his hand. "Come see what I found."

They followed the stream to the southwest and around a slight bend. Victoria smiled as a waterfall came into view—a stream of pure water falling from the cliff's edge into a clear, circular pool.

"Oh, Tony, this is perfect. After breakfast I'll return."

He laughed. "Be prepared. The water is icy."

"Hmm. At this point, I'd rather be clean than warm."

"You say this now, but I have no doubt you will change your mind as soon as your toe touches the surface."

When breakfast was ready, she called the men to eat. They asked the blessing and then dug in. Victoria watched them for a few moments and smiled. Eating seemed a serious business, and they had no time for small talk while they attended to their business. She ate slowly and waited for them to finish before asking, "Sam, after the accident, did you and Arnie say any words over my parents before we left?"

"No. We were in a hurry."

She looked to the place where they now rested. "Before we leave, I'd like to do this."

They agreed, and Arnie and Tim stood with the crosses they'd made. The rest of the group followed them to the base of the slide. After they'd planted the crosses in the ground, the group stood in a semicircle. No one spoke for several moments.

"Lord," Victoria lifted her face to the sky. "I don't know why you chose to take my parents from me when you did. You know how big the hole is their going has left in my life, and you know the anger I sometimes feel toward both you and them.

"Last night, Lord, you reminded me that your thoughts and ways aren't mine. I acknowledge this now, oh God, and I can only trust the deaths of my parents had a purpose."

She bowed her head. "My Lord, in the name of your Son, I ask you to forgive me of my doubts, anger, and lack of trust. I'm stubborn and willful sometimes, and I don't lead easily. You've said the trial of my faith is much more precious than gold, and I pray you would use these hard times to bring honor and glory to your name. Amen."

The men stood in an attitude of respect, their heads bowed, and their hats in hand. Suddenly, Hercules snorted, and a mule brayed. Victoria and Tony turned toward them as each animal looked up the canyon to the northeast, their ears pricking, tension tightening their muscles and spreading their nostrils.

Tony and Sam moved quickly to grab their weapons and then faded into the surrounding trees. Tony signaled Victoria to get her gun and to wait in the trees near the tent. Arnie and Tim moved toward the horses to calm them. Eventually, the animals returned to grazing but, now and again, they'd lift their heads and look up the canyon.

Victoria entered the tent and picked up the pistol and her mother's Bible. She then moved toward a large, upturned spruce tree. Soil and plant material still attached to the roots—the bare patch of soft earth beneath the upturned roots providing a good hiding place. She sat and listened for any unusual sound but, after an hour, decided to read until Tony returned. She kept the pistol within easy reach.

Since Christmas, Victoria had used the smaller Bible Elizabeth gave her, but she wanted to read the words her mother had written in the margins as she sat near the place where her mother had died.

She opened the cover, and the letter from Chancellor McDowell fell out. She'd forgotten all about his note in the rush to leave Denver. She unfolded it slowly and began to read.

Dear Miss Silverthorne,

After your visit, I looked through your father's documents and books in hopes I might find information that might aid you in your quest. I found the last two pages of a letter he had written, but the first part of the letter is missing, so I do not know to whom he wrote. I wish you the best on your journey.

Victoria glanced at the Chancellor's signature and then lifted the pages he'd enclosed. The paper had yellowed with age and some of the words had faded, but she could make out most of the writing.

… Maggie and I hope to visit the site soon. The directions in the diary seem clear enough. We hope Sam can help us locate … God willing. If we can find this Bible, we will truly have found a treasure beyond that of rubies. … first printing of the Spanish Bible, _El Cassiodoro de Reina, in 1569_ … Spanish Reformer … native of Seville. Can you imagine how … to hold this in your hands? … typographical ornament at head, two woodcut illustrations in the preface, and numerous woodcut initials … old full calf … joint tender but well-corded …

Shocked, Victoria moved away a bough and looked toward the wooden crosses. With just a few words written in her father's hand, she realized the treasure her parents had died for was an ancient Bible, not Spanish gold. Relief washed over her. As a historian and lover of old documents, the search for a Bible of great antiquity would have interested her father, more than elusive Spanish gold ever could have. She'd known Mark had been wrong in his assessment of their characters.

Why should your parents be any different?" he'd asked.

"Because they were Christians, Uncle Mark. They sought the things above, not the things beneath."

When Tony and Sam returned an hour later, she showed them the letters. She felt like singing, and the emotion must have shown on her face.

"Do the answers now satisfy you, Victoria?" Tony looked in her eyes, and she knew he really wanted to know if she was satisfied enough to return to Texas.

She plunged from happiness into uncertainty at his words. "Enough for now."

Victoria folded the letters and returned them to the Bible. She looked toward the pool but decided a bath could wait. She'd rather be safe than sorry, so she watched and waited.

Tony nodded and took his rifle with him as he walked toward the others. She noticed Sam still held his weapon, but gestured toward the northeast. Arnie signed something to Tim, who responded with "Yes."

Sam and Tony split up and found vantage points from which they could watch the canyon to the northeast.

What lurked in the forest? Victoria wondered. A man, or beast? If a man, why? What harm did he intend?

Victoria wished they could leave for Silverton today, instead of tomorrow.

FIFTEEN

As the first rays of sunlight peeked over the horizon, the group had already packed and were ready to depart. They intended to reach Silverton in one day, which meant they'd be spending many hours in the saddle and needed an early start. As they headed out of the canyon to the northeast, Tony and Sam rode with their firearms within easy reach. Observing their actions, Victoria slid the pistol into the saddle holster near the pommel. They hadn't told her what was wrong, but she knew the actions of the horses last night disturbed them. Tony eyes were never still. He scanned the trees and canyon walls, and he seemed ready to move at any given instant.

As they rode single file, she watched Tony and Sam cast for tracks. Did they look for animal or human prints? She shivered, and the mental image of the dark, unkempt man from Ouray flashed through her mind. She remembered the sense of darkness and evil surrounding him and the coldness and lack of interest he displayed when he watched the rescue operation on Red Mountain Pass. The look in his eyes reminded her of a prairie rattler ready to strike. The acid in her stomach churned at the thought of him on their trail.

"Lord," Victoria prayed as she rode, "please protect us from whoever lurks in the darkness."

Shortly after they started out, Tony stopped and looked at the ground. Sam dismounted, and together they knelt and studied the tracks.

"Two shod horses and a mule." Sam pointed. "The ones coming in are older than the ones going out, which is to be expected."

"Yes, the tracks appear to be only an hour old. We must ride carefully."

The dark-haired man had two horses and a mule. "Tony, can you tell how large the horses are by their tracks?"

He examined the prints in the narrow trail. "One is large, maybe sixteen hands by the length of his stride. The other, about fourteen."

Victoria nodded. The descriptions matched. *I wonder what he wants.* The response permeated her thinking immediately. *Gold.* She couldn't shake the feeling he'd followed them for the mythical Spanish gold he thought she had. She wondered if Lawrence Lucky or Larry Blunting were behind this? Her body chilled at the thought of Blunting sending out one of his criminals to follow her. After the talk at the mansion, she didn't believe Lawrence could be involved.

"Well," she muttered, "if gold is what he's after, he's probably disappointed."

When they finally reached the main trail, Tony studied the tracks they'd followed. He examined the surrounding area for other signs then turned Hercules toward Silverton.

Victoria ached from head to toe when they finally rode into town and checked into the hotel. After placing their bags in their rooms, they stopped by the fancy livery where they would board the animals for the night. She brushed Dorado as he sniffed her hair and leaned toward her for more scratching. "Good boy. You're worth your weight in gold."

When Victoria came down for breakfast, well past seven o'clock, she felt the heat of embarrassment climb into her cheeks when the men looked up at her as she entered the dining room. "I'm sorry. I didn't intend to make you wait. You must be starving."

"No importa, chica." Tony smiled and pulled out a chair for her.

They ate a leisurely breakfast and made plans to return to Texas. Tony laughed as Tim continued to ask many questions about, Miguel, Elizabeth, and the ranch—his excitement obvious to them all. Victoria hadn't heard Tony's laugh for a while, and the sound warmed her As she watched his eyes crinkle at the corners in an attractive manner.

Tony signed to Tim, "We have plenty of time to talk, Amigo, when we travel. Mamá and Papá will welcome you." Tony's signs still weren't as fluid as Arnie's, but Tim must have thought they were perfectly acceptable. He lifted his hand to shoulder height, palms outward and rotated his hands in the celebration or clapping sign.

Once they reached Ouray, they'd try to sell as much of the tackling and tools they'd no longer need for their descent into lower altitudes. Then they would travel by train the rest of the way home.

"Señorita?" Tony offered his arm. "If you have no other plans for the day, I will be happy to escort you on a walking tour of the Silverton shops again."

"Oh, Tony. I know how much you hate such activity, but I will accept your offer." She glanced toward the livery stable where Sam, Arnie, and Tim had entered, then looked around. "Look how gorgeous this place is." Victoria breathed in the fresh mountain air as they walked and closed her eyes for a moment. "So much color and texture. I wish I could paint like the artist in Montrose."

As they strolled the streets and talked, the world felt right, at least for now. They hadn't been this relaxed in each other's company for some time, and Victoria thought the time might be right to mention her plan.

"Tony …" She heard the hesitation in her voice and noted an immediate change in his demeanor. She swallowed and continued, "I've been thinking a lot about my future. You know—when I return to Texas." He stilled and stared at her face.

"I can't stay with Mary and John any longer. Not after John paid Lawrence Lucky to follow me." She grimaced and looked away. Tears threatened to choke her. "I'm twenty-one now. I never expected to live with the Keesons my entire life. The time has come for me to leave them."

Tony waited and she could see the muscle in his jaw clench.

"I've spent many hours thinking about what I can do. I'd like to open a business in Amarillo like the furniture shop I visited in Denver. I want to hang pictures of this area in the showroom. The artist said …"

Tony frowned, and Victoria recognized all the signs of anger.

"What's wrong? What did I say? Please don't walk away from me."

"I have not moved, Victoria."

"I know you're angry when you call me *Victoria* in that tone of voice and, though you haven't moved away from me physically, you just distanced yourself mentally. Why?" Tony said nothing, and her irritation rose. "I hate when you stop talking. I can't read your mind, so unless you tell me what you're thinking, I don't know what I've done to make you so angry. Please talk to me."

"Why do you push me away from you, querida?"

She shook her head as if to unblock her hearing. "You may know what you're talking about, but I don't."

He looked in her eyes but remained silent so long, she didn't think he would answer. Finally, he said, "For many years, I have tried to show you with my words and actions *me te amo*—I love you, Victoria, yet you speak to me about being good friends and moving to Amarillo. You tear the heart from me with your words."

"You love me?" Joy spread through her middle and she stepped closer. His hat brim shaded his eyes, and she wanted to see the truth of his words.

His eyes softened. "Have I not said so?"

"Why didn't you say something earlier? You don't know how much I agonized over my future."

"I thought you would understand, *mi amor*, because of the words of endearment I use when I speak to you, by my actions, and by the happiness I show when I am with you. Did these not speak of my love for you?"

"Not necessarily. I knew you were fond of me, but I thought you were just in the habit of being charming. You never told me what was in your heart."

Her words unlocked a flood of softly spoken Spanish. She looked in his eyes and listened to his words of love.

Excitement replaced the angry tenseness in his muscles. "Queen of my heart, will you marry me? Will you be content to put the responsibility for your welfare and your future happiness into my hands?"

She smiled. "Yes, Tony. I'll marry you. When?"

"Today."

She laughed. "What about the license and the preacher? Do you think a wedding can be arranged in the blink of an eye?"

"Tomorrow then. We will, at this moment, look for the justice of the peace or a local minister to perform the service."

"What about your parents?"

"I will send a message to them and the Keesons, to the Silverthornes, and to the Sebastians without delay. I will notify them of our marriage and our homecoming. Does this please you?"

"First, let's send a message to your parents and get their permission before you send telegrams to the others. This would please me even more."

Tony nodded. "You are wise. I will restrain my impatience for another two or three days, since I have waited this long."

During the next few days, they got the license, arranged for the church and minister, and spoke to a photographer. They spent time walking and talking together and often stopped by the church and knelt at the alter and asked for God's blessing on them and their marriage.

When the telegram came from Miguel and Elizabeth, Victoria unpacked the white blouse, gingham skirt, and petticoats she'd brought for a special occasion. She sent the blouse and skirt to the nearby laundry to be cleaned and pressed.

Victoria knelt by the side of her bed. "You gave me the desires of my heart, Lord, and I thank you. Help me to be the wife Tony needs. I pray for many long, joyous years together."

When Tony told Sam, Arnie, and Tim of their plans, they went to one of the clothing stores and bought fancier clothing. Dinner had a festive feel. The men had washed, shaved, and combed. They teased Tony and Victoria mercilessly.

"Arnie and me wondered when you were gonna pop the question." Sam smiled at Tony. Arnie nodded and grinned while Tim watched the conversation, a contented smile gracing his face. "We've seen this relationship buildin' for years. Mighty slow out of the corral, ain't you, Antonio?"

Tony laughed and held Victoria's hand under the table. "Sí, but do not be deceived, my friends. Though I started slowly, I will win the prize tomorrow."

Victoria blushed when she saw the promise in Tony's eyes. Excitement fluttered and somersaulted in her middle. Her life had suddenly changed. Tony would provide the love, security, support, and companionship she desired. Victoria didn't fool herself into believing their new life together would be without problems or conflict—experience taught her otherwise— but they'd weathered the storms before.

The group laughed, spoke of the journey ahead, and talked of plans for the following days.

After a while, Tony spoke, his voice serious. "My bride and I will be *ocupado* for the next two or three weeks, but we should leave for Ouray by the end of the month. Is this agreeable?"

They all nodded, and Victoria blushed again. How long until she got used to the idea of being a wife?

"Well, I'm thinkin' Tim, Arnie, and me can hold down the fort until you two come up for air," Sam said with a straight face.

Tony grinned.

The ceremony the next day was short, but lovely. Tony slid the diamond ring with the silver filigree crown onto her finger—the same ring she'd admired earlier when the jeweler had invited them into his shop. Tony kissed her fingertips and then her lips.

Sam, Arnie, and Tim witnessed their vows, and when the promises had been made and the paperwork signed, they stood together for photographs. The photographer took many others and promised he would have them ready within the week.

The group walked back to the hotel together, but the other three left them to "hold down the fort," while Victoria and Tony continued inside, past the dining room, and up the stairs.

"*Señora Morales*, do you desire food before we begin our new life together?"

Victoria shook her head. Food on such a quivering stomach would not be wise.

Tony unlocked the door and then touched her cheek with gentle fingers. "I have waited for this moment for many years, *mi esposa*."

She slid her hands around his neck and pulled his head down for a kiss. He inhaled sharply before picking her up and carrying her across the threshold.

For the next several days, they drank deeply and unashamedly from the cup of love the Lord had given them.

Sam figured the best way to "hold down the fort" would be to do a bit of fishing, but when a local advised them that no fish lived in the mineralized water full of mine tailings, he opted to sit on a bench in the shade near the hotel, his boots propped on a hitch rail, instead. He watched

Arnie try to teach Tim how to use a lasso and chuckled more than once to see their antics. Arnie was no cowboy.

When the gruff-looking man from Red Mountain Pass rode into town, Sam stiffened. He'd seen a lot of toughs and hard-cases in his day, and knew the man was trouble. The rider led an extra mount and pack mule. Sam studied the size and stride of the animals, and his senses sharpened. If he had a bent for wagering, he'd bet the set of tracks they found in the valley were made by these animals.

From under the brim of his hat, Sam watched the man without making eye contact. Though the rider glanced their way as he passed, he didn't seem to pay them any mind. When he examined all the horses standing at the hitching posts with care, and then turned his attention to the hotel windows and then to the people on the street, Sam stilled. He'd seen those cautious movements and careful attention to details before. Either this *hombre* was a law officer or a criminal.

Finally, the man walked toward the livery.

Sam put down his chair without a sound and then signaled for Tim and Arnie to follow.

Denver had filled with unsavory characters like the man they now watched. As the man strode across the dust-covered street, people made way for him and cast their eyes to the ground or to the heavens. It seemed obvious everyone sensed this man's mean spirit. Even the tougher elements left him alone. The three watched and followed for the next several days as the man entered hotels and spoke to the managers. Once, Sam overheard him describing Victoria, indicating she was "a friend," and he was supposed to meet up with her. Every hotel manager denied having such a guest until the gruff character asked at the Victorian Grand Hotel.

"Mrs. Morales? Yes, she's staying here at the hotel," the clerk said, and Sam cringed. "Would you like to leave a message, Mr. …?"

The man shook his head and asked instead for an available room.

When Victoria and Tony came down for breakfast that next morning, the clerk mentioned her friend.

"Which friend?" Victoria asked.

"Unkempt. Dirty. But that doesn't mean much in Silverton. Some of the richest miners don't look any different as others who work in the mines." Victoria shook her head. "I don't have any friends fitting this description. Did he leave a name?" Her heart pounded. "He registered for a room." The clerk pointed to a name in the ledger. Dan Black. Denver.

Victoria watched as Tony frowned and examined the signature. His mouth tightened and fierce anger and protectiveness shown from his eyes. She lightly touched his arm, attempting to divert his attention back to her.

Lord, please stop Tony from acting in his own power. You know how quick he is to act, and I'm not always sure he seeks your guidance first. We're learning how to give our lives to you, but you know how much we struggle. Please show us what to do.

The clerk watched their silent exchange.

When Tony finally spoke, his words sounded clipped and more accented. "You described a man who may have followed my wife from Denver. We believe he works for a notorious crime boss."

The clerk blanched, and his eyes widened. "The sheriff's office is right down the street."

Tony nodded his thanks, but Victoria knew Tony well enough to know he would only seek help from the sheriff if he couldn't handle the problem.

The man smiled. "Would you and Mrs. Morales be interested in directions to a secluded hot spring only an hour away? Few people know of this location."

Victoria smiled at Tony. "I would. Shall we?"

Tony hesitated before nodding.

While Victoria packed food, Tony went to advise the others of their plans.

"I good watcher." Tim smiled. "No people worry about deaf boy. Know we have closed ears, but many times think we have closed eyes. Strange people." He chuckled.

"*¡Cuidado, Timo!*" Tony made the sign for "careful" at the same time he spoke. Tim nodded his fist.

Dan sat in a chair near the saloon's window, a beer in front of him, when he saw Tony ride by on a big, chestnut gelding, leading the woman's saddled palomino.

He straightened and stared as the two mounted and left town. They traveled light, so he figured they'd return before nightfall.

He stood then and dropped a coin on the table. Now was his chance. Before he stepped out of the saloon doorway, he panned the street looking for the two men and the deaf boy who traveled with the couple. He knew they'd been watching him for the past several days. But the men had their backs to him now, watching the deaf boy perform tricks with his lasso, so he eased himself out the door and joined the crowd on the street.

He entered the hotel and slipped by the clerk. On silent feet, he climbed the stairs to the Morales' bedroom. The corner of Dan's lip curled at how easily he'd acquired the information. One look at the unguarded register when the clerk's back was turned told him what he needed to know. The locked door presented no problem to him either, since he'd picked many locks in his long, criminal career.

He made a thorough search of the room and contents yet was careful not to disturb anything. When he finished, he felt certain the map or diary wasn't in the room. The woman must carry the documents on her person.

Dan cursed and left, returning to his room a few doors down where he grabbed his saddlebags and rifle. Time to end the hunt. He left the hotel and mounted his horse that been ground-hitched in the shade of an adjoining building. He'd not bothered with the livery as he never knew when he might have to make a quick escape. Although, earlier, he'd made a point to visit the livery where the woman and her men kept their horses. He'd examined the prints the chestnut and palomino made and now cast tracks as he followed the trail the two had taken out of town.

———————————

Tim slid from behind a large potted plant in the hallway. He'd watched the big man enter and leave Victoria's room. When the man rode away, Tim reported to Sam, and the three rushed to the stable for the horses. "Not too close, or he'll see us," Sam signed. "We'll hang back and keep track of him with these." He indicated the binoculars hanging around his neck.

COLORADO TREASURE

Not twenty minutes out of Silverton, Dan discerned someone followed. He hadn't seen anyone, but his finely honed sixth sense had kept him alive for years. He paused in a grove of aspens and turned his head toward town. He caught a glimmer of sunlight off binocular lenses, and a primal sense of battle lust rose in his throat. He knew who followed: the three musketeers.

He spurred his horse deeper into the trees and, like a sore-headed grizzly, laid in wait for those who followed.

Sam, Tim, and Arnie stopped in a small meadow to get their bearings and to discuss whether they could get ahead of Black in order to warn Tony and Victoria. They dismounted and examined a crude map the hotel clerk had provided.

Sam pointed to the map. "We have to turn off somewhere here. What does the map say, Arnie?"

Arnie frowned. "I don't know. The man's writing looks like a bunch of chicken scratching to me. I cain't make heads or tells of the thing."

The two bent over the map while Tim scratched his horse's neck and watched. Suddenly, a stick broke under the weight of a heavy animal. Sam and Arnie stopped their perusal of the map and looked toward the trees. The heads of their horses snapped up, ears pointed in the same direction. Tim swung into the saddle, grabbed the reins of the other animals, and waited.

Dan watched from the shadows and listened to their conversation. He knew they had a map to the woman's location and intended to take it. He knew he'd have a fight on his hands from her man, and the map would give him an advantage. He'd watched the way the Texan moved and had observed his strength, agility, and quick responses. Defeating him wouldn't be easy, but he had no doubt of the outcome.

He spurred his horse into the sunshine and stopped. His gun covered the two older men and motioned for the deaf boy to stay back. "Bring the map here," he commanded, his tone cold.

"No," the one with thin shoulders said. "It ain't yours."

Dan cocked the hammer of his pistol and aimed at the man's head. "I said to bring the map to me."

The man looked at his other friend and he nodded. He ambled toward Dan. Twenty yards separated them, but the man continued to speak, "God said, 'Thou shalt not steal,' mister."

Dan laughed. "Shut up, you simpleton. There is no God, dummy. Even if he existed, who is he that I should obey him? I obey my own laws."

"That ain't a smart thing to say, mister. He hears you. Ain't you afraid?"

Dan glared. "Of course not. Now shut up and bring me that map."

Dan's horse suddenly flinched, jumped, and began to snort. Dan grasped the reins attempting to halt the plunging animal but, before he knew what happened, a swarm of mountain yellow jackets had risen from their hole in the ground at his horse's feet and were in his hair, on his face, and flying up the sleeves of his shirt. He dropped the pistol and screamed as he swatted the vicious wasps. The more he crushed the angry insects, the more of them appeared and attacked. The terrified horse bucked, plunged, and fell to the ground.

The three friends watched with open mouths at the scene before them. After a moment, Sam rushed to his saddlebags and pulled out a heavy white cotton shirt. He wrapped this around his face and ears, put the hat back on his head, and pulled the bandana over his nose and mouth. He laced down his sleeves and gloves with the leather ties strings from his saddle. Then he pulled his jeans out of his boot tops and laced his pant legs down so the insects couldn't get inside next to his skin.

Arnie and Tim realized what Sam intended, so they moved quickly and did the same. Then Arnie signaled for Tim to take the horses further away.

When Dan rolled off his fallen horse, Sam and Arnie pulled him to the tiny stream. He was unconscious, his face so swollen the man struggled for breath.

COLORADO TREASURE

"We've got to get him to the doctor," Sam signed. "Tim, while we get his horse, you pull out as many stingers as you can find then plaster his face with mud."

Tim nodded and went to work immediately.

They rigged a frame so the big man would stay in his saddle, lifted him, tied him to this support, and then lit out of the meadow as if their tails were on fire.

They rode directly to the doctor's office in Silverton, yelling for the physician before they dismounted. The doctor rushed out, took one look at the man, and said, "Carry him to the examination table."

Sam and Arnie unstrapped Dan and removed him from the saddle while Tim tended the animals. The doctor rushed to the cabinets for medicine and instruments.

Just as the doctor reached to lift Dan's eyelids so he could look at the pupils, Dan jerked, opened his eyes in terror, screamed, and pointed toward something in the corner of the room near the ceiling. He then sank back onto the table as his last breath left him.

"The righteous one called him to his accounting," Arnie whispered. "He left in the blink of an eye."

They stared at the dead man who had intended to do them harm, not knowing what to say. Goliath had fallen and fallen hard.

"Well, I've seen death by stinging a few times, though I'm thankful to say, not often," said the doctor, shaking his head. "He appears to have been stung more than thirty times. I'll conduct an autopsy to be certain, but I believe he was probably allergic to bee stings. Who is he?"

Sam answered, "I think his name is Dan Black. He registered at the hotel yonder. We came across him in the meadow about twenty minutes from here."

The doctor nodded and began preparing his utensils.

* * *

When Tony and Victoria returned later that afternoon and heard the news, she raised her face to the sky and whispered, "Thank you, Lord. Truly your grace is sufficient, and your loving kindness never ends."

176

SIXTEEN

On the twentieth day, before the sun rose, Victoria and Tony were packed and ready to go by the time the others brought the horses and mules to the hitching post in front of the hotel. Victoria had ordered breakfasts to go so they could eat further down the trail. By the time everything was loaded, the food tins waited to be packed just inside the top of the panniers.

Tony asked for God's blessings and protection as they returned home, and then held the stirrup for Victoria. He smiled and gave her a boost.

"*¿Lista, mi hermosa esposa?*"

"Yes, Tony, I'm ready." She patted Dorado's neck and watched the others mount.

They rode uphill for a couple of hours before they pulled off the trail and ate their breakfasts.

"The days are getting longer." Victoria looked at the sky. "I think we should push as far as we can before stopping for the night."

Tony nodded. "Home beckons. Shall we attempt eleven uphill miles today?"

"Yes," Tim agreed.

They made sixteen before they camped for the night.

"We can make the rest of the trip to Ouray in a day, Tony?"

"Sí. We ride downhill all the way from the top of the pass."

Victoria swallowed her apprehension. Her stomach tightened as she thought about descending the summit of Red Mountain Pass into Ouray. The ten miles from the summit to the town would be the longest she'd ever ridden, regardless of how quickly they descended.

The next day when they reached the summit and started downhill, Victoria glimpsed the vast depths to her left. Bile rose into her throat. What had Tony said? Think of something else. She closed her eyes and grasped the pommel. As she rode with her head turned toward the cliff face on her right, she tried to imagine their homecoming. What would Miguel and Elizabeth say to her? Would they be happy about the decision she and Tony had made? Would they be hurt they couldn't be at the wedding? Perhaps the pictures she carried would ease any hard feelings. What would she say to John and Mary the next time she saw them? Her stomach turned once more with this line of thought. Should she say anything, or pretend nothing had happened?

By the time they reached Ouray, Victoria had fought the nausea for several miles. The constant swaying motion, and the knowledge that she rode next to a yawning chasm served to tie her stomach in acidic knots. She didn't open her eyes until they started down the last incline into town. She almost fell off Dorado's back into Tony's arms.

"Victoria, your face is pinched and white. What is wrong, *mi amor*?"

"I'm going to be sick. I must get to a bathroom."

He signaled to the others to take care of their animals while he helped Victoria to the room. The same clerk waited on them, and when he saw her urgent need, handed Tony the key to their room.

The clerk shook his head. "Poor lady. Might be a good idea if you don't travel at high altitudes anymore."

She knelt in front of the privy and vomited until she felt like she was being ripped apart. Victoria cried while Tony watched, helpless. When the heaves stopped, he brought her a cold, wet towel to put on her forehead and a glass of water to rinse her mouth.

She shook with chills while Tony supported her to the bed where he helped her remove her clothes and then covered her with blankets.

"Shall I send for the doctor?" He sat on the edge of the bed and felt her forehead.

"No, let me rest for a while." She gave him a weak smile. "I feel better already."

"Rest. I will return shortly with your clothing and saddlebags." He kissed her forehead and left.

When Victoria warmed enough to quit shaking, she sat up. She longed for her toothbrush, tooth powder, and a hot bath.

Soon, Tony returned with her things, and she smiled. "Will you fill the tub, *querido*? Once I rid myself of the dust of the trail and the disgusting taste from my mouth, I will feel much better."

"Sí, claro," He strode toward the tub and turned on the faucets. Victoria sat up and slid to the edge of the bed to unbraid her hair.

Tony watched her for several moments before he approached and sat down beside her. "Permit me."

Victoria closed her eyes and enjoyed the feel of his gentle hands as they released her hair from the braid. The thick mass flowed over his hands and floated around her.

He touched one of the dark strands. "Never have I felt anything so soft as your hair and skin."

She smiled and pushed her hair aside so he could kiss her neck. He obliged.

Much later, when they were both clean, Tony tickled Victoria's face with the end of a lock of her hair. "Do you feel well enough to dine this evening, Señora?"

Victoria stretched and yawned. "I think so."

When they entered the lobby, the clerk stared at her face and smiled. "Glad to see you're feeling better, ma'am."

"Thank you."

Tony seated her, and they placed their orders. As they waited, they spoke of home and loved ones.

"Even though your parents gave their permission, do you think Beth and Miguel will be upset with us for not waiting to marry until they could be present, querido?"

Tony shrugged. "Papá and Mamá have known of my desire to marry you for many years now. They will be pleased that mi Señora has seen fit to grant the desires of my heart. They may have wished to be present, but they will trust our judgment."

Victoria reached across the table and took his hand. "I love you, Antonio Alejandro Morales, and I hope God will grant us a long and happy life together."

He kissed the palm of her hand, and then her fingers. "May this be so, *mi bella esposa*."

Victoria sipped her water as the waiter served meals to the diners at the next table. Catching a whiff of the medium rare steaks on their plates, her stomach instantly rebelled.

She dabbed at her mouth with the napkin and swallowed with difficulty. "Tony, please excuse me for a moment. I'm going to make a quick trip to our room."

She retained her composure until she was out of sight of the dining room then raced up the stairs. She had only seconds to spare before she heaved into the toilet bowl.

"What is happening to me?" she muttered and looked at her frowning face in the mirror. She was rarely sick, and the thought of all those miles yet to travel filled her with dread. What would she do if she suddenly felt sick on the train? She rinsed her mouth, brushed her teeth, and drank a glass of water before returning to the dining room. She needed to get out of these mountains before she died from heaving.

Victoria composed a smile for Tony as she walked toward him. She saw the question in his eyes as he stood to seat her.

"Is everything well with you, beloved?"

"Yes, I'm fine."

He studied her face. "*Bien*. Our dinner is served."

Victoria pleaded for the ability to get through the meal without vomiting again, and said a prayer of thanksgiving when she was able to get her soup and crackers down without mishap. She ate slowly and felt grateful she hadn't ordered a heavy dinner.

The next day, as they prepared to board the train, Tony spoke his concern when he saw the toll the mountain sickness had taken on her. "Are you prepared in the event the stomach tremors come upon you once more, mi amor?"

Victoria grimaced and nodded. "Yes, I brought several paper bags. I'll keep them with me at all times in case I'm not close enough to the toilet. For the sake of the other passengers, I'll try to vomit quietly and in a ladylike fashion."

"*Pobrecita*. Perhaps we should see the doctor before we board?"

"No, Tony. We don't have time. I'm feeling somewhat better. I'll be glad to reach the Texas plains."

Sam had found a buyer for their ropes, tackle, axes, and extra equipment they no longer needed, so they could travel lightly. The miner seemed glad to get such a deal, and they were glad to get rid of the load.

Victoria watched her men load the animals, and then they all found their seats on the northbound train to Montrose. They would retrace their earlier route to Pueblo, and from there, would ride the Fort Worth and Denver City rails to Amarillo. Tony intended to send Miguel and Elizabeth a message when they reached Pueblo indicating they should meet them with the buckboard.

Victoria continued to wonder what she would say to Beth. To relieve her concern, she turned to Tim. "In five days, we'll be home."

Tim raised both of his hands to shoulder height and rotated his wrists, fingers spread, in celebration.

Tony laughed. "My eagerness matches his. We have much to do when we get home."

"Yes, so much I'm already tired."

The train moved, and Victoria glanced at her fellow travelers. Fortunately, the train was less crowded, and no one lit a cigar, cigarette, or pipe.

To pass the time, Victoria told stories of her time in Denver. She told Tony of The Watchers, and of her network of spies. Tim added his piece, and the others asked several questions. Tim smiled at Tony's praise, and Victoria raised her eyebrows. "I thought you'd be upset. You're taking this information more calmly than I expected."

When Tony hesitated to speak, she straightened, urging him on.

He sighed before saying, "The third group of watchers you could not identify were friends of Papá. They watched as a favor to our family. They grew concerned when others began to follow you after Christmas, so they notified us."

Before Victoria could speak, he placed a finger across her lips. "This was the price paid for my sanity, mi amor. Though Papá said he would not help you, he also saw how disturbed I was when I thought of you being so far from our protection. He had a difficult time persuading me not to get on the first train to Denver once we knew you were watched by others."

Victoria's tight lips loosened into a grin. She had no trouble visualizing that conversation. "I'm sorry you had to endure so much anguish because of me." She reached for his hand and snuggled her hand in his. "If you'll forgive me, I'll forgive you for making me feel I lived in a fishbowl or in a luxurious prison."

"¿Perdón?"

"Once I knew I was being watched, my only choices were to stay hidden in the house, or to go out and risk I knew not what. To know someone watched my every move, made me afraid and angry. I didn't know why, and the uncertainty hung like a dark cloud over my head." She smiled at Tim. "Knowing Tim's spies watched made me feel better."

—⁂—

Tony pondered Victoria's words for quite some time. He had never thought his provision for her safety would cause her to feel incarcerated. He did not want his hard-won treasure to feel as if she were a prisoner of his love, yet he could not, and would not ignore his responsibilities, first as her friend and now as her husband, to protect, defend, and provide. Had he not done these things when she first showed up in his life as a frightened child? Had he not made vows before God and witnesses to do so now? He wondered how a man and woman established balance and harmony between his needs and hers. How could a man ever understand what dwelt in the heart and mind of a woman or what lay in his wife's heart? She did not think as he did, nor he as she.

He would talk to Miguel. Both his parents had achieved this balance, and he wondered how they had accomplished this. Even John and Mary Keeson seemed to have achieved some sort of felicity, which seemed truly a marvel.

That night, when they reached Salida and checked into their room, Tony sat on the bed and watched Victoria unbraid and brush her hair in front of the vanity mirror. The brush strokes seemed unhurried and deliberate.

"You've be abstracted ever since we boarded the train in Ouray, husband. Is something bothering you?"

"I have thought much about your words today." He wanted to put his troubled thoughts into words and, though he was hesitant and uncomfortable sharing his deepest fears, he knew he had to.

Victoria listened in silence and then spun on the stool to face him. "Would you like me to help you understand women in general, and me in particular, Tony? I can give you the gist in a few sentences."

"Can this be done so easily?"

"Oh, yes." She nodded.

He smiled.

"Number One." She held up one finger to accentuate her point. "Talk before you act. I can't read your mind, my love, and if I don't know why you are doing what you're doing, I have a hard time seeing your point of view. I usually misunderstand the motives behind your actions, and we end up angry with each other. Don't assume I know why you make the decisions you do. Talk to me. Explain. I know God has placed you in the leadership role in our home, and I know you'll be responsible to make the final decisions. I'm okay with this, but I also know He has given me certain abilities and insights too. Together we complement each other, and we can work together for the good of our marriage and family. Does this make sense, Tony?"

"Sí. Continue."

"Number Two." She held up two fingers. "Listen. Listen to the words I speak, but also listen to the emotions attached to the words. Don't judge until you've truly heard what I'm saying, and if you don't understand, ask. I will try to do the same with you, okay?"

He processed the points while she waited.

"Simple, right?"

Tony sighed. "I perceive this will be easier said than done, but I will do my best. I ask for your patience."

He stood up and walked toward her. When he removed the brush from her hand and began to brush her thick, black hair with gentle strokes, she closed her eyes.

When he stopped, she opened her eyes and must have read the desire in his. Without a word, she took the brush from his hand and led him toward the bed.

The next day, they boarded the Denver and Rio Grande Western to Pueblo. They intended to stay the night to give Victoria a chance to recover from last night's upset stomach and headache before they connected with the Fort Worth and Denver City line.

Many passengers traveled the Rio Grande Western, and Victoria looked suitably impressed when a train agent told her how many had come through that year. "When the mines do well, we do well."

She glanced around and noted the full passenger car. Tony made sure they were seated near the restroom and that all the windows were open.

Victoria ate a cracker and drank water before the train started to move, and she made sure to nibble on something through the long, monotonous ride. She had learned an empty stomach made her feel worse when the sickness hit. So far, she'd had only a couple of bouts with queasiness.

Arnie brought out his harmonica and played several lively tunes which encouraged other musicians to bring out their instruments and join him. Other passengers sang the words to the tunes, and their ability to stay on tune surprised her.

The music continued until they entered the Royal Gorge, and then everyone opened their windows and craned their necks to gaze with awe upon such magnificence. Some stood on the platform just outside the door and pointed toward the cliff walls as they chatted with their neighbors.

Victoria shared some of her crackers and cheese slivers with Tony, and they munched companionably. When she had finished, she stood and brushed the crumbs from her clothing before sitting again and looking at her husband. "We have so much to do when we get home. What do you think should be at the top of our priority list?"

Tony laughed. "That is a comment spoken from the depths of your personality, Victoria."

"What makes you say so?"

"I have never seen anyone with a mind as organized as yours. What would happen if you did not have this mental list, eh, querida?"

"I'd probably become as crazy as a cow who'd eaten loco weed." She paused. "Your mother said something similar to me. She said she thought John and I shared similar characteristics. When I cringed with horror, she said, 'Just look at the painful cleanliness of your room,' though she thought my love of beauty softened this character defect."

Tony laughed again, and Victoria tilted her head to one side. "I never thought to ask if you were a messy person before I married you." Her eyes teased. "Maybe I should have. I hope we don't come to blows because you are inconsiderate enough to track mud all over my clean floors or to drop your clothing all over the house in the expectation I will pick up after you."

He traced a finger down her cheek. When he spoke, his tone sounded serious, though his eyes smiled. "You need not fear I would ever strike you, my love, no matter the provocation. If I have never done so in all the years you made me continually insane, then I think I have demonstrated my abilities in the area of self-restraint, no?"

She nodded and held his hand. "And if I have demonstrated a Herculean effort not to slap you or throw something when you provoked me almost beyond the point of endurance, then I think I can continue to control myself. We'll just have to come to an agreement on expectations, won't we, love?"

"Yes," he agreed.

They talked for hours until they pulled into the station at Pueblo.

That night, as they all met up again for dinner, the table conversation centered around home and the loved ones awaiting them. Tim wanted to know what his new home looked like, where he would stay, and when he would begin working. Most of all, he wanted to know what Miguel and Beth would think of him.

"Have no fear, Amigo," Tony signed. "They will appreciate you as we do. They will value the contributions you will make to the ranch and our lives. You will be one of us."

Tim's eyes glimmered. "I teach them to sign."

Tony nodded and laughed, and Victoria shared his amusement at the thought of Miguel's attempts to learn sign language. He would hate the awkwardness of initial learning, but she had no doubt both Miguel and Beth would gain proficiency in time.

Tim grinned and looked around the table. "My birthday today. Fourteen. Best birthday of all."

"Happy birthday. We must celebrate." Victoria called the waiter and ordered a piece of chocolate cake for everyone. After dessert, they walked down the streets of Pueblo together and looked into the shop windows.

By the time they'd returned to the hotel, Tony and Victoria had bought Tim a shirt, a pair of jeans, new socks, and boots. Sam and Arnie bought him a bandana, silver spurs, and a new felt cowboy hat. When Victoria watched him stride down the street in his new clothes, her heart swelled with love. She had as much affection for him as she would have if he were her brother.

Victoria brushed tears from her eyes as she watched him walk with pride and self-worth. She promised herself she'd write to Cooky soon to share this moment with her, and to tell her Tim appeared to have grown another inch or two.

The chocolate cake didn't set well in Victoria's stomach, so she spent a restless night. Twice during the night, and once early in the morning, she had to race to the bathroom to empty both her bladder and stomach. Surely the altitude sickness should have stopped now that she had descended in elevation. What else could be wrong? This sickness seemed abnormal.

Victoria rummaged through her bag looking for the sodium bicarbonate, and her hand contacted the strap and rags she hadn't used for a while. Her hand froze, and her heart suddenly pounded in her chest. Calculating quickly, the breath left her lungs. With certainty, she knew now what the sickness meant.

Chilled and shaken, she returned to bed and snuggled in Tony's embrace.

In the morning, he followed her into the bathroom and waited as she knelt before the toilet, head in hands, groaning. "This sickness frightens me, Victoria. Shall I send for the doctor?"

Victoria looked up and shook her head before rising from her kneeling position and returning to bed. She faced him, her nose only inches from his. "I'll see the doctor in the morning before we go, querido, but I think I already know what he will say."

"What will he say?"

She pushed the lock of unruly dark hair from his brow and grinned. "He will tell me that your son or daughter wants his or her presence known to us."

She kissed him and turned away as his muscles tensed. She knew if she looked into his eyes, she'd see stark fear. Already the increased tempo of his heartbeat pounded against her spine.

"Victoria," he whispered near her ear, "I will be a papá?"

She turned back over and smiled.

"I have only begun to accustom myself to the idea of being a husband, and now ..." His hands trembled as he caressed her face. "I must speak to Papá inmediamente."

"Well, you can't fly, love, so you might as well relax. Goodnight."

SEVENTEEN

Victoria and Tony visited the doctor the next morning as soon as the office opened.

The elderly man smiled at Tony's uneasiness. "Relax, man. Women get pregnant all the time. They have since the beginning of time and will continue to do so in the future." He looked at Victoria. "Morning sickness is common in the first trimester. Some unfortunate women may experience digestive discomfort through all forty weeks before their baby is born. I hope this will not be the case for you."

"I hope you're right, doctor. I can't imagine vomiting for so long." Victoria grimaced.

"Unfortunately, nothing much can be done to prevent this. The sickness can hit you at any time of the day or night. I'd suggest you avoid greasy, spicy, and fatty foods. Fruits, leafy green vegetables, breads, and grains may help alleviate some of your symptoms. Salty crackers and food made with ginger have helped some women." He looked at Tony. "See she gets plenty of fresh air and water."

Tony nodded, and the doctor returned his attention to Victoria. "Eat a little before you get out of bed in the morning, then eat several small meals during the day. An empty stomach may aggravate the nausea. I wouldn't recommend three large meals."

"Doctor, I didn't expect to get pregnant this soon." Victoria's phrased her question as a statement.

He grinned. "When the timing and conditions are right, pregnancy results. My wife got pregnant a week after our wedding day."

Victoria and Tony rose to leave, thanking the doctor and shaking his hand.

"You'll soon get used to the idea of being a father, Mr. Morales, so don't worry so much," the doctor advised.

Tony escorted Victoria from the office with a light touch of his hand at the small of her back. He opened the door and seemed to tiptoe next to her.

"I won't break, Tony. I won't be so large I waddle for a few more months yet."

He smiled in recognition and understanding of Victoria's feelings then helped her board the train.

Tim flooded them with questions when they sat down.

"Whoa, Tim. Let me answer one question before you ask me another." Victoria chuckled and answered the questions in the order he'd signed them. "We'll travel all day and through the night. You'll see Amarillo tomorrow afternoon. Yes, passengers will get on and off. No, we won't sleep on beds in the train. We'll stretch our legs and buy food at some of the stops, but we'll sleep sitting up or slouching, like Sam does."

Sam chuckled.

Victoria longed for Mark's comfortable Pullman, but decided she'd rather be sitting on a hard seat and returning with Tony than sleeping in comfort and returning alone.

"How Amarillo different Denver?" Tim wanted to know.

"Not as big as Denver. Town is one of world's largest cattle-shipping centers. We'll smell Amarillo before we arrive." Victoria wrinkled her nose and continued, "Cows and horses come from the Texas Panhandle, South Plain, and eastern New Mexico and are shipped to markets back east. When I ate at a restaurant with Tony and his parents several months ago, I overheard men talking about new railroads being built within the next ten years to handle all the cattle. Tony's dad, Miguel"—she made the sign for intelligent—"knows much about Amarillo's history. He shared many things I didn't know."

Victoria turned to Tony. "Will you tell Tim about Joseph Glidden and his former partner, Mr. Sandborn?"

"You may have to help me with the signs. I do not know if I know enough to tell him everything."

Tim told him to finger spell the words he didn't know, and he would show him the sign.

Tony agreed and began his narrative. "My papá greatly admires these two business men. Together, they owned one of largest ranches in the area— The Frying Pan Ranch. Señor Glidden patented barbed wire and, to prove his invention worked, he and his agent, Señor Sandborn, bought 335,000 acres and fenced the property in barbed wire. They also bought 12,000 head of cattle and branded them with the *Panhandle* brand. I think Señor Glidden is now one of richest men in America because of his invention." He grinned. "Cowboys often prefer other, simpler names, Amigo. This you will learn soon. Cowboys called the brand 'the frying pan' because of the shape, and this is the name others began to use."

"Big numbers. Not understand big space, big cattle."

"Sadly, partnership ended, and they have begun to sell all cattle. I expect the property to be divided into pastures and leased to others soon."

"Amarillo Spanish name?"

"Yes. Word means yellow. Amarillo name of nearby lake and creek." Tony looked to Victoria to confirm his sign for creek. She nodded, and he continued. "Yellow flowers grow on banks of lake in spring and early summer. My papá speaks of time when name of town changed from Oneida to Amarillo. To celebrate, several residents painted their houses yellow."

Victoria admired Tony's rapidly developing skill with signs. He tried so hard to make himself understood to both Tim and her. After their talk at the hotel, he'd put extra effort in communicating with words before he acted.

He turned and caught her admiring gaze and then grinned and clasped her hand. "Of what do you think?"

"You. You're going to make a great father, Tony."

"Perhaps I will be as wise as my papá, no?"

"Both of your parents are the smartest people I know."

"Sí. My impatience to speak with them grows by the mile."

She leaned her head against his shoulder and eavesdropped on Tim's conversation with Arnie and Sam.

"Tony?"

"Hmm?"

"Do you think the townsfolk will accept Tim?"

He shrugged. "I have my doubts. Many continue to distance themselves from my parents because they do not believe brown skin and white should mix."

"Your mother said something to that effect when I visited her after you gave me the kitten, remember? I asked her if people truly minded that she'd married Miguel. She said they still minded, which is why they weren't often invited to others' homes. They believe she'd married below her station."

"She told you this?"

"Yes. She reminded them that Miguel had been a successful businessman and hacienda owner in Mexico long before he married her. If the truth were told, she said, she'd probably married above her station."

Tony smiled. "Those sound like my mother's words."

"When I asked her if she would make the same choice to marry Miguel, knowing how she'd be treated in the future, she said, 'Certainly. I can't imagine finding another man as honest, kind, and lovable as Miguel. Besides, look what I got from the deal—I got Anthony.'"

Tony grinned. "How did you respond to her statement?"

"I said, 'Some deal. Half the time he makes me crazy, the other half he—' and then I remembered the kiss you gave me in the barn, and I lost my train of thought."

Tony looked as if he also remembered the kiss and leaned in as if to repeat the action.

Victoria leaned back and traced the shape of his curled lips with her index finger. "Elizabeth said our ability to be best of friends one moment and throat-hold antagonists the next amused her. I assured her we were best friends most of the time until you decided you wanted to be *el patrón* and boss me around." She sighed. "The people in town won't accept our marriage, Tony. You know this, don't you?"

"Sí, my skin is browner than yours, though not as dark as my father's. Your hair is black, and your eyes are green. The people of the town have always shunned those who are unlike them."

She stroked his hand and whispered, "For your information, I love your skin."

"And I yours," he whispered next to her ear before nuzzling her neck.

As they rode through the night, Victoria rested her head on Tony's shoulder and looked out the open window at the star-studded sky. The rhythmic motion and sound of the train movements lulled her. She snuggled deeper in her blanket.

"I wonder if King David gazed at a night sky like this one when he wrote the nineteenth Psalm, 'The heavens declare the glory of God, and the firmament shows His handiwork.' or when he wrote, 'The heavens declare His righteousness, and all the people see His glory.'?"

"*Probablemente,*" Tony replied and snuggled her closer.

She sighed her contentment knowing tomorrow they would be home.

Victoria sealed the letters she and Tim had written to Cooky and George and placed them beside the ones addressed to Bella and Mark. They'd mail them as soon as they got off the train in Amarillo. Tim had enclosed the pictures along with his enthusiastic retelling of their adventures. Victoria wrote to Abby to share the news of her pregnancy.

> The doctor said the baby should be born near the end of January, Abby. Just think, yours will be born a month or two before mine. I hope the children grow up to be good friends.
>
> Every evening before bed, Tony reads the Scriptures aloud and then kisses me and pats the baby. He says 'goodnight, son or daughter.' He insists he wants the baby to recognize his voice from a young age.
>
> Well, I'd better close. We're pulling into the train station now. Write soon.
>
> Victoria

She sealed the letter and looked out the window, wondering if Miguel and Elizabeth were waiting for them.

"*Alla*. Over there. I see them." Tony pointed and waved.

Victoria spotted her in-laws as they returned his wave.

They collected their belongings and de-boarded. Victoria glanced in Tim's direction and noted his concern as he looked toward Miguel and Elizabeth. "You have nothing to fear," Victoria assured him.

"Father like Boss only older. Walks with same movements. Always watch. Always know. I think he strong like Boss." He studied Elizabeth and then said, "Mother of Boss reminds me of stream in Colorado mountains."

Victoria frowned. "How?"

"Stream pleasant. Arnie say quiet. Soothe nerves. Mother of Boss walks like queen. No hurry. No judgment." He smiled at her. "Maybe they like deaf boy."

She hugged him. "They will."

"Mamá. Papá." Tony shook Miguel's hand and embraced him and then bent and kissed Elizabeth's forehead. Then he took Victoria's hand in his and said, "And now, may I present to you mi hermosa *mujer*, Señora Victoria Morales!"

"Oh, Tony, you goose," Beth laughed and hugged Victoria. "I need no introduction to my beautiful daughter." She stroked Victoria's face. "Are you well? Are you happy, love?"

"More than you can know." She laughed and turned for Miguel's hug and kiss.

"So, little one, was your quest profitable?"

"Yes. I have much to tell you both, but first, I'd like to introduce a dear friend to you. He's come to make his life with us."

Victoria signed to Tim, and he stepped forward and offered his hand to Miguel.

Without a moment's hesitation, Miguel took Tim's hand and said, "You are welcome here."

Tim glanced at Victoria for the interpretation then smiled at Miguel.

Elizabeth hugged him. "Not only do I have a new daughter, I have another son to love. God is so good."

When Victoria translated her words, Tim agreed, "God very good. Better life for me."

Tony signaled for Tim to follow him and Miguel. They would help Sam and Arnie unload the livestock and gear. Victoria and Elizabeth watched from the shade of a nearby tree.

"I'm glad you're home, darling. I missed you so much." Elizabeth hugged Victoria one more time.

"And I missed you, Beth." She looked in her new mother's eyes. "Can you forgive Tony and me for marrying without your presence?"

"Oh, love, Miguel and I weren't angry. We knew you both had to do what you thought best, though I wish I could've seen you speaking your vows of love to each other."

Victoria opened the flap of her saddlebag and brought out the bundle of photographs. "I thought you would, so we got pictures. Here."

Elizabeth smiled as she studied each image and the marriage license with care. "I never thought you two would ever resolve your differences enough to marry. I'm so full of joy I want to sing and dance."

"Look at the ring Tony gave me." Victoria held her left hand toward Elizabeth just as Tony walked to them with Hercules and Dorado.

"Will you ride Dorado, or do you prefer to ride in the wagon with Mamá?"

Victoria touched Elizabeth's hand. "Forgive me, Beth, but I'd like to ride. I'm tired of sitting on a hard seat."

"Go ahead, love."

"I'll ride next to the wagon and tell you about our adventures."

"I look forward to this, love."

When the extra gear had been loaded into the buckboard, they mounted and waited for Miguel to click to the horses. Tony rode next to Miguel as the road space allowed to do so, and Victoria rode next to Elizabeth. Sam, Arnie, and Tim followed behind with the pack animals.

"Oh, how lovely this is." Victoria closed her eyes and lifted her face. "Riding in the warm Texas sun again feels so pleasant."

As they traveled, she told of their journey to Colorado, to the grave sites, and of their marriage in Silverton.

"Did you search for more gold coins while you were in the valley?" Beth asked.

"No, but Arnie and Sam searched up and down the stream where I found the coin. They didn't find anything. My guess is the coin I found must have fallen out of one of the settler's pockets when he went for water."

As they neared the town, Victoria indicated to Tim where the ranch sat from their current location, where Sam and Arnie lived, and where she'd lived with the Keesons until she'd left for Denver.

When she returned her attention to Elizabeth, her new mother said, "Mary and John expect us for dinner, love. She thought we'd appreciate not having to fix a meal when we returned home." Her words sounded like a warning, but what did the warning entail?

Victoria nodded but said nothing. She hadn't told Miguel or Beth of John's actions, and she hesitated to see the couple so soon. She would've preferred more time to think about what she wanted to say.

She glanced at Tony. He watched her but his shrug indicated he would support her decision if she wanted to avoid dinner and go to the hacienda instead.

When they dismounted in front of the store, the three boys took the horses for water and would then go to Sam's place to clean up. They'd return in a half hour.

Mary opened the door to the store when they stepped onto the boardwalk. "Come in, come in." She beckoned them inside and then smiled at Victoria. Her smile seemed genuine. "Come in, my dear. Seems like such a long time since I saw you last."

Victoria responded to Mary's sincerity with a hug. "I'm glad to be back, Mary."

John stood in the background and waited. She tilted her head, wondering if his stance indicated apprehension. She greeted him and his eyes met hers briefly before looking quickly away.

The travelers washed at the pump out back, and then waited in the living room for the others.

"Mary, another young man will sit at the table with us," Victoria advised. "Tim traveled with us from Denver and will live with us at the ranch." She smiled. "He's fourteen, and he and Arnie have become best friends."

Mary nodded and added another place setting and chair.

When Tim entered, Victoria signed and spoke the introductions. Mary and John seemed completely taken aback. Neither moved to greet him, so Tim stepped closer and extended his hand. He smiled, but the wariness in his eyes reflected his concern at their response. Victoria's heart ached. Yes, she had returned to her old life with a vengeance.

EIGHTEEN

John stared at the deaf boy Victoria had brought with her. He didn't understand her. Didn't she realize the townsfolk would ostracize her even more? She seemed to take joy in acting in ways she knew would set up people's backs. First, she'd bonded with Antonio Morales and his parents from the moment she met them. He'd tried to stop this relationship for her own good but had little success. Then, as she grew into a woman with such disturbing looks, she'd allowed the green-eyed fire to roast others when they made distasteful or unkind remarks. He tried to tell her to grow a thicker skin, but she hadn't listened. Soon, she'd begun to turn that intimidating look on him. When she often stared at him as if he were some kind of a bug that had crawled from under a rock, he could scarcely contain his anger. She made him feel so inadequate and useless.

Now that she was married, would she continue to challenge those who teased Arnie? Would she continue to go her own way? He had a sinking feeling she would. Victoria wouldn't back down for anyone, not even those who had more wealth and status. He often feared for her when she moved into this protective mode.

He turned his attention to Victoria and watched her sign to Tim. She hadn't always been so contrary. He remembered a time shortly after she'd come to live with him and Mary when she crawled on his lap to watch him make notations in his ledgers. She rested against him and asked questions. He'd patted her hand and answered with as much patience as he could muster. He knew this had been the right response when he'd seen how much his actions had pleased Mary. Over the following weeks, he'd taught Victoria to make letters and numbers. If he read aloud in the evenings, she would sit at his feet and listen with wide-eyed interest. Her admiration warmed him.

"Dad used to read to me," she explained. "I like to hear stories. Read more."

For a while, she'd taken him at face value. Now, she'd not only married that half-bred, Antonio Morales, but she'd also brought a misfit to live with them.

Elizabeth and Victoria helped Mary by bringing the food in from the kitchen. When Mary passed her daughter-in-law with a platter of beef steaks, Vicky sat her bowl of mashed potatoes on the table and said, "I'll be right back. Excuse me."

Elizabeth watched the hasty exit with a frown. Vicky's face had suddenly paled, and her lips had snapped together. She'd almost run from the room.

She glanced at Tony, who also watched his wife's abrupt exit. When his gaze met hers, he grinned and shrugged.

Joy raced through Elizabeth. A baby? She would finally become a grandmother?

"When?" she whispered.

Tony shrugged again. "Perhaps the middle of January."

Color had returned to Victoria's cheeks by the time she returned to the table, but Beth noted she picked at her food and avoided the steaks.

An hour later, they finished dinner and cleaned up. They said their goodbyes and started for the ranch. Elizabeth could barely contain her excitement. A grandchild. In January.

Victoria thought she might be more comfortable resting in the back of the straw-filled wagon, so she tied Dorado to the tailgate next to Hercules and waited for Tony to spread the blanket. He sat beside her and drew another blanket around them. She leaned against him and looked at the stars. "The moon is full, and the stars shine so brightly we almost don't need the lamps from Miguel's lanterns to see the road. This is a perfect night for a ride."

Tony nodded.

Perfection changed to pain the longer Victoria endured the rocking, bumping motion. She closed her eyes and tried to ignore the mounting nausea. "Stop, Miguel. Stop."

He pulled the horses to a stop, and Victoria lunged from the wagon.

Tony followed and waited until the retching stopped. He removed his bandana and wetted the material from the canteen he'd grabbed. "Pobrecita, I wish I could make this better."

She leaned against him and whispered, "If this doesn't go away soon, I know I'll feel better in less than nine months."

The last mile felt like pure torture. When Tony finally lifted her from the wagon and carried her to his room, Beth followed with a pitcher of water, a glass, and a spare nightgown. "Go help your father with the wagon and your bags, son. I'll take care of Vicky."

He nodded and left.

Elizabeth helped Victoria out of her clothes and into the nightgown. Then she sat on the stool, eyes closed, and allowed her mother-in-law to brush her hair.

"Hopefully, the sickness will leave soon, and you'll feel better."

Victoria's eyes snapped open. "You know?"

"Yes. Tony told me." She continued brushing.

"I'd imagined sharing the news with you and Miguel with more refinement."

Elizabeth hugged her. "I'm so happy, I don't know what to say."

"Well, you might start by thinking about what you want the baby to call you when he, or she, is old enough to talk."

At that moment, Tony walked in, and his mother rose to go. She hugged them both. "You've made me so happy, dear children."

She left and Tony led Victoria to his bed. "Rest now, querida. I have a surprise for you tomorrow, if you feel well enough to ride."

Birdsong awoke Victoria. She listened for a few moments, stretched, and then rolled over to see that Tony had already arisen and gone. She ate a couple of crackers and drank the water he'd placed on the nightstand before he left.

She washed and dressed in her riding skirt and boots. She'd have to find her trunks later.

Her new family sat around the table drinking coffee and chatting, but as soon as she entered, Miguel and Tony stood. Tony pulled out a chair for her.

"You look much better, darling." Elizabeth smiled and handed her a cup of hot chocolate.

"I feel much better, though I'll feel even better when I can have a bath."

Elizabeth nodded. "What would you like for breakfast? Miguel and Tony have already eaten."

"I'm not hungry. I'll eat later."

Miguel chuckled. "So, the little one is making his or her presence felt, eh hija?" He looked at Beth. "Did not Antonio announce his presence in a similar manner?"

"Yes, but only for a few weeks."

Tony touched her hand. "If you are ready, cariño, I will help you mount. Tim and Dorado await us."

Victoria watched from Dorado's back as Tony mounted Hercules and Tim hopped on Chester, one of the Appaloosa ranch horses. Miguel rode Santana, a young, black stallion he'd purchased in Mexico, and Elizabeth rode her favorite bay gelding, Sampson.

They rode a mile to the east before turning toward the valley where the creek flowed through a grove of trees.

"Are we going to the swing?" Victoria smiled. She hadn't been there for several years.

"Wait." Tony held up his gloved hand and smiled. "You shall see."

The valley spread before her, but the place had changed dramatically. Her jaw dropped as a red Spanish tile roof and white stucco walls came into view. The house of her dreams dozed in the sunshine. Victoria noted the orientation of the house. The eastern sun would shine into at least two of the rooms, and she could guess which ones they would be.

Victoria said nothing as Tony led her through the house and told of all the planning he and Miguel had done. Her letter and drawing had come at a critical time. They brought skilled craftsmen from Mexico to finish the job while Tony went for her in Colorado.

"They did a magnificent job, Papá," Tony eyed the details and seemed pleased.

Victoria stared at the fireplace and mantle and tears came. Tony had built this beautiful house to please her.

"Say something, mi amor." He took her hand. "Do you like your new home?"

She raised their intertwined fingers and kissed his. "I don't have any words in English or Spanish to tell you how beautiful this home is, or how much I love you. Thank you doesn't come close to telling you what is in my heart, Tony."

He smiled. "Your words suffice."

Miguel stood and signaled for him to accompany him and Beth.

"We will now leave so the two of you may enjoy your first day in your new home. You will find food and lemonade on the table. Your clothing and trunks are in the bedroom. *Adíos, hijos.*"

"Welcome home, *preciosa.*"

Victoria flew into Tony's arms, "My home is wherever you are, Antonio Alejandro Morales."

CHAPTER	SPANISH	ENGLISH
1	*¡Hóla, brujita!*	Hello, little witch
1	*Sí*	Yes
1	*al rato*	later
1	*señorita*	Miss
1	*Hasta pronto*	See you soon
2	*hija*	daughter
2	*¡Vaya con díos, hermosa mia!*	Go with God, my beautiful one
2	*Papá*	Dad
2	*sin duda*	Without doubt
2	*hijo*	son
2	*mi'jita (mi hija)*	my daughter
2	*Dorado*	Golden
2	*querido*	dear
3	*Mamá*	Mom
3	*en punto*	sharp
3	*caballero*	gentleman
3	*¡Muchísimas gracias!*	Thank you very much!
3	*Mira*	Look
3	*¡Basta!*	Enough!
3	*¡Hermosa mía!*	My beautiful one
4	*frijoles*	beans
5	*mi'jo (mi hijo)*	my son
5	*Nuestro Señor*	Our Savior
7	*oro*	gold
9	*¡Cariño mio!*	My darling!
9	*¡Qué hermosa!*	How beautiful!
9	*muy difícil*	very difficult
9	*Mucho gusto.*	Nice to meet you
9	*Amigo.*	Friend
9	*pequeña*	little one (female)
9	*Claro*	Clear(ly), of course
10	*Señora*	Mrs.

COLORADO TREASURE

CHAPTER	SPANISH	ENGLISH
11	*Buenas noches, hermosa mía.*	Good night, my beautiful (one)
11	*Hasta mañana*	Until tomorrow morning
11	*pequeña*	little one (female)
11	*Entiendo*	I understand
11	*Jesucristo*	Jesus Christ
11	*en realidad*	in reality
11	*¡No importa!*	It's not important!
11	*chica*	little girl
12	*¿Qué haces?*	What are you doing?
13	*¡Atrás!*	Back! Back up!
13	*¡Gracias a Dios!*	Thank God!
13	*Pues*	Well,
13	*¡Que magnifico!*	How magnificent!
14	*leon de montañas*	mountain lion
14	*Mi Señor,*	My Sir, My Lord
14	*El Salvador*	The Savior
14	*mi amor*	my love
14	*padres*	parents
14	*inmediamente*	immediately
14	*me te amo*	I love you
14	*ocupado*	occupied
15	*mi esposa*	my wife
15	*¡Cuidado, Timo!*	Be careful, Tim!
16	*¿Lista, mi hermosa esposa?*	Ready, my beautiful wife?
16	*mi bella esposa*	my beautiful wife
16	*Bien*	Well
16	*Pobrecita*	Poor little one
16	*¿Perdón?*	Pardon?
17	*Probablemente*	Probably
17	*el patrón*	the patron, the boss
17	*mujer*	woman
17	*Alla*	Over ther
18	*Adíos, hijos*	Goodbye, children

CHAPTER	SPANISH	ENGLISH
18	*preciosa*	precious (female)

ABOUT THE AUTHOR

DERINDA BABCOCK is an author and graphic designer. She lives in Southwestern Colorado near the base of the western slope of the Rocky Mountains. In her previous career as an English as a Second Language teacher, she worked with students of all ages and many different linguistic and cultural backgrounds. The richness of this experience lends flavor and voice to the stories she writes. When Derinda is not writing or designing, she continues her education. You can contact her at www.derindababcock.com/contact

OTHER BOOKS
THE DESTINY TRILOGY
Dodging Destiny
In Search of Destiny
Following Destiny

WATCH FOR THE REST OF THE BOOKS IN THE
TREASURES OF THE HEART TRILOGY:
Trouble in Texas
The Prodigal Returns

NOTE TO READER
If you enjoyed *Colorado Treasure* please consider posting an online review on Amazon, Barnes and Noble, and/or Goodreads. Thanks!